THE PATRIAN CHAMPION
STOOD OVER HIM . . .

as Captain James T. Kirk, on his own in the alien arena, dropped into a fighting stance.

The champion thrust his weapon at Kirk, and Kirk parried the thrust. The champion brought the staff around, twirling it so that the stunner tip was toward Kirk's body. Kirk brought up his staff to block, but the champion locked weapons with him, bearing him down.

Their faces were only inches apart as Kirk strained against his opponent's inhuman strength. . . .

Look for STAR TREK Fiction from Pocket Books

Star Trek: The Original Series

is a work of fiction. Names, characters, places, and
re either products of the author's imagination or are used
Any resemblance to actual events or locales or persons,
ad, is entirely coincidental.

POCKET BOOKS, a division of Simon & Schuster Inc.
1230 Avenue of the Americas, New York, NY 10020

© 1994 by Paramount Pictures. All Rights Reserved.

 is published by Pocket Books, a division of
Schuster Inc., under exclusive license from
t Pictures.

reserved, including the right to reproduce
or portions thereof in any form whatsoever.
mation address Pocket Books, 1230 Avenue
nericas, New York, NY 10020

671-88044-6

ket Books printing April 1994

8 7 6 5 4 3 2 1

STAR T

THE PAT
TRANSGRE

SIMON HAU

Copyrigh

This boo
Simon &
Paramou

All right
this boo
For info
of the A

ISBN: 0

First Po

10   9

POCKI
Simon

Printed

POCKET BOOKS
New York   London   Toronto   Sydney

For Andy and Trish

With special thanks to Bruce and Peggy Wiley, Pat Connors, Henry Tyler, Seth Morris, Scott Glener, the gang at The Fine Line in Tucson, as well as Robert Powers, Sandra West, Michel Leckband, Eve Jackson, and all the people at Bubonicon, in Albuquerque, N.M., whose convention I sadly had to miss due to the deadline pressures of this book—thanks for understanding, guys. Maybe next year . . .

THE PATRIAN
TRANSGRESSION

Prologue

THE POLICE FLIERS swooped down like predatory birds, descending at a steep angle in tight formation. It was almost midnight, and the streets of the city were deserted. The red and yellow lights on the exteriors of the vacant office buildings switched to blue, closing off the airspace as the police pursuit craft entered the area. They came in dark, lights off, sirens silent, and they came in fast.

Lt. Joh Iano gave quick, last minute instructions to the strike team over his helmet comset as they touched down, then the gull-wing doors of the sleek, dark gray pursuit flier opened with a muted whine. Iano and his partner came out running, their weapons held ready. Behind them, the rest of the strike team moved quickly into position, their faces invisible behind the polarized visors of their black helmets.

Each officer wore body armor and carried a high-capacity riot rifle in addition to his issue sidearm. The rebels would not be taken without a fight. They never surrendered, preferring to die rather than fall into the hands of the police. This time, Iano was determined to capture some of them alive.

The raid had been planned quickly, but Iano wasn't taking any chances. He had several of the fliers peel off from the formation as they came in for a landing, blocking off the street on both sides, and he made sure that the rear of the building was covered as well. They were going to hit hard and they were going to hit fast. This time, the rebels were not going to get away.

As the officers lined up in assault formation, Iano quickly checked with the units at either end of the street and behind the building. Everyone was in position. It had taken months of trying to infiltrate undercover officers into the rebel movement, but it had finally paid off. The tip about the cell meeting came in earlier that evening. It was to be a major planning session, and some of the rebel leaders would be in attendence. If they could capture the leaders, they could break the back of the entire rebel underground.

Iano was about to order his men in when a panic-stricken voice came over his helmet comset. *"We are under attack! We are under attack!"*

Iano winced as a piercing scream came over his helmet speakers, followed by the crackle of frying circuitry. At the same moment, the main body of the strike team came under fire. Out of nowhere, bright beams of force lanced through the night and struck the strike team as it was drawn up in assault formation. Iano heard screams coming over his helmet speakers as officers died all around him, incinerated by the deadly beams. He brought his hands up to his head and staggered. It was an ambush, and they had walked right into it.

For a moment Iano was disoriented. He glanced around in all directions, trying to see where the fire was coming from. It seemed to be coming from all over. However, they couldn't even see who was firing at them, and Iano had no idea what sort of weapons they were using. He'd never seen anything like this. The panic-stricken officers still standing scattered and started firing in all directions, their rifles emitting sharp pops and high-pitched whines as the projectiles left the barrels, but the deadly beams kept right on coming, cutting them down where they stood. As Iano watched, numb with shock, bright auras of glowing light wreathed the officers who were struck, then they simply disappeared.

"Pull back! Pull back! Retreat!" he shouted into his comset as he ran back toward his pursuit flier. One of the beams missed him by inches and he felt the intense heat of its passage as he ran. What in the name of Ankor were the rebels using? He had never seen such devastating weaponry. He plunged into his flier and started its engines, shouting for his partner. Seconds later he saw him sprinting toward the flier. Then one of the beams stuck him. Iano heard an agonized scream over his comset as his partner became wreathed in an incandescent glow, then he saw him start to fall. His partner was gone before he could even hit the ground.

Iano screamed. The doors came down and, still screaming, he slammed the stick back hard. The flier rose straight up into the air, turning as it gained altitude. Through the canopy, Iano could see several other fliers getting off the ground, but one by one they were struck by the deadly beams and they exploded into blazing fireballs, raining wreckage down onto the street below. He saw the beams crisscrossing in front of him, and he aimed the nose of the flier straight up, then shoved the stick forward and hit the throttles.

Iano was thrown back against his seat as the engines whined and the flier shot straight up, climbing rapidly, leaving the scene of carnage far behind. He kept going up and up until he left the air traffic lanes and was high above the city, then he came out of his climb and banked sharply, bringing the flier around.

"All units, report!" he said into his comset, breathing hard and trying to control his shaking.

There was no response.

"Repeat, all units! *Report!*"

Silence.

Iano sat numbly in his pilot's seat, unable to believe what had just happened. They were all gone. All of them. The entire strike team, thirty officers, all killed. He was the only one left alive. His breathing came in sharp gasps and he could not stop trembling. What kind of weapons *were* those?

It had been a trap, a devastating, horrifying ambush, worse than anything he had ever experienced. They took out the units blocking off the street. They were ready for the units covering the rear of building. They knew the raid was coming and had set up a devastating field of fire, covering all positions; a field of fire such as he had never seen. Disintegrator beams. The technology for weapons like that simply did not exist on Patria! Yet thirty officers had died in a matter of mere moments. He could not deny the evidence of his own senses. They never even had a chance. Iano alone was left alive, and as he piloted his flier back toward headquarters, his mind echoed with the dying agony of those men, and of his partner. And he knew that a part of him had died as well.

"Lieutenant, are you absolutely certain—"

"I *told* you what I saw!"

"Lieutenant!" Commissioner Karsi said sharply. "Do not forget to whom you are speaking!"

Iano clenched his fists and took a deep breath, trying to control himself. "Forgive me, Prime Minister. I meant no disrespect. But the facts, as far as I know them, are all there in my report."

It was almost dawn, and they were sitting in Prime Minister Jarum's office, overlooking the central government district. The prime minister got up from behind his desk and went over to the window. The sky was turning light. He had not slept, and he was tired. The heated debate at the Council meeting had run very late into the night, and just as he was about to leave for home, Commissioner Karsi had called with the news of the rebel ambush.

"Energy weapons," the prime minister said grimly. "For the second time in as many days."

"The *second* time?" Iano said, staring at the prime minister.

"You did not hear that, Lieutenant," Commissioner Karsi said.

"What difference does it make?" the prime minister asked wearily. "Thirty officers killed, right here in the city, only several blocks away from the government district. There is no possible way that we can keep this quiet now. The rebels have taken that option away from us. He might as well know. In a matter of hours, everybody else will too."

"There was an attack on a power distribution station just outside the city yesterday," Commissioner Karsi told Iano. "The entire southern district was affected. We managed to shift the load to another station, and we kept it quiet by reporting it as a malfunction and shutting down the area for public safety, but it was no accident. The rebels attacked with energy weapons. The entire station was destroyed. Fortunately, no one was killed."

"And you kept this quiet?" Iano said with disbelief.

"Only a handful of people outside the Council knew," the prime minister replied. "We did not wish to start a panic."

"So you kept it secret, even from the police?" Iano said. "It was nothing more than a practice run for the attack on us tonight! They wanted to see how their new weapons worked! Well, they work just fine! Thirty officers died tonight because none of them had any idea what they were going up against! You might as well have killed them yourselves!"

"That will be *enough,* Lieutenant!"

"No, Commissioner, he is more than entitled to his anger," the prime minister said. "The error was ours. We overreacted. We should have allowed you to inform the people under your command." He turned to Iano. "You should know, Lieutenant, that Commissioner Karsi protested our decision vigorously. However, we felt we needed more time to debate the issue, and we were concerned that news of the attack on the station would get out. Now it appears that we have run out of time. The rebels have struck again, using the same weapons, and this time people have died. We cannot fight against weapons such as these. We have nothing in our arsenals to match them. Their technology is clearly not of Patrian origin. I have already called another Council meeting for this morning. We can no longer afford to debate the issue. The time for isolation is past. We shall have to appeal to the Federation."

"How do we know these weapons are not coming from the Federation?" Iano asked.

"There are those in the Council who have asked that very question," the prime minister replied. "However, the Federation has been very forthcoming in their ongoing exchange of information with us. We know what sort of weapons they have. They have not supplied us with the details of their manufacture, for which caution I can hardly fault them, but they have been very open in describing how they function and just what they can do. I find it difficult to believe that they would be as forthright with us as they have been, while at the same time arming our rebels in an attempt to destabilize our government. Such an act would violate their Prime Directive of Cultural Noninterference."

"But we have only their word concerning this so-called Prime Directive, do we not?" Iano said.

"No, Lieutenant, we have considerably more. It is not generally known, but since we began our flights of interstellar exploration, we have been in subspace communication with a number of other alien cultures as well, some of whom are allied with the Federation and some of whom are not. And they have each confirmed the Federation's policy in this regard. We have entered a new age, Lieutenant. Not only are we not alone in the universe, but we are only one among many intelligent civilizations, most of whom are advanced far beyond us. That is both a fascinating and a frightening discovery. And we are now learning just how frightening it can be. We have been extremely cautious, and we have kept much of the details of these communications secret, but events have now escalated beyond our ability to control them. We cannot deal with this new threat on our own. It is obvious that what happened last night was only the beginning. We are very badly in need of help."

"And what makes you think the Federation will provide that help?" Iano asked.

"There is no guarantee that they will," the prime minister replied. "But we have nothing to lose by asking."

"With all due respect, Prime Minister," Iano said, "we may have a great deal to lose."

"Again, Lieutenant, that same concern has been expressed by a number of the Council members," Prime Minister Jarum said. "However, the fact remains that if the Federation chose to exercise dominion over us, there would be little we could do to stop them. Their technology is vastly superior to ours."

"Yes," Iano said. "They have energy weapons."

"True," the prime minister agreed. "But if they wanted to subjugate us by force, they could do so easily. They would not need to arm the rebels. Someone else is doing that."

"Who?" Iano asked.

"We have our suspicions," the prime minister replied. "Discussing them now would be premature."

Iano stared at the prime minister thoughtfully. "If some other alien culture is providing the rebels with these weapons, then what prevents *them* from attacking us directly?"

"Good question, Lieutenant. I think what prevents them is the Federation. If they moved against us openly, while we are in negotiations with the Federation, then that could provoke the Federation into joining the conflict on our side."

Iano sat there silently for a moment, allowing the full implications of the prime minister's words to sink in. "Interstellar warfare," he said at last. "With us caught right in the middle."

"Correct, Lieutenant. And I must do everything within my power to make sure it does not come to that."

"But if we turn to the Federation, we may be inviting just such a conflict," Iano said.

"Perhaps not," the prime minister replied, "if we request their aid under cover of a formal diplomatic contact. It will have to be handled with the utmost care. But the fact is, we simply have no other choice. With weapons such as these, there is nothing to stop the rebel underground. Nothing at all."

Captain James T. Kirk pulled down the shirt of his dress uniform to smooth out any wrinkles, then stepped through the door into the transporter room. His senior officers were already waiting for him. Mr. Scott, Dr. McCoy, and Mr. Spock had all been summoned to the transporter room to join Kirk and greet the special envoy, who would arrive momentarily. Kirk had also ordered the bosun's mate to be on hand, to officially pipe the envoy aboard. They were all in their dress uniforms for the occasion.

"Well, you're certainly pulling out all the stops," McCoy said as Kirk came in. "You'd think we were receiving a fleet admiral, instead of some member of the Federation diplomatic corps."

"This special envoy to the Patrian Republics has been charged with an important mission, Bones," Kirk said. "It can't hurt to start this thing off on the right foot and create a good impression. Diplomats often have tender sensibilities."

"Right," McCoy said. "So how long you think it will be before you threaten to throw *this* one in the brig?"

Kirk glanced at McCoy with irritation. "That's *not* what I would call a helpful attitude."

"Just who are the Patrians, anyway?" McCoy asked. "How much do we know about them?"

"We have been monitoring their progress for the past twenty years, Doctor," Mr. Spock said, "as their rapidly developing culture has approached the capability for interstellar travel. They have already colonized the three habitable planets in their own system, and their technological development is almost on a par with that of many Federation worlds. However, politically, their society is an unstable one. The Federation had refrained from making contact with them until such time as the Patrians could manage to solve their own internal difficulties. Recently, they have perfected an interstellar drive and started making exploratory forays outside their own system. In the process, they became aware of the Federation and initiated contact themselves."

"In other words, they've jumped the gun and forced the issue," McCoy said.

Spock raised an eyebrow. "In essence, yes. To date,

all contact with the Patrians has been by subspace communications. The initial talks have been conducted at long range, in an atmosphere of cautious prudence. Now, the Patrians have finally agreed to direct contact, and the *Enterprise* will be the first Federation vessel to visit Patrian space."

"So, in other words, they're prime candidates for Federation membership," McCoy said.

"Or for acquisition by the Klingon Empire," Kirk replied. "There's a lot at stake in this mission, Bones. It could easily go either way."

"But I thought we just agreed to a truce with the Klingons," McCoy said.

"Yes," Kirk said wryly. "But if our negotiations with the Patrians fail to result in an alliance, the Klingons would be free to make their move. And we'd be helpless to do anything about it."

"Why?" McCoy asked.

"An attack on a culture that is not part of the Federation could not, from a strict standpoint, be regarded as a break in the truce, Doctor," Spock explained. "If the Klingons moved against the Patrian Republics, and the Federation tried to intervene, then *we* would be the ones breaking the truce and the Klingons could, with some justification, accuse us of initiating open warfare."

And at stake was nothing less than Patrian autonomy, Kirk thought. The question was, could the Federation envoy convince them of that? Ironically, at the moment of the greatest technological triumph in their history, the Patrians were also facing the greatest crisis in their history. With their own culture struggling for political stability, they were suddenly confronted with the most important decision they had ever faced—ally themselves with the Federation, or face conquest by the most imperialistic and warlike race in the known universe.

It was not for nothing that Starfleet had chosen the *Enterprise* as the flagship of their diplomatic overture. They wanted to send in their best, and being chosen for this mission was an honor. Kirk could only hope that they would send the best from their diplomatic corps as well. Ordinarily, that would have been Sarek of Vulcan, but Sarek's skills were required in the ongoing peace talks with the representatives of the Klingon Empire.

Kirk's thoughts were suddenly interrupted by a message from the bridge. "Bridge to Captain Kirk," said Lieutenant Sulu.

"Kirk here. Go ahead, Mr. Sulu."

"Sir, we have rendezvoused with the *Lexington* and they are ready to beam aboard the Federation envoy."

"Are we ready, Mr. Scott?" Kirk asked.

"Aye, sir, I'm giving them the coordinates right now," Scott replied from the transporter console.

"Very well, Mr. Scott." Kirk nodded to the bosun's mate. "Stand by to pipe our visitors aboard, Mr. O'Dell. Tell them we're ready, Mr. Sulu."

A moment later, as O'Dell blew the bosun's pipe, two shimmering, blurred images appeared on the transporter pads and resolved themselves into the figures of a male and female, both human, both in civilian dress. The woman was a young Asian, perhaps in her late twenties, strikingly beautiful, tall and slim and perfectly proportioned. The man appeared to be in his late forties, clean-cut, fit, and distinguished-looking, with firm, well-chiseled features and hair that was prematurely going gray. Kirk recognized him at once. He stared with astonishment, then broke into a wide grin. As Mr. O'Dell piped them both aboard, Kirk stepped forward, all appearance of formality gone.

"Bob!" he said. "I can't believe it! *You're* the envoy?"

Robert Jordan stepped down off the staging area. "That's *special* envoy to you, Jim," he replied with a grin, holding out his hand.

Kirk shook it warmly. "Damn it, why didn't you let me know?"

"And miss seeing the expression on your face? Not a chance. I wanted it to be a surprise."

"Well, it's the nicest surprise I've had in a long time," Kirk said sincerely. "Welcome aboard the *Enterprise.* Allow me to present my senior officers, Commander Spock, Dr. Leonard McCoy, and Lieutenant Commander Montgomery Scott."

"It's an honor to have you aboard, sir," Spock said.

"You two obviously know each other," McCoy remarked.

"We were classmates at the Academy," Kirk said. "In fact, we roomed together during our last year."

"Well, then I'll bet you have some interesting stories to tell," McCoy said to Jordan with a grin.

"My lips are sealed," Jordan replied with a smile. "After all, I have my position to consider now." He turned toward the young woman standing behind him. "Allow me to present my assistant, Secretary of Protocol Kim Li Wing, of the Federation Council on Intercultural Affairs."

Kirk turned toward the young woman. "Welcome aboard the *Enterprise.*"

"Thank you, Captain," she replied.

"I hope you don't mind my asking," Kirk said, "but how does this old reprobate rate a department secretary of a Federation council for his assistant?"

"It comes with his ambassadorial rank," she replied.

Kirk turned to Jordan with surprise. *"Ambassador?"*

"I've been appointed first Federation Ambassador to the Patrian Republics," Jordan said. "I guess that means you'll have to call me sir, Jim."

"Why, you old—" Kirk caught himself and cleared his throat. "Congratulations, sir. They couldn't have picked a better man for the job."

"Thanks, Jim. That means a lot, coming from you. We've got a lot of catching up to do, but it's been a long and tiring journey. If you've got quarters prepared for us, we'd appreciate a chance to rest and refresh ourselves."

"Of course," Kirk said. "Mr. Spock will show you the way."

"If you would follow me, Ambassador," Spock said.

"If there's anything you need, don't hesitate to ask," Kirk said.

"Thanks, Jim. Right now, I just think we do with a little down time. We'll talk later, old friend."

"I'll be looking forward to it," Kirk said.

They followed Spock out of the transporter room.

"Well," McCoy said, as the doors closed behind them, "imagine that. James Kirk hitting it off with a Federation diplomat. That's got to be a first."

"Can it, Bones," Kirk said with a grimace. "Thank you, Mr. O'Dell, you're dismissed. Mr. Scott, have the bridge inform the *Intrepid* that the ambassador's party has arrived safely and we will be getting underway."

"Aye, sir."

"How did a graduate of the Academy wind up in the diplomatic corps?" McCoy asked as they left the transporter room.

"He left the service," Kirk replied. "We lost touch after that. He never got beyond first lieutenant. I thought he was making a big mistake, throwing away a promising career. But I guess he knew what he was doing. He was always interested in politics." Kirk smiled and shook his head. "Ambassador Jordan. That's going to take some getting used to."

"Look on the bright side," McCoy said. "At least you know you've got someone you can work with."

"Yes, I must confess, I was a little worried about that," Kirk said. "On a sensitive mission like this, an officious bureaucrat with an inflated sense of self-importance could have been a real pain in the posterior. But Bob Jordan served his time in Starfleet, and he was a damned good officer. That's one Federation official who knows how the other half lives. We're not going to have any problems with him."

"Well, that will certainly be a welcome change of pace," McCoy said. "Now if you don't mind, I'm going to get out of this uniform. I never did care much for these tight collars."

"Neither have I," Kirk said with a grin. "I'll bet Jordan had himself a good laugh, thinking about me rolling out the red carpet for him. He always hated official functions. I remember one time . . . well, maybe I'd better not tell you that one. He is an ambassador now, after all."

"With a beautiful department secretary for an assistant, no less," McCoy said.

"Yes, I . . . did notice," Kirk said. "And I noticed *you* noticing, as well."

"Hard not to notice a woman like that," McCoy said.

"Yes, indeed."

"And you can wipe that smirk off your face," McCoy said. "She's young enough to be my daughter."

"True. But she isn't."

"I've got work to do," McCoy said gruffly.

"Right," Kirk said with a perfectly straight face.

He watched McCoy turn and head back down the corridor, then stepped into the turbolift. "Bridge," he said, then smiled. With a man like Bob Jordan in charge of this mission, things were bound to run smoothly. That would, indeed, be a welcome change of pace. The way things were shaping up, this mission could wind up being nothing more than official escort duty and an opportunity to catch up on old times with a good friend.

Chapter One

"STATUS REPORT, MR. CHEKOV," Kirk said as he came onto the bridge.

"We are approaching the Patrian system, sir," the helmsman replied in a thick Russian accent. "We should be coming out of warp and slowing to impulse power for rendezvous approach in approximately three point twenty minutes."

"Very good, Mr. Chekov," Kirk said, taking his seat. "Lieutenant Uhura, stand by to open hailing frequencies on entering Patrian space. Let's do this one by the book."

"Standing by, Captain," Uhura said.

Since coming on board, Bob Jordan and Secretary Wing had remained closeted in their quarters. They had also, apparently, comandeered Mr. Spock, who still had not returned. Kirk had resisted the impulse to call Spock and summon him to the bridge. For the time being, he could afford to spare his first officer. Besides, he had a fairly good idea what Spock was doing at the moment. Doubtless, Jordan was having Spock brief them on the ship's operation and routine. It had been a while since he had served aboard a starship, and he probably wanted to be brought up to speed. In his place, Kirk probably would have done exactly the same thing.

"Captain," Chekov said, "I have that information you requested."

"Very good, Mr. Chekov," Kirk replied as he sat down. "A brief summary, if you would be so kind."

Chekov called up the data on his screen. "Secretary Kim Li Wing was born in the city of Beijing, of mixed American and Chinese parentage. Her father is Dr. Kam Sung Wing, Director of the Sun Yi Institute of Xenoanthropology. Her mother was the late Dr. Anna Stanford Anderson, formerly the Director of—"

"The Federation Council on Intercultural Affairs," Kirk said. He was impressed. "I should have guessed. That, Mr. Chekov, is what I would call one hell of a pedigree."

"Yes, sir. Shall I go on?"

"Please."

"Secretary Wing was educated at the Sorbonne, in Paris," Chekov continued, "and completed her graduate studies summa cum laude at Princeton, with a doctorate in xenoanthropology. She served her foreign service internship on Vulcan, as first assistant diplomatic attaché to the Federation ambassador. For the past two years she has served as Secretary of Protocol on the Federation Council on Intercultural

Affairs, and adjunct lecturer in xenopolitical studies at Starfleet Academy."

Kirk was impressed. "She sounds like a highly capable and intelligent young woman."

"Indeed, Captain," Chekov said. "Her IQ is measured at—"

"If it's all the same to you, Mr. Chekov, I really rather wouldn't know," Kirk said. "It might give me an inferiority complex."

Chekov grinned. "It *is* considerably higher than yours, Captain."

"*Thank* you, Mr. Chekov," Kirk said. "That will be all."

"Yes, sir," Chekov said, exchanging smiling glances with Navigator Sulu.

"Sir," Lieutenant Uhura said, "I am picking up a subspace signal from a Patrian vessel at the scheduled rendezvous point."

"Slow to impulse power, Mr. Sulu," Kirk said. "Put it up on the main viewer, Lieutenant."

As the ship came out of warp drive and slowed to impulse power, Lieutenant Uhura punched up the subspace signal on the main viewscreen.

"Attention Federation vessel. This is Commander Anjor of the Patrian starcruiser *Komarah*. Please respond."

"Hailing frequency, Lieutenant," Kirk said.

"Go ahead, sir," Uhura said.

"This is Captain James T. Kirk, of the Federation starship *Enterprise*. We have on board the special Federation envoy to the Patrian Republics, the honorable Ambassador Robert Jordan. We are awaiting your instructions, Commander."

The face of the Patrian commander appeared on the main viewer. He was almost completely human in appearance, save for a ridged brow, yellow eyes with vertical pupils, and no hair. His eyes, like those of a reptile, possessed nictitating membranes in place of eyelids, and his skin was a dark, almost golden hue. Despite his somewhat ophidian appearance, he had a handsome, almost regal look about him. A career military man through and through, Kirk thought.

"Greetings, Captain Kirk," he said. "We have been dispatched to escort your ship and the Federation envoy to a station in orbit above our homeworld, Patria One. If you would be so kind as to match your speed to ours, we shall lead you in and give you the proper approach coordinates."

"Thank you, Commander," Kirk said, noting that Anjor was not using a translator. He had learned the language, and though his speech was heavily accented, he spoke it well. "Mr. Chekov, match speed with the *Komarah,* if you please. Mr. Sulu, stand by to receive approach coordinates."

"Standing by, sir," Sulu replied.

"Approach coordinates coming in, sir," Uhura said.

"Thank you, Lieutenant," Kirk said. "Patch them through to the navigation console, please."

"Right away, sir," Uhura replied.

"Approach coordinates received and locked in, Captain," Sulu said.

"We await your pleasure, Commander," Kirk said.

"Thank you, Captain," Commander Anjor replied. "It would be my pleasure, once we have achieved orbit, to receive you and your senior officers, as well as the ambassador and his party, of course, at a small formal reception aboard my vessel to mark this historic first meeting."

"We would be honored, Commander," Kirk said. "On behalf of Ambassador Jordan and my officers, I accept your gracious invitation. Do you have transporter facilities on board?"

"Regrettably, Captain, we do not possess the technology for teleportation," Commander Anjor replied. "However, we would be pleased to dispatch a shuttle for you."

"No need, Commander," Kirk said. "We can beam directly over to your vessel if you would advise us of a suitable location. We can scan your ship and compute the proper coordinates for our arrival."

"That would be perfectly acceptable, Captain Kirk," Anjor said.

"Sir," Sulu said, "I am scanning a main shuttle docking area aboard the *Komarah* that should serve."

"Commander—" Kirk said.

"I heard, Captain," Anjor said. "I shall have the main docking port prepared for your arrival."

"Thank you, Commander," Kirk said. *"Enterprise* out." He turned to Uhura. "Lieutenant, please inform the ambassador that we have achieved rendezvous with the Patrian ship *Komarah* and are proceeding to station in orbit above Patria One. Inform him also that we have been invited to a formal reception aboard the Patrian vessel once we have achieved orbit."

"Yes, sir," Uhura said.

The turbolift doors slid open and Kirk's first officer stepped out onto the bridge.

"Ah, Mr. Spock," Kirk said. "I thought I'd lost you."

"I was with the ambassador, Captain, conducting an informal briefing at his request," Spock replied. "I had assumed you would call if I was needed on the bridge."

"Yes, of course," Kirk said. "Well, what did you make of him, Mr. Spock?"

"Ambassador Jordan seems to be a forthright and capable man, Captain," Spock replied. "Though it has been years since he has served aboard a Starfleet vessel, he still has an excellent working knowledge of ship's operations and routine. He had requested an informal briefing, but I found his knowledge already quite extensive. And Secretary Wing struck me as a highly intelligent and versatile young woman. Her knowledge of Vulcan customs and traditions is impressive. Humans, as you know, have great difficulties in reproducing Vulcan speech, and yet Secretary Wing managed as close an approximation as I have ever heard or even imagined possible for a human. And though she graciously apologized for her inability to effect the correct pronunciation, I found her knowledge of the Vulcan language flawlessly fluent. I must say, Captain, I was very much impressed."

"Sounds like Jordan's picked himself a first-rate assistant. She seems to be a young woman of singular accomplishment," Kirk said.

"Indeed," Spock replied. "While we spoke, we played dimensional chess. She said it helped her to relax."

"Dimensional chess helps her *relax?*" Kirk said. He had played the game with Spock on a number of occasions, and since the Vulcans were the acknowledged masters of the game, he was convinced that Spock occasionally gave in to him a little. Nevertheless, he found the game demanded an almost brutal level of concentration that was mentally draining and exhausting.

"She defeated me two times out of five," Spock said, "once using a cleverly disguised version of the Karaluk gambit. I had thought I recognized it, but I must frankly admit that I did not think a human would be able to execute its intricate complexities." He raised one eyebrow, as close as he usually came to an emotional response. "Clearly, I was wrong."

"I wish I'd been there to see it," Kirk said with a smile.

"Captain?" Uhura said.

"Yes, Lieutenant?"

"I have a message from Ambassador Jordan. He requests that you and all the senior officers who will be attending the reception aboard the *Komarah* meet with him for a briefing as soon as possible."

"Very well, Lieutenant. Please inform the ambassador that we shall meet him in Briefing Room One in five minutes. Attending will be myself, Mr. Spock, Dr. McCoy, Mr. Chekov, and Mr. Scott. Kindly inform Mr. Scott and Dr. McCoy of the briefing. Mr. Sulu, you will have the conn in our absence."

"Yes, sir," Sulu replied. If he was disappointed at the prospect of missing the reception, he did not show it. Someone had to stay behind to take charge of the bridge in the captain's absence, and that Kirk felt confidence in him was no small compliment to his abilities.

Ambassador Jordan and Secretary Wing were already waiting for them when they arrived at the briefing room.

"Ambassador," Kirk said with a smile, seeing Jordan sitting at the table as soon as he came in. "We came as soon as we could. I hope you have not been waiting long."

"No need for apology, Captain Kirk," Jordan replied with mock formality, then grinned. "Actually, you're not late. In fact, you're two minutes early. It's been a while since I've been aboard a starship, and I wasn't sure how long it would take to reach the briefing room. I did not want to keep you and your officers waiting."

"That's very kind of you," McCoy said.

Jordan glanced at McCoy and smiled. "Thank you, Dr. McCoy. I see that everyone is present, so we might as well begin. Please, take your seats, gentlemen."

They all sat down around the conference table.

"I have a few prefatory remarks, and then I'd like to turn this briefing over to Secretary Wing," Jordan said with a nod in her direction. He cleared his throat and got to his feet.

"Gentlemen, you have received your orders, and it should probably go without saying that this is a highly important diplomatic mission. However, I cannot stress enough just how strongly the Federation council feels about this. Quite aside from the fact that the Patrian Republics represent an intelligent, technological, and cultured race worthy of Federation membership, there is the question of their place in the balance of power between the Federation and the Klingon Empire, not to mention the Romulans, who, as always, remain as something of a wild card in this sort of situation. Doubtless, you are all aware that truce negotiations are currently proceeding between the Federation and the Klingon Empire. There have been those who have been so bold as to refer to them as 'peace talks,' though personally, I feel that such a designation would be somewhat premature."

"That's putting it mildly," Kirk said wryly.

"Yes, well, as a diplomat, I'm supposed to put things mildly," Jordan said. "However, I'm sure you can guess my true feelings on the matter. Prior to leaving on this assignment, I spoke with Ambassador Sarek, who is heading up the ongoing negotiations with the Klingons during the ceasefire. The Klingons will not consent to any face-to-face negotiations, and the analogy Sarek used to describe the talks to me was that of a fencing match between two champions, in which each moves warily, attempting a small feint here and there in an effort to draw out his opponent or reveal a weakness, with neither yet ready nor willing to commit to a decisive action."

"In other words, they're merely going through the motions," Kirk said with a grimace.

"Yes, that was more or less my interpretation too," Jordan said. "However, whether or not these motions, as you put it, will amount to anything, they must be gone through just the same, not only on the chance that something productive may come of it, but because failing to do so would only play into the Klingons' hands. And whether or not the Klingons are sincere, the fact is that we do, at least for the moment, have a ceasefire, and that is no small thing."

"Indeed," McCoy said. "Any chance at peace, no matter how slight, is certainly worth taking."

Secretary Wing glanced at him with approval and nodded.

"Quite so," Jordan said. "Which brings us to our current situation. I realize, Jim, that your orders did not contain much more than the most general background information, for which I apologize, but the Patrians quite unexpectedly agreed to direct contact, and the Council decided to move on this with all possible speed. There really wasn't time to assemble a full briefing package for you. In fact, except for Secretary Wing and myself, there really wasn't anyone else qualified to do it, and we had our hands full just getting ready for this mission."

"I understand," Kirk said. "My crew and I stand ready to assist you in any way we can."

Jordan nodded. "In all probability, Jim, your involvement will be minimal, and purely in the nature of formality. However, you must be prepared to be flexible, as we really have no idea what the Patrians may or may not request of us."

Kirk merely nodded. Jordan was only stating the obvious, but it was his show, and not Kirk's place to point that out. Perhaps all Jordan wanted was a certain reassurance. He seemed a little nervous, which was certainly understandable, under the circumstances.

"That's all I have to say for now. Secretary Wing?" Jordan said, resuming his seat.

"Thank you, Ambassador," she replied. She remained seated. "Gentlemen, you are, of course, familiar with the proper protocol in such situations, but there are a few idiosyncrasies peculiar to the Patrians, of which you should be made aware. We have exchanged a considerable amount of information about each other via long-range, subspace communications, and we have found that in many ways their society is similar to ours, but certain customs differ. For example, the Patrians do not shake hands. Their hands, unlike ours, are taloned, and the extending of a hand as we would for a handshake could be interpreted as an aggressive or offensive gesture. Now, they have learned something of our social customs, as we have learned something of theirs, and it is entirely possible that a Patrian may, out of courtesy, extend a hand to you in greeting. If that occurs, you should, of course, respond in kind and accept the proferred handshake. Otherwise, the Patrian equivalent is to hold up both hands, like this, and incline the upper body slightly." She demonstrated, holding up her arms, bent at the elbows and close by her body, the backs of the palms facing out.

McCoy grinned. "That looks like the way a doctor holds his hands after scrubbing up for surgery," he said.

She smiled. "Yes, I suppose it does, at that. It makes for an excellent analogy, Doctor. I hope you don't mind if I use it."

McCoy grinned again. "Be my guest."

"The purpose is to show that the talons are re-tracted," she continued, "and the hands, facing toward you and away from the person being greeted, are not in position for attack. Patrians also do not laugh the same way we do, though they do seem to have a somewhat self-deprecating sense of humor. Their laughter is a sort of snorting sound, rather like this. . . ." She demonstrated, making a sound through her nose that sounded remarkably like a pig grunting. It took Kirk and the others by surprise, and they could not resist chuckling.

"I hope we're not going to be expected to do *that*," McCoy said.

She smiled. "No, Doctor, the Patrians know how we laugh, and understand the concept, though they find the sound of our laughter as amusing as you seem to find theirs. I have illustrated merely so that you would know what they are doing if they should suddenly break out in snorting grunts. I might add that the way they do it is much louder and rather more bestial sounding than the way I have demonstrated it. I cannot quite reproduce the sound. Their language is difficult to master, though not quite as difficult as the Vulcan tongue," she added, with a nod toward Spock. "I have learned it to some degree of fluency, as we have exchanged linguistic programs, but since Federation ships all carry a supply of universal translators, you will not need to trouble yourselves about that. I suggest we present them with a number of translators from your stores, Captain, to aid them in the manufacture of their own."

"We can let you have as many as you need," Kirk said.

"I think one case should be sufficient," the ambassador replied.

"Scotty?" Kirk said.

"I'll have a case ready for you, sir," Mr. Scott said.

"Good. We can bring it with us to the reception as a gesture of goodwill," Jordan said. "Please continue, Secretary Wing."

"Thank you, sir. Now, as to the Patrian diet, we have exchanged information regarding the chemical composition of various items of our respective diets, and thus far we have ascertained that nothing the Patrians eat would be injurious to humans. I have taken the liberty of programming your ship's food synthesizers with the necessary data, so that you may try some samples of their food prior to the reception." She reached forward and turned on the communicator in the console set into the briefing room table. "May we have the dietary samples brought in, please?"

A moment later the briefing room doors slid open and a crewman entered, carrying a large tray, which he set on the table before them.

"The Patrians are primarily vegetarians," Secretary Wing said. "These are chemically accurate replications of certain items in their diet, based on the information they've provided us, but we may encounter certain variations in taste, appearance, and texture due to local growing conditions and the lack of the actual items themselves for replication purposes. Still, these should be fairly close approximations. Help yourselves, gentlemen."

McCoy reached for a bowl that contained something that resembled a cross between asparagus and celery. He picked out a stalk and bit off a small piece. "Crunchy," he said. "Very fibrous. Takes a lot of chewing."

"How does it taste?" Kirk asked.

McCoy grimaced. "Like plywood."

Spock selected something from a plate that held what looked like fruit of some sort. It was green and orange, and shaped like a grapefruit. "Does one peel the skin, or simply eat it?" he asked, examining it curiously and taking an experimental sniff.

"That is a fruit called *kaza*," Wing replied. "Patrians eat it with the skin, but I have found that peeling it, as you would an orange, makes it more palatable."

Spock peeled the fruit, revealing a reddish pulp beneath, tore off a segment and popped it in his mouth. "Curious," he said.

"What does it taste like, Spock?" McCoy asked.

"I can find no adequate comparison," Spock replied. "It is, however, very tart, quite juicy, and rather refreshing."

"Would this be what they drink?" Scotty asked, reaching for a carafe containing an amber-colored liquid.

"It is called *geeza,* Mr. Scott," Wing said. "A sort of wine they prize quite highly."

"Ah, that's more to my liking," Scotty said, pouring himself a glass and taking a healthy slug. He swallowed, and then his eyes popped out and he screwed up his face in a grimace of profound disgust. "Och, sweet mother of God!"

"That bad, Mr. Scott?" Kirk asked.

"It takes like brine flavored with rotten herring!" Scotty said. "Here, Captain, you try it."

Kirk held up a hand as Scotty held out the glass to him. "Uh, no, thank you, Mr. Scott. I will defer to your undoubted expertise."

Chekov was chewing on something that looked like a salad of mixed greens and vegetables.

"How does that taste, Mr. Chekov?" Kirk asked.

Masticating furiously, Chekov grimaced wryly. "It is . . . interesting, Captain," he said.

"And?" Kirk prompted him.

"And . . . very, very chewy," Chekov added.

"But how does it *taste,* Mr. Chekov?" Kirk pressed him.

Chekov took a deep breath and swallowed with some effort. The expression on his face spoke volumes. "I . . . don't think you really want to know, sir," he replied.

Chapter Two

THE OFFICERS' MESS aboard the starcruiser *Komarah* was somewhat spartan in its accommodations compared to the *Enterprise,* but Kirk reminded himself that the Patrians had only recently begun building starships. This was a first generation vessel. Nonetheless, the Patrians had gone all out for the occasion.

When the ambassador's party had beamed aboard the Patrian vessel, Kirk saw that the entire complement of the *Komarah* had been drawn up in formation in front of the shuttles in the docking bay. They were all resplendent in what he assumed were their fulldress uniforms, black with gold trim and insignia, and as they had materialized, one of the officers barked out a command and the entire crew snapped to, stamping their feet three times—left, right, left—in perfect unison, and giving voice to a cry that would have done justice to a battalion of marines. They were invited to inspect the troops, and Commander Anjor led them up and down the lines, clearly proud of his men. At least, Kirk assumed they were all males. He could recognize individual differences in their features, but if there were females among them, he could not tell which ones they were.

From the docking bay they were conducted to the officers' mess, where a long table was laid out for a meal. Waiting for them was a delegation of Patrian officials, headed by Elder Rohr Harkun, and representatives of the scientific team that had participated in the initial first contact and exchange of information leading to the meeting.

There was a brief, formal presentation ceremony, during which the Patrians spoke in an awkward standard Terran, while Jordan replied and Secretary Wing translated his remarks in their own tongue, apparently impressing them greatly with her mastery of it. The case of universal translators was presented, and Mr. Scott demonstrated their use. The Patrians were clearly delighted with the gift, and used the translators for the remainder of the occasion, which made things a great deal easier for all concerned. Finally, Kirk realized with a sense of apprehension, it came time for the meal.

They all took their seats around the table, and Commander Anjor had drinks poured. "We understand that, in your culture, it is customary to mark an occasion such as this with a ceremonial libation called a 'toast,'" he said, rising to his feet and raising his goblet. "In honor of our guests, then, I would like to"—he hesitated, groping for the right word—"present a toast?"

"We say *propose* a toast, Commander," Kirk said.

"Thank you, Captain," Anjor replied. "I would like to propose a toast, then. To our new friends from the United Federation of Planets, may this historic first meeting mark the beginning of a new age in peace and cooperation between our cultures. To this, I drink."

Scotty glanced down at his goblet with an expression of dismay. He looked up and met Kirk's gaze with a pained look on his features. Kirk gave a slight, barely perceptible shrug of resignation and nodded at him to drink. The expression on Scotty's face was pitiful. He looked toward the ceiling, as if offering up a silent prayer, then closed his eyes and tossed back the liquid in one quick gulp. Kirk took a deep breath, prepared to suffer the same fate. Suddenly, Scotty's eyes opened wide with complete astonishment and an expression of happy disbelief came over his features.

"It canna' be!" he said, utterly amazed.

"Mr. Scott," Kirk said with sudden concern.

"Captain, this here's scotch whiskey! And single malt too! But I canna' tell from where!"

Kirk sniffed his own goblet, while McCoy and Chekov both drank from theirs. It was, indeed, scotch. Kirk took a sip. And a very fine scotch too, he thought.

"Now *that,"* McCoy said with emphatic approval, "is what I call a drink!"

"Does it meet with your approval, Captain?" Commander Anjor asked anxiously.

"It does indeed," Kirk replied. "I'm frankly astonished. However did you manage it?"

Obviously pleased with himself, Commander Anjor explained, "It was my own idea, Captain. You see, unlike your Federation, we do not possess an equivalent of your Starfleet Academy. Experience is our teacher. We all enlist in the service at the lowest levels and work our way up through the ranks. I began my own career as a ship's cook, and consequently, I was especially interested in the data relating to your diet. While we do not possess your synthesizer technology, of which I am most anxious to learn more, I noticed in the data transmitted to us that one of your popular libations, the one you call 'whiskey,' is derived from a type of plant that is remarkably similar in chemical composition to one of our wild native grasses. I could not resist the temptation to experiment."

"Experiment?" Mr. Scott said. "You call this an *experiment?* Why, this stuff's smoother than a baby's bottom!"

Anjor frowned. "I . . . fear I do not understand."

"You may consider it a very high compliment, Commander," Kirk explained with a smile, "from an acknowledged expert in the field."

"Truly?" Anjor said, obviously very pleased.

"Aye," Scott said emphatically. "Would it be too much trouble to have another taste, sir? Simply to reaffirm my judgment, you understand."

"Bring a container of Distillation number twenty-nine for Mr. Scott, please," Anjor said to one of the crew members serving the meal.

"Distillation number twenty-nine?" Kirk said. "Am I to understand that there were Distillations one through twenty-eight, as well?"

"I was not satisfied with my early results, Captain," Anjor replied. "I could not judge by the taste, you understand, so I had to go purely by chemical analysis. I feared that I had failed utterly, because there was simply no time to duplicate your unique aging process. And even though this particular distillation matched the required chemical composition, none of my crew would try it more than once. It made some of them quite ill. They assured me it had to be all wrong. They simply could not believe that you would drink such a vile concoction."

"Commander Anjor!" Elder Harkun said, distressed at his remark.

"Please forgive me, Captain," Anjor said hastily. "I truly meant no offense."

"None taken," Kirk said. "It might amuse you to know that Mr. Scott had a very similar reaction to your wine."

"Indeed?" Anjor said. He glanced at Scott, and then erupted into a series of grunting snorts that, had they not known it was laughter, might have sounded quite disconcerting. Kirk and the others joined him, laughing in their own way, which produced not a few curious reactions among the members of *Komarah*'s crew.

"Do I understand correctly, then," Mr. Scott said, "that this has not been aged in any way? That is to say, this stuff is *freshly distilled?*"

"It is no more than a week old, Mr. Scott," Anjor replied. "I must admit, I had some serious reservations about serving it to you. I was absolutely certain that it would not cause you any harm, you understand, but I thought that it was still taking a risk, as regards the taste."

"Well, I, for one, am glad you took it, sir," Scott said, pouring himself another gobletful from the container that had been set before him. "And I'd be most anxious to have your recipe."

"It would be my pleasure to give it to you, Mr. Scott, along with a generous supply of the ingredients," Anjor replied.

"Why, thank you, sir!" Scott said. "I'll be mighty curious to see if I can match your excellent results. But a whiskey this good should have a better name than Distillation number twenty-nine."

"With your permission, then, I shall it call it 'Scott's whiskey,'" Anjor said.

Scotty beamed. "Scott's whiskey! Aye, that has a ring to it! I'll drink to that!"

"It is fortunate that your experiment has turned out well, Commander," Elder Harkun said. "But you took a great deal upon yourself. You should have cleared it with us first. It could have created an unpleasant incident."

"Forgive me, Elder Harkun," Anjor said, "but my study of the dietary data with which we were supplied indicated that while our guests would have been able to consume our food without any ill effects, they would probably not have found it very pleasing."

"With all due respect, Elder Harkun," Jordan said, "I think the commander showed admirable initiative."

"Perhaps," Elder Harkun replied, "but nevertheless, he has overstepped his bounds."

Anjor looked uncomfortable, because at that very moment his crew members were bringing in some dishes for the dinner. "In that case, Elder Harkun, I fear that I am about to further incur your displeasure."

As the covers were lifted off the dishes set down before the men of the *Enterprise*, Kirk caught an unmistakably familiar odor.

"Good Lord!" McCoy said as he stared down at his plate. "Is that what I think it is?"

"I'll be damned," Kirk said. "It's steak!"

"Commander . . ." Harkun said tensely.

Anjor suddenly looked even more anxious than before.

"Now *this* is what I call a proper meal!" Scott said, inhaling the odor deeply and digging in with gusto.

Kirk took an experimental bite. It wasn't beef, that much was for certain, but it had a similar flavor, and it was excellent, cooked medium rare. "This is really very good, Commander," he said sincerely. "My compliments."

Anjor sighed with relief. Elder Harkun merely shook his head, apparently at a loss for words.

Spock ate sparingly, sticking to the Patrian fruits, but he watched with interest as the others dug into their steaks. "I am curious, Commander," he said. "We were informed that your people are primarily vegetarian. Surely, you do not raise cattle. What sort of creature did this meat come from?"

"It is the flesh of a creature that we call the *zama,"* Anjor replied.

"What?" Elder Harkun said, nearly dropping his goblet. He looked utterly aghast.

Kirk glanced from Harkun to Anjor. "What is a *zama?"* he asked.

Secretary Wing cleared her throat slightly. "According to the comparison analysis we made from the Patrian zoological data, it is a sort of giant rodent."

"You mean . . . a *rat?"* Chekov said, his fork frozen halfway between the plate and his mouth.

"Roughly speaking, yes," she said, calmly eating her steak. "And a rather large one, I should imagine."

The nictitating membranes slid over Elder Harkun's eyes. Despite the physiological differences, Kirk had no trouble reading his expression.

"It is a type of . . . vermin," Commander Anjor said, a little awkwardly. "However," he added quickly, "biologically, according to the data we received, it *is* remarkably similar to your beef mammals."

"Fascinating," Spock said. "And what of the dish that resembles a potato? What sort of plant is that?"

"Actually, it is not a plant," said Anjor. "It is a baked grub."

Chekov's jaws froze in the act of chewing. Elder Harkun looked as if he wanted to crawl under the table.

"Well . . . rat or not," McCoy said, "this steak is delicious. And if anyone had ever told me that I would enjoy eating grubs, I would have said they were crazy. But I'll be damned if it doesn't taste just like a baked sweet potato."

"Allow me to commend you on your culinary artistry, Commander," Kirk said. "You must have been one hell of a ship's cook."

Anjor's chest swelled with pride. "I am pleased that my efforts have met with your approval. It has been quite some time since I have worked in a ship's galley. I feared that I had lost my touch."

"You may soon have ample opportunity to reacquire it, Commander," Elder Harkun said.

"Please, Elder Harkun," Jordan said, "do not hold this against Commander Anjor on our account. Perhaps his actions may have been a bit irregular, but they were certainly well-intentioned, and highly successful. He has produced a truly remarkable meal. I would say that he has executed something of a diplomatic triumph."

"Thank you, Ambassador," Anjor said with an uncertain glance at Harkun.

"Well," Harkun said, relenting, "since the meal seems to have gone so well, thanks to Commander Anjor's admittedly unorthodox efforts, perhaps this would be a good time to turn our talk to more serious matters. No doubt, Ambassador, your Federation council was somewhat surprised when we seemed so anxious to effect this meeting, especially after having been so cautious in our dealings with you from the beginning."

"Caution in making first contact with an alien race is certainly understandable, Elder Harkun," Jordan said. "Especially since the Federation represented a number of races that were alien to you."

"Quite so," Elder Harkun said. "And you have been very forthright in your communications with us, for which we are most grateful and appreciative. It has resulted in a significant exchange of information, which, I am sure, shall be of benefit to both, or perhaps I should say *all,* of our respective cultures." He inclined his head toward Mr. Spock, who returned the gesture.

"There are many benefits to membership in the Federation, Elder Harkun," Jordan said. "I hope to have the opportunity to acquaint you with some of them."

"I was hoping you would say that, Ambassador Jordan," Harkun replied, "because we find ourselves in the rather delicate position of asking for just such a benefit, as evidence of your intentions. With your permission, I shall come directly to the point."

"Please do," Jordan said, while the others listened with interest as the plates were cleared away.

"Doubtless, you are aware that our society has been troubled with some internal political difficulties," Harkun said. "We both understand and appreciate your stated desire to refrain from involving yourselves in our internal affairs. However, recently there have been certain developments which, quite frankly, would make such an involvement not only welcome, but indispensable."

"That would, indeed, be a delicate matter, Elder Harkun," Jordan said. "Our Prime Directive prohibits us from any sort of cultural interference. Could I ask you to be a little more specific?"

"Certainly," Elder Harkun said with a nod. "There are those within our society who, while a minority, have no compunction against using violence to achieve their stated goals. And lately they have escalated their violent acts of rebellion against our people and our government to a point where we find ourselves ill-equipped to deal with them."

"If you are asking us to help you suppress terrorist activities in your society," Jordan said, "then I am afraid that would come under the heading of cultural interference, and our Prime Directive would forbid that. You must understand, Elder Harkun, that the purpose of the Prime Directive is to protect and preserve cultural autonomy. The Federation cannot involve itself in the internal political problems of other cultures. Doing so would not only destroy the integrity of the Federation Accords, but it would set a dangerous precedent as well."

"Yes, I understand that," Elder Harkun replied. "However, if I have read your Federation Accords correctly, then this particular case would prove an exception, and I believe your Prime Directive would not be violated."

"Please go on," Jordan said, looking a bit anxious.

"We have recently become aware of another 'federation,' so to speak, an empire of worlds united under the government of a race known as the Klingons."

Kirk and his fellow officers all stiffened. "You have had contact with the Klingon Empire?" he asked tensely.

"Please, Captain," Jordan cautioned him with a stern glance. "Allow Elder Harkun to continue."

In other words, Kirk thought, shut up and stay the hell out of it. Quite right too. It was not his place to speak out now, unless his opinion was solicited. But mention of the Klingons had brought about a marked change in the mood of the proceedings.

"Let us say that it appears as if the Klingons have been in contact with us," Elder Harkun replied, "or more specifically, with the violent rebel faction of which I have been speaking. Recently, the rebels have started using energy weapons of a highly advanced nature, weapons that we are not yet capable of manufacturing. Our authorities are not equipped to deal with such weapons. Their like has never been seen on the Patrian worlds before, and we are convinced that they are of alien origin. At this point, regrettably, I fear I must admit that there are certain dissident voices within our government speaking out in opposition to Federation membership for the Patrian Republics. Some of them have claimed it is the Federation that has been clandestinely supplying the rebels with these weapons."

"Nonsense!" McCoy said.

"As you were, Doctor," Kirk said softly, noting Jordan's warning glance.

McCoy frowned, but kept silent.

"I quite agree, Dr. McCoy," Elder Harkun said. "The majority of us do not believe the Federation would do any such thing. Even if most of us were not already convinced of your goodwill, supplying the rebels with energy weapons simply would not serve your interests. It would be illogical."

Mr. Spock nodded in agreement.

"We believe these weapons must be coming from the Klingons," Elder Harkun said. "The Federation and the Klingon Empire are in active opposition to one another, is this not correct?"

"We have been at war for many years," Jordan replied. "The Federation stands for a union of mutual, voluntary cooperation between its member worlds. The Klingon Empire stands for conquest. We are currently engaged in a mutual ceasefire, while negotiations for a lasting truce have been proceeding. However, there is reason to believe that the Klingons are not sincerely interested in a lasting truce, merely a temporary ceasefire that will serve their immediate needs."

"I think I begin to understand," Elder Harkun said slowly. "Your agreement for a temporary cessation of hostilities allows the Klingons to concentrate their attention elsewhere while these truce negotiations are proceeding. And we are the ones caught in the middle. If our negotiations do not lead to Federation membership for the Patrian Republics, then the Klingons shall seek to add us to their empire. If the Federation should attempt to intervene, then it shall be guilty of breaking the ceasefire agreement. And if the Federation does not intervene, then there is nothing to prevent the Klingons from attacking us with their vastly superior weapons."

"I would describe that as an astute and accurate analysis of the situation, Elder Harkun," Jordan said. "It would certainly seem to be in the Klingons' interest to disrupt our negotiations and add to your internal instability."

"Yes, I can see it would," Elder Harkun said. "The question is, how is such a situation governed under your Prime Directive?"

"If the Klingons are, indeed, supplying energy weapons to a terrorist faction in your society," Jordan replied, "then clearly, your culture has already been interfered with. Under such circumstances the Prime Directive would allow Federation involvement only insofar as to restore the status quo."

"Then that means you can help us?" Elder Harkun asked anxiously.

"As a political delegate, I am not empowered to speak for the Federation in this particular regard without further instructions," Jordan replied. "However, I believe that Captain Kirk is." He turned to look directly at Kirk.

Kirk glanced at Jordan quickly, but the ambassador's expression was completely neutral. There was no hint of how he should proceed. Lacking any hint from Jordan, he decided to go by the book.

"What the ambassador means, Elder Harkun," Kirk said, "is that Starfleet regulations allow for a contingency where Starfleet officers may act to prevent such interference, providing a formal request for assistance has been made, and, of course, that irrefutable proof of such interference has been demonstrated."

"I understand," Elder Harkun said. "Commander Anjor?"

The Patrian commander signaled to a crewman stationed at the door. The crewman opened the door, spoke to someone outside, and a moment later two other crewmen entered, each carrying a case. They laid the cases down on the table and opened them, revealing a collection of weapons that were instantly recognizable to the men of the *Enterprise*.

"These were confiscated in a raid on a rebel storehouse by our law enforcement officials on Patria One," Elder Harkun said.

"Klingon disruptors," Kirk said, staring at the weapons. He reached out and picked one up, examining it. "Still fully charged," he added, passing the disruptor to Spock so that his first officer could make an official confirmation in the report. He glanced at Jordan once again, but still saw no clue in his expression as to how he should proceed. Jordan was apparently leaving this one up to him.

"Well, so much for Klingon sincerity," Kirk said to the others. "They wouldn't dare act openly so long as the Federation and the Patrian Republics are in negotiations, so instead they supply weapons to the Patrian terrorists in an effort to disrupt their government and cause the negotiations to collapse."

"This puts things in a different light," Ambassador Jordan said, keeping his tone carefully neutral. "I shall have to report this to the Federation council as soon as possible. In the meantime, Captain Kirk, under the provisions of Starfleet regulations governing the prevention of cultural interference, I would like to request that you assemble an investigative team to work with the Patrian authorities and determine all the facts of this situation."

"With your permission, Ambassador," Kirk said, "I will personally take charge of the team, and I will be joined by the officers present, with the exception of Dr. McCoy and Mr. Scott, who will take command of the *Enterprise* in my absence."

"Jim, I'm coming along," McCoy said. "This will be the first time humans have ever set foot on Patria, and there are health considerations involved here. After all, someone's got to come along in case you get the sniffles or something."

"Good point," Jordan said, nodding. "Very well, then. I shall inform the Federation council of our decision regarding this matter and await further instructions. In the meantime, we shall assist the Patrians in their investigation to the best of our ability."

"You have our grateful thanks, Ambassador Jordan," Elder Harkun said. "Captain Kirk, how soon can you and your officers be ready to meet with our authorities on Patria One?"

"Within the hour," Kirk replied. "With your indulgence, we shall return to our ship and change into our duty uniforms, and I shall make arrangements for our landing party to beam down to whatever location you deem appropriate. Additionally, my ship and its crew will stand by to provide whatever further assistance you may require. These weapons are getting through to your rebels somehow, and we will do whatever it takes to stop the shipments. The *Enterprise* can assist your vessels in patrolling this sector while the negotiations are proceeding."

"Excellent," Elder Harkun said. "I feel, now, that we may proceed with our talks in an atmosphere of mutual cooperation. Ambassador, with your permission, I shall take my leave now to communicate with my superiors on Patria One and advise them to anticipate the arrival of Captain Kirk and his party. If it is convenient, we may reconvene for the beginning of our formal talks within twenty-four of your hours."

"That would be fine, Elder Harkun," Ambassador Jordan said. "And it would give us both ample time to prepare and communicate with our respective superiors."

"Good," Harkun said. "Captain Kirk, you may expect to receive a communication from Commander Anjor shortly, with further instructions."

"We'll be standing by, sir," Kirk replied.

The reception broke up, and the crew of the *Enterprise,* along with the ambassador and Undersecretary Wing, returned to their ship.

As soon as they stepped off the transporter pads, Kirk turned to his officers. "Gentlemen," he said, "you have one hour. We'll meet back here." Then he turned to the ambassador. "I'd like a word with you in private, Bob."

"Of course," Jordan said, appearing distracted.

Kirk turned to the transporter chief and said, "Give us a few minutes, will you, Chief?"

"Aye, sir."

As soon as they were alone, Kirk turned to Jordan. "You didn't exactly give me any help back there."

"I thought you were doing fine," Jordan replied.

"But you might have given me some *hint* about how you wanted me to handle that," Kirk said with some exasperation. "A look, a nod, anything! This whole thing just went from a support effort for a diplomatic mission to active duty in a matter of minutes!"

"Which is exactly why I allowed you to pick up the ball and run with it," Jordan said. "I can appreciate your position, Jim. I went to the Academy. As a starship captain, I'm sure the very last thing you want is to have a Federation bureaucrat breathing down your neck. I have no desire to make things difficult for you. However, we are in a rather delicate position here, so let's just do this by the book, okay?"

"This sort of situation isn't exactly something that is covered by the book," Kirk said. "Suppose the Patrians want us to give them phasers? What then?"

"Well, in my current position, I don't really have the authority to make a decision of that sort," Jordan said. "I'd have to contact Federation Headquarters and consult with them. And that could take time. However, as the ranking Starfleet officer, you have considerably more latitude in that regard. I'll leave the decision up to you. As far as this investigation is concerned, I would like you to keep me advised of your progress with regular, daily reports. And if anything of significance should occur, I want to hear about it immediately. If I am not available, due to being engaged in talks with the Patrians, you may report to Secretary Wing. But I do want you to keep me posted."

"I'll do my best," Kirk said.

"I expect nothing less from you," Jordan replied with a smile. He moved toward the door, then stopped and turned around. "Oh, and one more thing, Jim. Good luck."

He left the transporter room, and the doors closed behind him. Kirk frowned. Maybe Jordan was just trying to allow him the maximum amount of latitude, as he had said, but on the other hand, what he'd just done was a perfect example of passing the buck. That did not sound like the Bob Jordan he knew. Perhaps he had misread the situation, but it seemed to Kirk that Jordan had thrown the whole thing into his lap. And that meant that if anything went wrong, Jordan could duck responsibility, and his own neck would be on the chopping block.

Kirk shook his head. No, he thought, it was just his old feelings about bureaucrats coming up again. He'd seen that sort of thing too many times before, but this was Bob Jordan, his old Academy roommate. He had been a Starfleet officer, and he didn't play those kinds of games.

Still, Kirk felt a nagging doubt as he left the transporter room and headed back to his quarters. This had just become a mission in which one wrong decision could have disastrous consequences. And Bob Jordan didn't seem to want to make decisions.

They all met in the transporter room an hour later, as scheduled. Mr. Spock, Dr. McCoy, and Mr. Chekov had changed into their duty uniforms, as had Kirk. They quickly performed a last minute check of their equipment, which included universal translators, tricorders, communicators, and phasers. As McCoy checked his weapon, he glanced at Kirk with a frown.

"Should we be taking phasers, Jim?" he asked. "After all, this is supposed to be a diplomatic mission."

"Good point," Kirk said. "We wouldn't want to ruffle anybody's feathers. However, we're supposed to be assisting in what is essentially a criminal investigation, and we were not asked to go unarmed. If the Klingons are involved, then there's a lot more to this than just diplomacy. We have no way of knowing what we may run into. If the Patrians object, we can always disarm."

"I would not like to give up my phaser if there's a chance that Klingons are around," Chekov said.

"Nor would I, Mr. Chekov," Spock said. "Our scanners do not report any Klingon power sources in the area, and our sensors have not picked up any Klingon life-form readings on the planet surface. Nevertheless, if we are going to be investigating terrorist activity, it would be prudent to take proper precautions."

"I agree," Kirk said. "Mr. Scott, the ship is yours. Take good care of her while I'm gone."

"You can count on that, sir," Scott replied emphatically.

They took their places on the transporter pads.

"Energize," Kirk said.

They materialized in what looked like a large briefing room. The walls were dark and there were no windows, but there were light panels set into the ceiling, giving off a subdued illumination. The floor was tiled in some sort of stonelike material, and there was a large, U-shaped table in the center of the room. Save for what appeared to be several large, metal sculptures placed around the room, there were no other decorations. Several Patrians were waiting, seated at the table, and as the men of the *Enterprise* materialized, they all rose to their feet.

"Welcome," said one of the Patrians, coming

around the table. "I am Mohr Jarum, Prime Minister of the Patrian Council of Advisors. Which of you is Captain Kirk?"

"I am, Prime Minister," Kirk said, stepping forward. He raised his hands in the Patrian greeting and bowed slightly. The prime minister returned the gesture, then held out his hand.

"Now, if you will allow me to greet you in your way?"

Kirk took his hand, noting that the talons were retracted, and shook it firmly.

"Allow me to present my officers, Prime Minister," Kirk said. "Commander Spock, my chief science officer and second-in-command; Ensign Pavel Chekov, ship's helmsman and assistant science officer; and Dr. Leonard McCoy, our chief medical officer."

"It is a pleasure to welcome you to Patria One, gentlemen," the prime minister said. "And may I, in turn, present our chief law enforcement officer, Commissioner Tohr Karsi, and one of our top criminal investigators, Lieutenant Joh Iano. You will be working with Lieutenant Iano on this investigation."

"Lieutenant," Kirk said, knowing those probably were not the exact titles, merely equivalents selected by the universal translators.

"Iano will suffice," the burly Patrian said in their own language. "I have some knowledge of your standard Terran, Captain."

"You seem to speak it very well," Kirk remarked, noting that he was clearly not of the same stamp as the others. He seemed more fit, and he had a firm, direct, no nonsense manner about him. He was about the same height as Kirk, but heavier, and most of that weight seemed to be muscle.

"I learn quickly," Iano replied.

"I suppose that would be an asset in your job," Kirk said.

"As in yours, no doubt," Iano said. He glanced at Spock. "You are different from the others."

"That is because I am not human," Spock replied. "I am a Vulcan."

"Forgive me, but I know nothing of your race," Iano said, gazing at Spock curiously.

"There is nothing to forgive," Spock replied. "I know very little of yours."

"A most logical reply," Iano said.

"You will find that Vulcans are nothing if not logical," McCoy said. "Unlike us humans, they do not display emotion."

"Very commendable," Iano said.

"Something tells me you two are going to get along," McCoy said wryly.

"Please, gentlemen, be seated," the prime minister said. They took their places around the table. "I do not know exactly how much Elder Harkun has told you, but we have prepared a presentation that should brief you on the situation we are facing. Commissioner?"

Karsi rose to his feet and took a small control unit of some sort from his pocket. He dimmed the lights with it, and a moment later a panel in the wall opposite the table slid aside to reveal a large monitor screen. The screen began to glow, and a second later an image of a city street scene appeared. It showed the site of what was obviously some sort of an explosion, probably only moments after it occurred. A building was damaged and in flames, people were shouting and running about, sirens were blaring, and wounded were being brought out of the building and tended to in the street. Except for the people, Kirk thought, it could have been a scene right out of Earth's history tapes.

"These images were recorded by a news crew," Karsi said, turning down the sound. "What you are looking at is the aftermath of an explosion right here in our capital city, in the heart of our business district, merely a short distance from where we sit. It occurred at midday, when the streets were at their most crowded. Twenty-seven people were killed in the blast, and more than twice that number were wounded. The victims were not government officials, but ordinary citizens."

"What caused the explosion?" Kirk asked.

"A bomb that was planted in the building, probably sometime during the early morning or the previous night," Karsi replied. "It was detonated by a timing device. Up until recently, it was the favorite weapon of the rebels, designed to cause terror among the citizenry and promote outrage against the government."

"A weapon of intimidation and coercion," Chekov said.

"Travel halfway across the universe," McCoy remarked softly, "and you only wind up coming right back where you started from."

"I beg your pardon?" Karsi said.

"We have had such incidents in our own history, as well, Commissioner," Kirk said, watching the screen grimly. "More than a few, I regret to say."

"What is the stated purpose of these rebels?" Spock asked.

"They have a number of grievances with our government," Karsi said, "but the latest concerns our contact with the Federation. They are opposed to the negotiations for Patrian membership in the Federation and maintain that it will bring about an end to Patrian independence. Shortly after it was reported that we had made contact with the Federation and had established subspace communications, they escalated their activities to an unprecedented level."

The image on the screen changed to that of a firefight taking place at night in the city streets. Kirk and the others stiffened as they watched. The Patrians were using some sort of projectile weapons, but the rebels who had them pinned down were firing disruptors, and with devastating effect.

"What you are seeing, gentlemen, is the only visual evidence we currently have on record of the new energy weapons being used by the rebels," Karsi said.

"Cossacks," Chekov said through gritted teeth as he watched the horribly one-sided battle.

"Our authorities responded to an anonymous report of a rebel storehouse at this location," Karsi noted. "It was a trap, and they walked right into an ambush. There was a news crew on the scene, and they recorded the entire incident. Note that no one in the news crew was fired upon, the better to ensure that our people would see this on their viewscreens at home. Note also the pinpoint accuracy of these energy weapons. These officers never stood a chance."

The men of the *Enterprise* watched in tense silence as, one by one, the Patrian police officers were killed. Their weapons were no match for the disruptors. The whole thing took no longer than about thirty seconds. They were caught in a deadly crossfire from the upper floors of three separate buildings. They never even saw who was firing at them.

The images on the screen faded and Karsi turned the lights back up. "That is what we are facing now, gentlemen," he said. "Our people are defenseless against such weapons. And what you have just seen is but one example of what we are now up against. There have been many more. So far, they have been confined to this city, which leads us to believe that the rebels may not have an extensive supply of these new weapons. However, if they should get more . . ." His voice trailed off, significantly.

"There are those in the Council who seem to be in sympathy with the rebels," the prime minister said, "at least insofar as our contact with the Federation is concerned. They are respected politicians, but they are distrustful of your motives. They are presently in the minority, but their influence seems to be growing and their voices are making themselves heard. Their arguments possess a certain logic, at least to those who are not in possession of all the facts. They claim that such terrible weapons have never been seen on Patria before and that, obviously, they are of alien manufacture. Where, they say, but from the Federation could the rebels have received such weapons? What further proof, they ask, is needed to demonstrate the hostile intentions of the Federation? They claim that under the guise of establishing diplomatic relations with us, the Federation is actually gathering intelligence that will enable them to subdue us, while secretly supplying weapons to the rebels in an effort to destabilize our government."

"That is not logical," Spock said. "If these rebels are opposed to contact with the Federation, then why would the Federation wish to supply them with weapons?"

"I quite agree, Mr. Spock," the prime minister said. "It is not logical. However, when emotions are running high, our people do not think logically. We have reached a major turning point in our history—contact with other intelligent beings. That is the sort of thing that frightens many people. I, myself, have tried to point out the contradictions in the arguments of the opposition, but they merely reply that the rebels are only seeking to confuse the issue. They claim that the rebels' stand against contact with the Federation is nothing more than obfuscation, that they are actually in league with the Federation because you have promised them positions of power when our government finally falls and you take over."

"Paranoia's hard to argue with," McCoy said.

"There is, perhaps, one argument we could make that would resolve the issue," the prime minister said. "And that is if you were to supply us with energy weapons of our own that we could use against these disruptors, as you call them."

There it is, Kirk thought. Just as he'd expected. And Jordan had left this hot potato sitting squarely in his lap. Well, he wasn't prepared to make that kind of decision, at least not yet. It was just too risky.

"I understand your concern, Prime Minister," Kirk said, choosing his words carefully, "but that is not something I could do under the current circumstances. You must understand that we are dealing with a highly sensitive issue here."

"I see," the prime minister said, obviously disappointed. "I understand your position, Captain Kirk, but unfortunately, it plays right into the hands of the opposition. You have your orders, of course, but they will claim that it is merely a Federation ploy to coerce us into joining you and thereby subjecting ourselves to your authority."

"But that's not how the Federation works," McCoy protested. "Each of the member worlds retains its own sovereign form of government, with an equal voice in the Federation council. The Federation is a democratic union, not a dictatorship."

"I believe you, Dr. McCoy," the prime minister replied. "My problem is, how do I convince those who do not?"

"The member worlds of the Federation enjoy the benefits of shared technology, Prime Minister," Kirk said. "And those benefits go beyond mere weapons technology. However, the question of Patrian membership in the Federation is one that will be resolved by the diplomats, and not by us. Our role here is to establish the facts of the situation and assist you in your investigation to the best of our abilities, within the limits of our authority and yours. We cannot give you weapons, but we will help you discover how the rebels are getting theirs."

"If you would do that, Captain," the prime minister said, "then it would certainly help prove that the Federation's motives are benevolent, rather than imperialistic." He rose to his feet and offered Kirk his hand. "I will leave the matter entirely in your hands, Captain Kirk."

"Just a moment, Prime Minister," Kirk said. "I'm not sure I understand. We were requested to *assist* your authorities."

"I think it has been amply demonstrated that the current crisis is beyond our ability to solve, Captain," the prime minister replied. "I have, therefore, determined that the best way the Federation could assist us in this matter would be for you to take charge of this investigation personally."

"With all due respect, Prime Minister," Kirk said, "this is a Patrian *internal* matter. As an officer of the Federation, I would really have no proper jurisdiction—"

"Captain," the Prime Minister interrupted, "I am *granting* you the proper jurisdiction, so you may rest assured on that account. Ambassador Jordan has assured me of your complete cooperation, and you are clearly more qualified to deal with this situation than anyone in our administration. You have had experience with these sort of weapons before, and you obviously know and understand a great deal more about the Klingons than we do."

"That may be true, Prime Minister," Kirk said, "but as an outsider, I have no knowledge of your laws and—"

"According to our laws, this is a police matter, but the solution clearly calls for a military man," the prime minister replied. "Regrettably, there is no one in our military even remotely qualified to conduct an investigation of this nature. You, on the other hand, possess all the necessary qualifications. And I think having a Starfleet officer in charge of this investigation will provide a dramatic demonstration of the sincerity of the Federation's motives in this matter."

Yes, and if we fail, Kirk thought, then the blame will rest with us, instead of your administration. It makes for a very convenient political solution. You're covered, either way.

"I will leave you to discuss the details of your investigation with Commissioner Karsi and Lieutenant Iano," Prime Minister Jarum said. "If there is anything you need to help you in your task, Captain, please do not hesitate to ask. You shall have my full authority behind you. We have done all that we could, to the best of our ability. We now place ourselves in your capable hands. If the Federation can help us solve this problem, then doubtless it will have a salutory effect on our negotiations. Thank you, gentlemen," he said, holding up his hands in the Patrian salutation, "and good fortune to you."

As he left, McCoy turned to Kirk and said, in a low voice, "I think we've just had a demonstration of the Patrian equivalent of passing the buck."

"Yes," Kirk said softly. "He's just dumped the responsibility for the whole thing squarely in our laps. And it looks as if we're stuck with it."

Commissioner Karsi turned to the men of the *Enterprise.* "Gentlemen, I shall issue orders instructing all my officers to assist you and Lieutenant Iano to the best of their abilities," he said. "Lieutenant Iano is authorized to speak in my name in any manner relating to this investigation. Are you carrying any weapons?"

Kirk removed his phaser from his belt. "These are called phasers, Commissioner," he said. "They are energy weapons, in principle not unlike disruptors. They possess both lethal and nonlethal settings. However, if you would prefer that we not carry them—"

"No, retain them, by all means," Karsi said. "If you should encounter any of the rebels who are armed with these disruptors, they shall doubtless serve you far better than any of our weapons could. As to the authorization for your use of them, my interpretation of the prime minister's remarks is that it will be left up to your own discretion. I shall leave it to Lieutenant

Iano to advise you on matters pertaining to our laws. He has my complete confidence. Now, if you would excuse me, I have other pressing matters to attend to. Gentlemen, it has been a great honor and a privilege to meet you, and I would personally like to thank you all for your help in this matter. I am confident that it will advance the cause of mutual cooperation between the Federation and the Patrian Republics."

Karsi gave them a slight bow and left the room.

"Well," Iano said gruffly, speaking to them in their own language, "so much for the formalities. It looks like you're in charge, Captain. Shall we get to work?"

Chapter Three

THE LIFT WAS NOT ENCLOSED; it was merely an open platform that rose up quickly in the smoothly finished shaft. The mechanism, as near as they could tell, appeared to be magnetic. As they ascended, Kirk questioned Iano about the rebel terrorists.

"What can you tell us about the organization of these people?" he asked.

"Not very much, I regret to say," Iano replied. "We have managed to capture some of the rebels, but few allow themselves to be taken alive. They are quite willing to die for their cause. We do know that their organization is structured in small groups, so that the members of one group have contact only with the groups immediately above and below them, and perhaps one or two others at the same level. If the integrity of one group is compromised, it is immediately cut off from all the others, and the groups with which it was in contact are quickly dispersed and reorganized."

"The cell structure," Chekov said, nodding. "It is similar to the manner in which anarchist groups were organized in Earth's ancient history."

"Anarchist?" Iano said.

"The word is derived from *an archos,* in the old Terran Greek language, meaning 'without a leader,'" Spock explained. "Specifically, the term 'anarchy' describes an absence of government, usually accompanied by political confusion and disorder. Typically, anarchist movements have been revolutionary in nature, and often violent."

Iano nodded. "That would be an accurate description of the rebels," he said. "They are fanatics, dedicated to the dissolution of our government and the complete collapse of social order."

"The prime minister mentioned that these rebels had a number of grievances against your government," Kirk said. "That is, aside from its contact with the Federation."

Iano made a sort of hissing noise that Kirk took as a sound of derision. "They dislike authority," he said. "They are opposed to the police and to a strong central government. They claim that the government has become oppressive, and invasive of the individual rights of citizens, and their stated position calls for a return to the decentralized, local governments of the past. In truth, they are simply criminals who seek to dignify their lawless activities with political rhetoric."

The lift stopped and the doors opened onto the roof of the building, which served as a landing pad for the police vehicles. A number of the sleek-looking, steel-gray craft were parked on either side of the roof, in diagonal formation. Iano took a remote control unit out of his jacket pocket and clicked it twice. One of the craft's engines started with a muted whine, and it slowly rolled out of formation where it was parked. Iano clicked the control again and it stopped, then its gull-wing doors swung open with a muted whine.

"We're going in that?" McCoy asked, eyeing the craft uncertainly.

"We are not going to find the rebels at police headquarters, Dr. McCoy," Iano said. "Our work is out there, in the streets." He pointed out over the city.

The sun was setting and night was falling on the city. The rooftop of the building afforded them a panoramic view of the sprawling Patrian capital. In many ways it resembled an Earth city circa the late twenty-second century. The Patrians had a penchant for constructing tall, cylindrical buildings resembling gigantic tubes. Many of these were surmounted with ornamental spires of various designs, others were flat-roofed, while still others were domed. Some were constructed in tight clusters with interconnecting passageways between them, while others stood alone, scratching at the sky, or rose above a collection of encircling buildings of lesser, varying height, giving them the aspect of smooth, crystalline formations.

"It is a beautiful city," Chekov said as he gazed out across the capital. The lights were coming on in most of the buildings, not only interior lights, but exterior lights as well, in different colors of green, blue, red, and orange. The entire city seemed to glow like an aurora borealis.

"Like most cities, its beauty is only skin deep," Iano said. "Perhaps men such as you can never truly feel at home in such an environment. Here, there are boundaries, while out there, in space"—he looked up at the sky—"there are no limits."

Kirk glanced at Iano with surprise. The policeman's words had closely echoed his own thinking. "I suppose you could look at it that way," he said, "but there are always limits. Even in space. And where none exist, people tend to make their own."

"It has been my experience that people are better off when limits are imposed upon them," Iano said. "People need the limits of the law, without which they would tear one another to pieces. We may be from different worlds, Kirk, and yet we do have at least one thing in common. We are both custodians of the law."

Kirk smiled. "You may have a point, though I must admit, I've never really thought of myself as a policeman."

"Then perhaps you should," Iano said, beckoning them toward the police vehicle.

They got inside and sat down in the contoured, individual seats. It felt not much different from sitting in one of the *Enterprise's* shuttlecraft, except that the police flier was smaller and narrower, about half the width of a shuttlecraft and roughly two-thirds the length. The seats had not been designed for human anatomy, but the Patrians were humanoid and had roughly similar dimensions, so they were not uncomfortable for Kirk and the others. Iano touched a button on the console and lowered the gull-wing doors. He grasped the joystick and the whine of the engines grew louder. Then he pulled back on the stick and the flier gently rose into the air, hovering, its wheels automatically retracting. Banking sharply, Iano flew out over the side of the roof, and the craft described a graceful arc out and away from the building as it picked up speed, swooping down toward the crowded streets below.

"This reminds me of the old aerobatic fliers we had back at the Academy," Kirk said, smiling at the memory as Iano leveled off about forty feet above street level, flying between the buildings.

"Well, I could do with a bit less of the aerobatics," McCoy grumbled as Iano banked the flier around a corner so sharply, it seemed to stand on edge.

"Forgive me, Doctor," Iano said, as he leveled off at about thirty feet. "Are you experiencing discomfort?"

"Oh, nothing serious," McCoy replied in a grumpy tone. "I just think I left my stomach back there somewhere."

"You'll have to excuse my chief medical officer," Kirk said. "He never feels entirely comfortable unless there's something he can complain about. Isn't that right, Bones?"

McCoy gave him a sour look. "I'm a doctor, not a stunt pilot," he said gruffly.

"My apologies, Bones," Iano said. "I will try to avoid turning so quickly in the future."

Kirk smiled at Iano's appropriation of his nickname for McCoy. He glanced at McCoy out of the corner of his eye and saw him frowning, but he did not correct the Patrian.

"I would appreciate that, Lieutenant," McCoy said. "Some of us aren't so sensitive to the discomfort of others."

"Surely, you can't be referring to me?" Kirk said. He raised his eyebrows and feigned a look of utter astonishment that McCoy should even make such a suggestion.

Iano gave a slight snort, which they interpreted as a chuckle. "You two remind me of the way my partner and I sound when . . ." His voice trailed off.

"Is something wrong?" Kirk said.

Iano made a soft, brief hissing noise. "Sometimes, I still forget," he said. "My partner was killed recently."

"I'm sorry," Kirk said, sincerely. "How did it happen?"

"The rebels," Iano replied, his voice laced with bitterness. "He was killed in an ambush. I saw him die. They used their new weapons. He was completely vaporized. There was nothing left of him."

"A tragic loss," Chekov said sympathetically. "It sounds as if the two of you were very close."

"He was my partner," Iano replied simply, as if that said it all. And, in effect, it did. Each of the *Enterprise* officers knew exactly what that meant.

"And you have sought no replacement?" Spock asked.

"I prefer to work alone now," Iano replied curtly. Then he quickly added, "However, the department is certainly grateful for whatever help the Federation may provide."

Kirk and Spock exchanged glances.

"In other words, we were sort of crammed down your throat," McCoy said, articulating what the others thought.

"Crammed down my throat," Iano repeated. "An accurate metaphor."

"You realize this wasn't exactly our idea," McCoy said with a grimace.

"What the doctor means," Kirk quickly added, "is

that we're perfectly willing to help in any way we can, but it was never our intention to take control of this investigation."

"Please do not misunderstand me," Iano said. "I was not implying that the Federation was forcing itself upon us. It is just that I would have preferred to handle this case myself."

"I can certainly understand how you feel," Kirk said, "but the impression we received from the prime minister was that the Patrian authorities were in over their heads."

"I see," Iano said. "Captain, you are correct in your impression. There are, indeed, those in our government who believe that we are 'in over our heads,' as you say. However, there are also those who believe that we Patrians should handle our own problems."

"No one is suggesting that you shouldn't," Kirk replied. "The whole point of the Prime Directive is to allow cultures the right to solve their own problems and make their own choices."

"Only in this case, it looks as if the Klingons are trying to make some of those choices for you," McCoy added.

"And that places the burden of counterbalancing their influence on the Federation," Iano said. "So where does that leave your Prime Directive? It would seem to be effectively neutralized by the involvement of the Klingons. To effect a balance, the Federation must become involved, and that leaves us Patrians caught right in the middle. We become merely another battleground in the war between the Federation and the Klingon Empire. So much for our right to choose our own destiny."

"The situation is, indeed, regrettable," Spock said,

"but the blame does not rest with any shortcoming of the Prime Directive. The Klingons have no respect for the sovereignty of any culture but their own. They are not now, and never have been, bound by the Prime Directive. The Federation has the latitude to intervene where the autonomy of another culture has been threatened, providing a request for such assistance has been made. However, if your government were to determine that it did not desire the involvement of the Federation, their wishes would be respected. Unfortunately, that would still leave you with the problem of what to do about the Klingons."

"Then it doesn't seem as if we have any choice, does it?" Iano said. "The Federation will respect our right to determine our own destiny, but if we exercise that right and choose not to join the Federation, we stand the risk of being conquered by the Klingons. And if we join the Federation, then the Patrian Republics become only a small part of a much larger body, merely a voice in a chorus."

"A *democratic* chorus," Kirk said, "where each voice, no matter how small or how large, bears equal weight. And where no one voice stands alone."

"But what if someone *wants* to stand alone?" Iano asked. "What then?"

"If that is what the Patrian Republics want," Kirk said, "then the Federation will respect that. But I'm afraid the Klingons won't."

"Where exactly are we going?" McCoy asked.

"Accommodations have been arranged for you," Iano said. "I thought, perhaps, that you'd like to see them and make certain that they're suitable before we proceed with the investigation. And at the same time, I can arrange for you to have access to all the reports of this investigation to date, so that you can familiarize yourselves with the situation."

"That would be very helpful," Kirk said. "You realize, of course, that we shall have to be returning to our ship from time to time."

"I had assumed as much," Iano replied. "Your quarters can serve as a base of operations for you. The building has been designated a legation, headquarters for yourselves and the Federation ambassador while you are on Patria One. You will be able to use it as a point from which you can transport to your ship. The grounds are protected to the best of our ability, and several police officers have been assigned to function in full-time support positions at the legation for the duration of your stay here. There shall always be someone on duty to serve as liaison between you and the department."

"That's very thoughtful, Lieutenant," Kirk said. "Please convey our appreciation to Commissioner Karsi."

"I shall," Iano replied.

"I would like to detail several members of my crew to work with the Patrian officers who have been assigned as our liaisons," Kirk said.

"As you wish," Iano said. "Quarters will be prepared for them if additional space is needed. However, I believe you will find that the legation can accommodate your personnel quite adequately. That building up ahead is where you will be staying."

Rising up ahead of them in a large, central city square was a tower complex that loomed high over the surrounding buildings. It took up an entire city block and was surrounded by well-manicured gardens and miniature parks. The walls of the large, circular building were constructed of a glassy, rosy-hued substance. Iano banked around it, gaining altitude as he climbed toward the landing port on the roof of the tower.

"My superiors are anxious that you be made as comfortable as possible during your stay here," Iano said. "This is one of the finest residence complexes in the city. I believe your word for it would be . . . hotel. The top three floors have been set aside for your personal accommodations, and the two floors beneath them have been prepared as security areas for our police personnel."

The quarters prepared for them as their base of operations were on a par with the most luxurious accommodations found in the Federation's most exclusive resorts. They consisted of several large, multiroom luxury suites, one of which had been completely refurbished as a large and fully equipped conference room, with communications and computer consoles as well as furnishings specially designed to accommodate humans. The Patrians, it seemed, had gone all out and spared no expense. Iano explained that the entire staff had been subjected to an exhaustive security check, and that no one could get in or out of the building without passing a number of security checkpoints.

They've gone to a lot of trouble to make us feel secure, thought Kirk. And the fact that they felt the need to go to all that trouble said a great deal about the situation they were facing.

"I'll inform the staff of your arrival," Iano said, "and see to it that everything is properly prepared for you. I shall also go and see that everything is in readiness on the lower floors of the legation, where your liaison personnel will be headquartered. In the meantime, perhaps you'd care to examine the facilities and let me know if there's anything else you may require. I will return shortly."

"Well, I must say, they certainly are hospitable," McCoy said after Iano left. "We *each* get one of these suites?"

"It certainly looks that way," Kirk said. "However, I have a feeling we're going to earn them."

"Captain," Spock said, "have you noticed anything about Lieutenant Iano that struck you as a bit . . . unusual?"

"What do you mean, Spock?" Kirk asked. "Unusual in what way?"

"His knowledge of idiomatic English, for example," Spock replied.

"I think it's quite good," Kirk said.

"Indeed, Captain, it is excellent," Spock said. "We have observed that the Patrians learn quickly. Commander Anjor's command of standard Terran was more than reasonably fluent, considering the relatively short amount of time he had in which to study it. However, Lieutenant Iano's fluency is not only markedly superior to that of Commander Anjor's, but seems to be improving rather rapidly."

Kirk frowned. "I'm not sure I get your point, Spock. What are you suggesting?"

"Merely that there may be more to Lieutenant Iano than meets the eye. He seemed puzzled at first by several figures of speech that were used in our conversation, and yet he used a figure of speech himself, just moments later, when he said that the Patrian Republics would be no more than 'a voice in the chorus' if they joined the Federation."

"Yes, I seem to remember that, now that you mention it," Kirk said.

"So? What's so unusual about that?" McCoy asked. "He's merely concerned about the future of his society and his culture. That seems perfectly normal."

"Yes, Doctor, it does indeed," Spock said. "However, that is also quite beside the point. The point is that the figure of speech, 'a voice in the chorus,' harkens back to classical Greek drama, something for which Lieutenant Iano would have no frame of reference. If the language programs transmitted to the Patrians were not deficient as to such things as figures of speech and cultural idiom, than why would Lieutenant Iano act as if they were? And if they were, indeed, deficient in that regard, then where would Lieutenant Iano have learned the reference for 'a voice in the chorus'?"

McCoy frowned. "I hadn't thought of that," he admitted. "He did pull that one right out of the air, didn't he?"

"And there is another interesting aspect to Lieutenant Iano's speech," Spock said. "When we first met him, he spoke standard Terran very formally and correctly, without employing any contractions. And yet, after only a short while with us, he is using contractions fluently. It is, of course, possible that he has a gift for languages, but he does seem to be learning at a rather unusual rate."

"In other words, you think he knows a lot more than he admits to," Kirk said.

"But . . . if that were the case, why would he bother to conceal it?" Chekov asked, puzzled. "It makes no sense. What purpose would be served in his misleading us?"

"That, Mr. Chekov, is a very good question," Kirk said.

"Why don't we just put it to him bluntly?" McCoy asked.

"No, I don't think so, Bones," Kirk said. "At least, not yet. We're in a somewhat delicate position here. We have to consider not only our immediate problem, but the larger question of Patrian membership in the Federation. It seems there are elements of Patrian society who are opposed to it. We don't want to do anything that could give them any ammunition."

"But if Iano's being less than honest with us . . ." McCoy said.

"We don't really know that for a fact," Kirk said. "But even if it's true, put yourself in his position. I don't think he really wants our help on this investigation. You hit the nail right on the head when you said we were crammed down his throat by his superiors. We don't like it much when bureaucrats try to tell us how to do our jobs, why should Iano be any different? And can we blame him if he's not? We're being cautious because we don't know very much about him. Isn't he in exactly the same position?"

"So then . . . what are we supposed to do?" Chekov asked.

"We'll just have to play it by ear," Kirk replied, shrugging. "Officially, we may be running the show, but he's got a much bigger stake in this than we do. It's personal for him. He lost a partner. We all know what that means. We have to remember that there's more at stake here than the matter of Klingons supplying the Patrian rebels with disruptors. The Patrians will be watching the way we handle this. While the negotiations are proceeding, they'll be judging the Federation by what we do and how we do it."

"Well, that's a comforting thought," McCoy said dryly. "Nothing like a little pressure, is there?"

"If this is pressure," Chekov said, indicating their luxurious quarters, "I think I could handle it."

Iano returned a few moments later with two Patrian police officers. He performed the introductions. "Officers Jalo and Inal will be in charge of liaison support during your stay here," he said. "They will be quartered three floors below you, along with their support team, and one of them will always be on duty. They both speak standard Terran with reasonable fluency, and will be able to provide you with whatever you require."

"I'd like to bring some of my own people down to work with them," Kirk said.

"Certainly, Captain," Iano replied. "At your convenience."

Kirk snapped open his communicator. "Kirk to *Enterprise*. Come in."

"Scott here, Captain," came the reply. "Go ahead, sir."

"Scotty, I'd like you to detail two crewmen to beam down to these coordinates to work with the Patrians as liaison support. I think a yeoman and a communications specialist should fill the bill."

"Aye, Captain. Should they be armed?"

"Issue phasers, Mr. Scott. And you might have them bring along some universal translators, just in case. The Patrians will be able to supply them with whatever else they may require." He looked around at the suite and smiled. "I think they'll find it relatively painless duty. Have them beamed down to these coordinates as soon as possible."

"Aye, sir, right away."

"Kirk out." He snapped his communicator shut. "Our people should be transporting down in just a little while," he told Iano.

"Officer Jalo will stand by to brief them when they arrive."

"Oh?" McCoy said. "Are we going someplace?"

"We have a job to do," Iano said. He turned to Kirk. "That is, *I* have a job to do. It is, of course, *your* decision, Captain."

He isn't used to having someone else running the show, Kirk thought. And he doesn't like it one damn bit. "If you have a course of action in mind, Lieutenant, by all means, let's pursue it."

"I was planning to 'follow up a lead,' as I believe you humans would put it," Iano said. "I could easily go by myself, but I would be pleased to have you and your officers accompany me. If we encounter rebels armed with disruptors, we may be grateful for the numbers. Especially since your people are armed with phasers."

"You think there's a chance we could be attacked?" McCoy asked as they headed for the lift.

"I would be very much surprised if the rebels were not aware of your presence here by now," Iano replied. "We have taken security precautions, but we should remain on our guard whenever we are away from here. Officers Jalo and Inal will have all the records of the investigation available for your people as soon as they arrive. In the meantime, I will brief you as best I can while we proceed."

As they made their way up to the roof, Iano quickly filled them in.

"At the moment, I am seeking a suspect named Rak Jolo," Iano said. "According to my information, he is known to frequent a gaming club known as the Arena. I had intended to visit the club and make inquiries. Unless, of course, you prefer another course of action."

"There's no need to tiptoe around our sensibilities, Lieutenant," Kirk said as they reached the roof and began walking toward the police flier. "You're the one who's been doing all the work on this case. We still have a lot of catching up to do."

"By gaming club," McCoy said, "are we talking about gambling?"

"Gambling?" Iano said. "Ah, you mean games of chance in which wagers are placed. Yes, I believe you could call this a gambling club, although I do not know if it would correspond with the sort of gambling you have in your culture. But you will see for yourself. And you may even place a wager or two, if you like."

"This ought to be interesting," McCoy said with a grin. "What sort of games are they? Cards? Dice? Computer simulations?"

"Life and death," Iano said as they got into the flier. "They are games of life and death."

Iano piloted the flier in silence, banking gracefully and soaring between the buildings. Other airborne vehicles moved past them, both above and below, and it became evident that the colored lights on the buildings marked traffic lanes. Some of the airborne vehicles below them were larger than the others, and

Kirk guessed that these were slower-moving public transports, while others were small, one-person skimmers as well as larger vehicles, flying above them in the faster lanes.

Even with the lights on the buildings marking off the traffic lanes at various levels and changing color to indicate when movement from one lane to another was permissable, Kirk could not see how so many vehicles could occupy such crowded airspace without collisions. Perhaps each individual vehicle was equipped with some sort of collision avoidance system, a computerized tracking program that sensed the momentum and direction of vehicles in its vicinity and automatically incorporated the data into the navigation system. Either that or the Patrians possessed astonishingly quick reactions, for they saw no accidents.

The traffic had grown considerably heavier now. They were in a much more congested part of the city. Kirk couldn't help but wonder if any of the vehicles they passed in the air traffic lanes carried Patrian terrorists, and if those terrorists might be carrying disruptors. One good shot was all that it would take. It was one thing to face a Klingon battle cruiser in space, even if the ship was cloaked—because they had to decloak before they could fire, and there were ways of spotting a cloaked ship—but this was something else again.

Here, they were not in space, but in a teeming city, surrounded by thousands of innocent civilians, any one of whom could be a terrorist. Any one of the airborne vehicles they passed, or that passed them, could suddenly draw even with them and fire without warning, then lose itself into the crowded traffic patterns. Any civilian on the street could open up with a disruptor at a police vehicle skimming overhead, then disappear into the crowd. For the first time, Kirk began to get an appreciation of just what the Patrian authorities were up against. And now, just what he and his officers were up against. It was an extremely unsettling feeling. That was the true horror of terrorism, he thought. It wore an ordinary face, and it hid among other ordinary faces, and it could strike at any time.

Iano slowed as he banked around a building and descended to about fifteen feet above the teeming street level, slowing down considerably so they could get a good look at their surroundings.

"This is the oldest and most crowded section of the city," he said. "And also the most crime-ridden. This part of the city never sleeps. It's here that the rebels have been the most active. They've struck at targets of opportunity throughout the capital, but always in a radius from this area. The rebels find a haven here among the other criminals. An assassin's favorite environment is always a crowd. My job—perhaps I should say *our* job—will be to force them out into the light of day. And I think your presence here may accomplish that very thing."

He pushed forward on the stick and the flier began to descend.

Chapter Four

THE SUN HAD GONE DOWN several hours ago, but the streets were bright as day. Everywhere they looked there was a symphony of colored lights. Hundreds of elaborate signs flashed invitations to enter dozens of different emporiums. Raucous, amplified, pre-recorded messages blared their pitches out into the night. It was a cacophony of sights and smells and sounds, reminiscent of some of the Federation's wildest and most wide-open cities, such as Bangkok, Bradbury City, New York, or Elysium.

Traffic in the air lanes was heavy, and pedestrians thronged the streets below. McCoy was startled as a formation of what at first glance looked like guided missiles swooped down past the police flier on his side, practically brushing it with their tail fins.

"What in the world!" He recoiled instinctively, taken aback at what seemed a near miss by a flock of

photon torpedoes, but then he abruptly realized that there were helmeted riders aboard those missile-shaped rockets, tucked in tightly behind small windshields as they darted in and out of traffic alarmingly. "Don't people believe in speed limits around here?" he asked irritably.

"Most people do," Iano replied. "However, the police are generally exempt."

"Those were police?" McCoy asked.

"We call them suicide squads," Iano said. "They are special volunteers. We have had a number of terrorist attacks in which the rebels have employed rocket sleds. They are far more maneuverable than our pursuit fliers, and as a result, make it easier for the rebels to escape. The suicide squads maintain a visible presence in the city, in an effort to discourage such tactics. It is difficult to fire a disruptor and avoid high speed pursuit at the same time. On the other hand, police officers on rocket sleds make very tempting targets to rebels on the ground. And those sleds are dangerous in heavy traffic. The collision avoidance systems of the other vehicles often do not register them. It takes a rather special breed of police officer to volunteer for such duty. They tend to be somewhat reckless, and they often enjoy baiting the rest of us, as you've just seen. It is all a game to them. Some games, of course, are more dangerous than others."

"Such as these life or death games you were talking about?" Kirk asked.

"The most interesting games are always the ones with the highest stakes," Iano replied.

"Exactly what are we talking about here?" McCoy asked. "Surely, you don't mean the stakes are *literally* life or death?"

"That is the most intense sort of competition, Bones," Iano said. "If you win, you could become very wealthy. If you lose, you could die."

"What the hell kind of game is *that?*" McCoy asked.

"You do not have such sports on your Federation worlds?" Iano asked.

"I certainly wouldn't call them sports," McCoy replied.

"In all fairness, Doctor," Spock said, "I feel I should point out that while blood sports may be somewhat controversial, they do exist on Federation worlds. Earth's history, for example, shows evidence of many different kinds of blood sports, from the gladiatorial games of ancient Rome and the jousting competitions of medieval England to the *buskashi* games of the Afghan tribesmen and the *kumite* martial arts competitions of the Orient, among which death matches were not unknown. To this day, the sport of boxing remains quite popular, and it could certainly fall under the category of a blood sport."

"Blood sport," Iano repeated, slowing down and guiding the flier toward the street below. "An interesting term. And I suppose it would apply to such games as we are about to witness. These games are also somewhat controversial, but they are not illegal. At least, not yet. If they were outlawed, then I, for one, would not complain. The games are often troublesome. Still, there is much support for them. And they bring in a great deal of revenue."

"You mean you tax them?" Chekov asked.

"There are licensing and registration fees for the game masters, and competition fees and waiver charges for the players," Iano replied. "The government also takes a percentage of the bets, though private wagers escape the tax, as it would be practically impossible to regulate them. Rather large sums of money often change hands on private wagers as a result, though they are technically illegal."

"Fascinating," Spock said.

"It sounds a lot like the procedures used with betting on thoroughbred horse races back on Earth," Kirk said.

"Horse races?" Iano asked as the flier came to a stop. "Ah, yes. You are referring to the large, domesticated mammals once used for transportation on your world, and now bred primarily for sport and private ownership as pets. We have an animal that functions in a rather similar role, a large, bipedal reptile called a *razzik*. However, you will not see any *razziks* in the city. There is not enough space for them here."

Iano opened the doors of the flier and they stepped out into the street. When they had all exited the vehicle, Iano closed the gull-wing doors and activated an electronic force field that would protect the flier while it was unattended.

"When we return, take care that you do not approach the flier until I have deactivated the force field," Iano cautioned them as he put away his remote control unit. "It could cause serious injury."

"Aren't you worried about somebody brushing up against the flier accidentally?" McCoy asked, noting the heavy pedestrian traffic on the street around them.

"No," Iano said. "It is a police vehicle. People should know to keep away from it."

As Iano started across the street, McCoy glanced at the others. "Charming fellow, isn't he?" he said.

"Well, I don't think he's any happier being stuck with us than we are being stuck with him," Kirk said as they started after him. "But like it or not, we need him. We'll just have to make the best of it until we find out how those Klingon disruptors are reaching the rebel terrorists."

"That could take a long time," Chekov said dubiously.

"Think positive, Mr. Chekov," Kirk said. "The rebels are against contact with the Federation. Violently so. That means there's a good chance our presence here will force their hand."

Iano was waiting for them at the entrance to what was apparently a gaming house. "Your presence here will undoubtedly create considerable interest," he said as they approached, almost as if he were replying to Kirk's remarks, though he couldn't possibly have heard them with all the noise in the street.

"Yes, we've already noticed," Kirk said, looking around. They were attracting a great deal of attention. A crowd was gathering, and people were staring and pointing at them excitedly. "It's one of the things I'm counting on," he added. "The assassination of a Federation starship captain and his officers could create a serious diplomatic incident, one that certainly would gain the rebels a great deal of notoriety."

"In other words, we make a target that's hard to resist," McCoy said with a grimace.

"I had considered that as well," Iano said. "However, I would not wish to expose you to any unnecessary risk."

"I don't mind a little risk if it gets the job done, Lieutenant," Kirk said. "My officers understand that too."

Iano nodded. "Of course," he said. His gaze lingered on Spock for a moment and he looked as if he were about to say something else, then apparently changed his mind. "The gaming houses in this district tend to attract what you humans would call 'a rough element,'" he said. "In the event that there is any trouble, you have the authority to employ deadly force if necessary."

"Only if it's absolutely necessary, Lieutenant," Kirk replied, beckoning him to lead the way.

"Thank you, Captain," Iano said. He looked at the others, and his gaze once more lingered briefly on Spock. Again, for a moment, it looked as if he wanted to say something else, but then he turned and went through the entryway into the gaming house.

"Curious," Spock said, raising an eyebrow.

"What is it, Spock?" Kirk asked.

"I am not yet certain, Captain," Spock replied, "but I have a suspicion about Lieutenant Iano that may explain a few things and put our present situation in an altogether different light. However, for the moment I would prefer to keep it to myself, until I have something more than merely an unsubstantiated theory. I could be wrong."

"Yes, you could be, but you rarely are," Kirk said. "What's on your mind, Spock?"

"Perhaps we should discuss that later, Captain," Spock replied. "Lieutenant Iano has already gone inside, and we *are* attracting a great deal of attention out here in the street."

"Yes, I see your point," Kirk said, looking around at the excited crowd, which was rapidly growing larger.

They went through the arched entryway into the gaming house. A number of the curious onlookers followed them in from the street.

The light inside was very dim, and it was even

noisier inside the club than it was outside. Loud music assaulted them, quite unlike anything they had ever heard before, filling the interior of the dark and cavernous establishment. It sounded like a strange mixture of howling wind, crashing surf, and weird, rattling, percussive noises, like hundreds of sticks being struck together. Kirk might not even have recognized it as music, except that it had a powerfully rhythmic ebb and flow, rising and falling steadily in an eerie manner that was almost hypnotic. Black seemed to be the dominant color scheme throughout the place, though not so much a color, Kirk mused, as an absence of color.

They stood just inside the entrance, at the top of a flight of stairs that led down to the floor of the establishment. Below them, bodies writhed in intricate, sinuous dance patterns on the main floor as the disturbing music swelled and faded repeatedly. The image that leaped unbidden to Kirk's mind was that of snakes writhing.

"Fascinating," Spock said as he gazed down at the tableau spread out before them.

"It looks like a scene from Dante's *Inferno*," Chekov said.

"It's just another nightclub, Mr. Chekov," Kirk replied, spotting the bar at the side of the room. It was located against the wall, in a lounge section that was on a slightly higher level than the dance floor. "A different world, a different race, and different customs, but the basic idea's still the same."

"Not quite the same, Captain," Spock replied. "The ambience here seems a great deal less social than ritualistic. These people are not merely dancing. They appear to be quite deliberately working themselves up into a frenzy."

"For what purpose?" Kirk asked with a puzzled frown.

"For the games, Captain Kirk," Iano replied. "It seems we have come just in time to witness the start of the festivities. This way . . ."

As they started to descend the stairs, the music rose in pitch and a section of the floor began to move. A slablike monolith began to rise out of the floor, and some of the dancers immediately stepped off it, while others continued to undulate on the slowly rising platform, waiting until it rose higher before leaping off into the waiting arms of the crowd below. As Kirk watched, the large, dark, rectangular monolith continued to come up out of the floor. He had no idea what it was supposed to be.

No one paid any attention to the men of the *Enterprise* as they came down the stairs with Iano. That seemed puzzling at first, until Kirk realized that the Patrians probably couldn't even tell that human aliens—and one Vulcan—had suddenly come among them. In the dim light of the nightclub, one silhouetted, humanoid form looked much like any other at first glance. Besides, everyone's attention seemed to be on the slowly rising monolith.

As they came down to the main level, a second black monolith began to come up out of the floor, taking some of the dancers with it as it rose. When it had risen to about half the height of the first monolith, a third one started to rise, and then a fourth, and then a fifth and sixth, until finally there were seven rectangular monoliths in all, each approximately four feet square by twelve feet high, each separated from those closest to it by a distance of about five feet. Two of the monoliths stood side by side, then there were three in a row, staggered in relation to the first two, and then the last two stood parallel with the first two. Seen from above, Kirk realized, six of the monoliths formed a circle, with the seventh monolith in the center.

As he looked up, Kirk saw that there were three upper galleries encircling the room, from which spectators could look down onto the main floor. Iano, however, was not leading them toward the stairs that led up to the gallery levels. Instead, he took the shorter, wider flight of steps that led up to the lounge, near the bar. He approached one of the tables and simply stood before it, looking down at those who were seated there. They glanced up at him and immediately vacated their seats without a word. Iano beckoned Kirk and the others to the table.

As they sat down, Kirk glanced apologetically at the people they'd displaced. The Patrians, in turn, stared at the men of the *Enterprise* with fascination and perhaps even a little fear. "It really wasn't necessary to make those people move," he said.

"Perhaps not, but it was convenient," Iano replied. "This table will afford you a good view of the proceedings. At the same time, its location allows us to see everyone who comes in or out of this establishment."

"What is this place called?" Chekov asked as he glanced around.

"It is known as the Arena Club," Iano replied.

"What exactly are those things?" McCoy asked, indicating the monoliths.

"The towers? You shall see in a moment," Iano

replied. He signaled a server, who apprehensively came over to their table to take their order.

Kirk and the others declined to order anything. As Iano spoke to the server, she stared at the officers of the *Enterprise*. Up to this point, the differences between Patrian males and females had escaped Kirk's human eyes, but now he saw that Patrian females were slightly smaller in stature, had a less pronounced brow ridge, and were of a more pale, slightly mottled hue. In general, Patrians seemed to move with a very sinuous grace, but the females were even more so. Kirk watched appreciatively as she moved away.

Suddenly, the music stopped. *"Ladies and gentlemen,"* an amplified voice announced through a public address system, *"welcome to the Arena Club! Let the games begin!"*

As the audience broke out in spontaneous cheering, Kirk and the others followed the announcements through the tiny and practically invisible remote earpieces of their universal translators. One by one the dark monoliths out in the center of the main floor lit up, each with a different color, as the audience cheered. It was an unnerving sound. The cheering of the Patrians was a sort of throaty, whistling sound, vaguely reminiscent of the sounds made by the bull roarers of Australian aborigines.

"Presenting . . . the challengers!" the announcer shouted over the public address system. *"Wearing blue . . . challenger Azk Yalu!"*

A Patrian male dressed in a bright blue skinsuit shot up through the center of the blue-lit tower to emerge at its top, waving some sort of staff.

"Wearing orange . . . challenger Zyl Barg!"

Another male in a similar skinsuit, only in bright orange, shot up through the orange-lit monolith and emerged on top, waving a staff like the first competitor.

Kirk realized there had to be a retractable hatch at the top of each tower. The monoliths were hollow, like small lift tubes, and when they were illuminated, it was possible to see through them. Each competitor apparently entered the tower from a basement and was then fired up through the tube by some sort of spring-loaded or compressed-air launching platform. As each competitor cleared the open hatch at the top of the tube, the hatch quickly slid shut, allowing the competitor to land on top of it.

"Very dramatic," he said.

"It grows even more so, Captain," Iano replied. "That is the entire point, after all."

By now all six challengers had appeared atop their respective towers. All were dressed identically, except in different colors, and all carried the same type of staff, which appeared to be made from some sort of metal, with a round ball at one end and a squared-off, lancelike projection at the other.

"What are those metal poles?" Chekov asked.

"They are fighting staffs, Mr. Chekov," Iano replied. "The rounded end is simply a mace, to strike with. The other end contains a device capable of delivering a strong electrical shock."

"How strong?" Kirk asked, curious.

"Strong enough to stun," Iano replied. "Repeated applications are capable of causing death."

"And this is your idea of a *sport?*" McCoy said, in a tone that clearly conveyed his disapproval.

"Take it easy, Bones," Kirk cautioned him.

"And now, ladies and gentlemen," the announcer said, *"your champion! Wearing white . . . the undefeated . . . the indomitable . . . Zor Kalo!"*

The crowd roared as the champion came shooting up out of the center tower and landed on top of it, brandishing his staff. He was clearly the crowd favorite.

"Kalo is a professional, the finest fighter in the games," Iano explained. "He has never lost a match."

"Before we begin our games tonight, ladies and gentlemen, we have an important announcement. We are honored and privileged tonight to have among us as our special guests . . . the commander of the Federation starship, Enterprise, *Captain James T. Kirk, and his senior officers. Please join us in extending a warm welcome to our distinguished foreign visitors!"*

As a bright spotlight hit their table, Kirk rose and beckoned the others to do the same. He held his hands out to the crowd in the Patrian greeting, and the others did likewise. The ovation lasted almost as long as the one they gave the champion. Iano nodded at them with approval as they resumed their seats. Kirk realized he must have given the server a message for the announcer to introduce them.

"Well, if the rebels didn't know we were here before, they'll certainly know now," Kirk said.

"That was what you wanted, was it not?" Iano said. "The Federation is here to establish diplomatic relations. I thought I would give you an opportunity to . . . diplomatically relate."

"Remind us to thank you when your terrorists shoot us in the back," McCoy said.

As the signal was given for the commencement of the game, the audience roared and the men of the *Enterprise* watched with fascination as the combatants squared off against one another. Their fighting staffs were about six feet long, while the closest towers were separated by about five feet. This gave each combatant a reach of about one foot into the area of his nearest opponents. The tops of the towers were about four feet square, so a combatant could quickly move back out of reach. However, the way the towers were arranged, each combatant was within striking distance of at least three other opponents, and this was assuming that everyone kept to their own tower, which, as Kirk and the others soon saw, was not the way the game was played.

"The object of the game," Iano said, "is to be the last one standing on the towers. There is no time limit, nor any rules. A player can do whatever he wishes to dislodge the others."

"You mean they try to knock the other players off the towers? But then what is to prevent them from falling onto the spectators below?" Chekov asked.

"Nothing, Mr. Chekov," Iano said. "Observe."

Standing at the central position, the champion, Kalo, could strike at any of the six challengers, but that meant each of them could also strike at him. Consequently, he wasted absolutely no time in making his first move. As soon as the reverberating, electronic tone that signaled the start of the match was sounded, Kalo used his fighting staff to vault from his centrally positioned tower over to the green-lit tower of one of the challengers. He struck the challenger dressed in green with both feet, knocking him backward off the tower and into the crowd. The man's cry was drowned out in the roar of the crowd as he dropped his staff and fell back into their waiting arms. They buoyed him up, passing him around so that he seemed to bob on their shoulders like a cork on water.

"They will toss him about like that until they grow weary of him," Iano explained. "Then they will let him down. If he is lucky, he will merely go home with a few bruises."

"What do you mean, if he's lucky?" McCoy asked.

"On occasion, if the crowd is worked up enough, it can become rather violent," Iano said. "Unpopular competitors have sometimes been found dead on the floor of the arena after the games are over. And not always in one piece."

The game had only just begun, and one competitor had already been eliminated. Another had been stunned. As Kalo had launched his attack, the challenger in orange, Barg, struck out at a red-suited opponent to his left with the stunner tip of his fighting staff. There was a crackling discharge as the red-suited challenger jerked violently and collapsed to his knees, barely avoiding falling off the tower. At the same time, the challenger closest to him, in a purple suit, had turned to meet the threat of Kalo, who had vaulted to the green tower next to him. Barg took advantage of this by immediately leaping to the red tower, kicking his stunned opponent off into the crowd below and attacking the purple-suited challenger from behind, striking him at the base of the spine with the stunner. The purple-suited fighter cried out as he spasmed violently and toppled from the tower.

At the same time, the challenger in blue, Yalu, had

engaged a yellow-suited challenger on the tower next to him. He parried a thrust with the stunner tip of his opponent's staff, they exchanged several quick thrusts and parries, and then Yalu connected with a blow, striking his opponent's head with the ball end of his staff. Blood flowed freely down the face of Yalu's opponent as he staggered heavily, leaving himself wide open for Yalu's next blow, which knocked him down into the crowd below.

McCoy jumped up, but Iano reached out and grabbed him by the arm, shaking his head.

"That man might be seriously hurt!" McCoy protested.

"You would never reach him," Iano said. "And you would be at considerable risk yourself down there in that crowd. The fighter knew the risks when he signed up for the match. Besides, there is nothing you can do, in any case."

The game was violent, fast-moving, and completely unpredictable. Within only a matter of moments four of the competitors had been eliminated and only three combatants were left. And there was yet another wrinkle in the game that made it still more dangerous.

As each competitor was eliminated, his tower, illuminated in a color corresponding to his suit, went dark. In the dim light of the arena, illuminated only by spotlights playing down on the combatants, the brightly lit towers had provided not only platforms from which to fight, but easily spotted areas of retreat. Now, four of those towers had gone dark, and in the heat of combat, the competitors could not easily tell exactly where they were.

"The competition has now entered the stage where

the champion has a slight advantage," Iano explained as the match progressed. "With four of the challengers eliminated, there are four unoccupied towers the remaining competitors can use for additional freedom of movement. However, with those four towers blacked out, they are difficult to spot. For us, sitting here, and for the spectators, it is easier to make out the blacked-out towers. For the competitors, engaged in fast-paced combat as they are, it is extremely difficult. At most, they can risk only a quick glance. Having fought in the arena before, the champion has a better idea where those darkened towers are in relation to the others. He has the experience of his previous matches to benefit him. The challengers must rely primarily on memory and instinct. And on luck, of course."

"So then it would be to the advantage of the challengers to team up and eliminate the champion as soon as possible, before turning their attention to each other," Kirk said.

"Very good, Captain," Iano said, nodding. "I see you devise strategy very quickly. That would indeed be the smartest thing for the challengers to do at this stage of the match. However, in the heat of combat, few people think so clearly. And when there is a considerable amount of prize money at stake, there is also the complicating factor of greed. Observe . . ."

Kirk saw that Iano was right. Instead of uniting—at least temporarily—to eliminate the greater threat, the two remaining challengers each thought only of themselves and continued to fight solo, directing their efforts not only at the champion, Kalo, but at each other as well. Barg, the challenger in the orange suit, struck out at Kalo, the white-suited champion, but even as he did so, Yalu, in the blue suit, launched an attack at him and Barg was forced to pivot sharply, breaking off his attack on Kalo as he brought his fighting staff up to parry Yalu's blow. This gave Kalo time to jump to one of the other darkened towers, putting himself out of reach of his two remaining challengers.

Kirk saw exactly what Iano had meant about experience in the game being an advantage to the champion. With a spotlight on him, Kalo had to leap blindly out into the darkness, using only his judgment to determine where he was going to land. The spotlight followed him, of course, but only after he had already initiated his leap. If he had misjudged it, the spotlight would illuminate him as he missed the tower and fell into the crowd below. However, Kalo had judged his jump perfectly and landed squarely in the middle of the darkened tower where the purple-suited challenger had stood.

The match slowed down now and became less of a fast-paced melee than a tension-impregnated dance. The champion's strategy, Kirk soon realized, was to keep putting distance between himself and the challengers. He was relying on his greater familiarity with the relative positions of the darkened towers, forcing the two challengers to choose between concentrating their efforts against each other or making risky jumps to the darkened towers in order to reach him. Kirk found the competition utterly compelling and he couldn't take his eyes off the fighters.

He felt his own pulse start to race as he became vicariously involved in the combat, and he found himself rooting for the champion, who was fighting intelligently and against the odds, trying to win one more match. Kirk watched the way he moved, with a fluid, athletic grace, and he started to anticipate the way Kalo judged the possibilities.

Then he glanced at Iano and noticed that the lieutenant wasn't really watching the match. The Patrian police officer was carefully scanning the crowd around them, an alert, intense expression on his face. Kirk glanced at Spock and nodded. While McCoy and Chekov watched the match, McCoy with an expression of dismay and Chekov with rapt interest, Kirk and Spock began to watch the crowd.

It was easy to get caught up in the excitement of the match, Kirk realized, but they were playing another, more dangerous game of their own. He could not afford to allow himself to be distracted. Anyone in the crowd could be a rebel terrorist. And in a place like this, an attack could come from anywhere, without warning.

Suddenly, in a bold move, Yalu parried a thrust from Barg and leaped toward the centrally positioned white tower. Barg, positioned once more on his own illuminated tower, turned to the center as Yalu leaped, but at the same time, Kalo executed a leap in the same direction, timing his jump perfectly so that he landed on the white tower at the same time as Yalu. Before Yalu could fully recover his balance, Kalo threw a hard body block into the startled challenger, knocking him backward off the tower, and in almost the same motion, he hurled his fighting staff, stunner tip first, at Barg. Caught completely by surprise, Barg was struck squarely in the chest by Kalo's thrown staff and there was a crackling discharge as the stunner tip made contact. Barg cried out and spasmed wildly, then lost his footing and toppled back into the crowd. The audience roared as the champion raised his arms over his head in victory.

"Fascinating," Spock said.

"Fascinating?" McCoy repeated. "You call that *fascinating?* If you ask me, it's barbaric!"

"Nevertheless, Doctor, it is a contest that involves speed, strength, agility, coordination, and quick thinking," Spock replied. "And no small degree of fighting skill. As such, I find it fascinating."

"It does get the blood up to watch such a competition," Chekov said.

"I believe it does at that, Mr. Chekov," Kirk admitted. "Lieutenant, I . . ." His voice trailed off as he saw the faces of the crowd all turning toward him, and he suddenly realized that the victorious champion, Kalo, was pointing at him and holding out his staff. "What's going on?" he asked.

"Interesting," Iano said. "I do believe you're being challenged, Captain."

"What?" McCoy said.

The spotlight struck their table. Kalo was looking straight at Kirk and beckoning to him. The crowd grew even more excited.

"Is this your doing?" McCoy asked Iano angrily.

Iano shook his head. "No. But you must admit it is an interesting development."

"Well, I've never been one to turn down a challenge," Kirk said, getting up.

"Jim! You're not seriously thinking of accepting?" McCoy said with alarm.

"Why not?" Kirk replied. "We came here to be noticed. And what better way to be noticed than to become the center of attention?"

"That man is a professional!" McCoy said. "A champion!"

Kirk smiled. "Oh, I don't think he'll hurt me, Bones. He's just making a gesture. And we are here to establish diplomatic relations, after all." He turned toward the champion, held up his hands in acknowledgment, and bowed slightly. "How do I get down there?"

As if in answer to his question, an attendant suddenly appeared at his side, beckoning him to follow.

"I think I had better go with you," Iano said, gazing at the crowd uneasily.

"No, Lieutenant, you stay here and keep an eye out," Kirk replied. "Mr. Spock will accompany me."

"Watch yourself," Iano said.

Kirk nodded. "I intend to."

Spock got up and they accompanied the attendant to the basement, where they were led to the bases of the towers and Kirk was given a fighting staff. He hefted it experimentally. It was a relatively simple device, weighted for balance. There were no controls of any sort. The stunner device at the tip was automatic, working on contact. The attendant beckoned him toward the entrance at the base of one of the towers. Kirk turned to Spock.

"As soon as I'm up there, get back up with the others," he said. "Keep your eyes open."

Spock nodded. "Be careful, Captain."

Kirk smiled. "I'll be all right. This will be a good opportunity to make some points for the Federation, show them we're good sports. But don't watch me. Keep your eyes on that crowd. I'm going to make a good target up there."

"I am aware of that, Captain," Spock replied.

"Right. Well . . . here goes."

He stepped into the tower, holding the staff upright by his side. The attendant pointed up. Kirk glanced up and suddenly felt himself launched through the hollow tube with a loud hiss of compressed air. A second later he came up through the open hatchway at the top, rising several feet above the tower as the crowd roared all around him. He looked down quickly and saw the hatch slide shut, then his momentum stopped and he began to drop. He landed lightly on top of the tower and looked around.

All the towers were now illuminated, though only he and the challenger stood upon them. The noise of the crowd was deafening. This was going to be a special treat for them. Their champion was going to fight a human, something they had never seen before. He glanced at Kalo.

The Patrian looked much bigger up close than he had from a distance. He was taller than Kirk by almost a foot, and powerfully built. He stood on his tower a short distance away, facing him, and held his staff out straight in front of him, across his body and parallel to the ground. Kirk took up the same position.

"Ladies and gentlemen," the announcer said, *"in an unprecedented event, we are proud to present a special exhibition match! Captain Kirk, of the United Federation of Planets, commander of the* Starship Enterprise, *which is currently visiting our world for the purpose of*

establishing diplomatic relations with the Patrian Republics, versus the undisputed, undefeated champion of the arena games, the one and only, Zor Kalo!"

The crowd went wild.

"For the purpose of this special exhibition match, all the towers will remain illuminated," the announcer said. *"And out of deference to the Federation challenger, who is a stranger to our games, there will be a special time limit of three minutes. At the end of the elapsed time, the tone will sound, signaling the conclusion of the match. Are the competitors prepared to start?"*

Kirk turned toward the announcer's booth and nodded. Kalo simply held up his staff and shook it. Kirk smiled at the champion. Then the electronic tone sounded to signal the start of the match.

Kirk immediately crouched into a fighting stance. The champion attacked at once. He thrust his staff at Kirk, ball end first, and Kirk parried the thrust. Kalo immediately brought the staff around, twirling it impressively, and swept the stunner tip toward Kirk's body. Kirk executed a sideways parry, blocking it with his own staff. The crowd roared in appreciation.

Then the champion made a feint and suddenly vaulted from his tower to Kirk's, landing right in front of him. Startled, Kirk brought up his staff to block. Kalo locked staffs with him, bearing him down. The Patrian was astonishingly strong. The crowd shouted encouragement as the champion tried to force Kirk down. Their faces were only inches apart as Kirk strained against his opponent's strength.

"You are being lied to, human!" Kalo said. "Can you understand me?"

"What?" Kirk said, taken aback.

Kalo suddenly swept his feet out from under him and Kirk went down. Kalo raised his staff, stunner tip aimed at Kirk, and brought it down. Kirk rolled out of the way in the nick of time, coming close to the edge of the tower. He quickly shifted his grip on his staff and swung it hard, sweeping Kalo's feet out from under him with the ball end. Kalo went down and the crowd could not believe it. The champion had almost fallen! Kirk quickly scrambled to his feet and launched himself at Kalo.

The champion got up to his knees and brought up his staff to block Kirk's blow. Kirk pressed against his staff, trying to keep him from rising. "What did you say?"

"I said, you are being lied to," Kalo replied. No one could hear them above the roar of the crowd. Kirk could barely hear what the champion was saying. "Do not trust the police!"

Kalo suddenly twisted his staff, hooking Kirk's and throwing him off balance. Kirk staggered toward the edge of the tower. Then he felt Kalo's mace strike him in the back from behind. He grunted with the shock of the impact. The champion had not pulled his blow. Kirk found himself propelled toward the lip of the tower. Instead of fighting the momentum, he used it and leaped.

He landed on the green tower, recovered, and quickly turned to face the champion. Kalo was taking this thing seriously! Or was he? The Patrian was immensely strong, and it occurred to Kirk that he probably could have struck much harder. He could easily have knocked him right into the crowd. Instead he had impelled him toward the other tower. And what did he mean about being lied to and not trusting the police?

As Kalo swung at him again, Kirk blocked the blow and struck one of his own. They stood near the edges of their towers, striking and parrying, to the immense enjoyment of the crowd, then Kalo vaulted to the purple tower. Kirk leaped at the same time he did, landing on the same tower and driving into him. They both went down, falling dangerously close to the edge.

"What do you mean, don't trust the police?" Kirk asked. "Who are you? Are you with the rebels?"

"You are being used!" Kalo said. "They are lying to you about the energy weapons! The underground is not to blame!"

Kalo brought his knee up hard into Kirk's stomach. The breath whooshed out of him as he doubled over, and Kalo regained his feet. He came at Kirk again, and Kirk just barely got his staff up in time to block the blow.

"Iano is a telepath!" Kalo said, his face inches from his. "He can read your thoughts! Be careful!"

"A telepath!" Kirk said. And then Kalo butted him with his head. Kirk staggered back, and Kalo reached out and caught him just as he was about to fall off the tower into the crowd below. He pulled Kirk toward him sharply.

"We have no quarrel with the Federation," he said. "You are our only hope!"

"But what about the disruptors?" Kirk asked. He drove his fist into Kalo's stomach. Kalo doubled over and pulled Kirk down with him. They both went down together.

"We have no such weapons!" Kalo gasped as he struggled to catch his breath.

"And the Klingons?"

"We have had no contact with them!"

"How do I know you're telling me the truth?" Kirk asked, breathing heavily.

"How do you know that Iano is?"

Kalo struck Kirk in the face and broke away from him. They both came up to their feet.

"We have to talk!" Kirk said.

"Too dangerous," Kalo replied.

"I can protect you!"

"And who shall protect you?"

Kalo feinted a jab, and when Kirk moved to block it, he reversed his staff and lightly tapped Kirk on the shoulder with its stunner tip. There was a crackling discharge and Kirk cried out as the shock went through him. Stunned, he dropped his staff and went down to his knees, clutching his shoulder.

Back at their table, the officers of the *Enterprise* tensed as they saw their captain go down. Spock noticed that Iano was staring at the two competitors intently. Suddenly, he spun around, rose to his feet quickly and, in one smooth motion, drew his weapon and fired. There was a loud, popping report, followed by a high-pitched whine as the projectile left the barrel of Iano's massive pistol. A man near the bar cried out as the shot took him in the chest, exploding and throwing him backward. People immediately started screaming and scrambling to get out of the way, in case there should be any further shooting. Immediately, Iano turned back toward the arena, but Kalo was nowhere in sight. Neither was Kirk.

McCoy was the first to react. "My God!" he said, and moved quickly to the side of the Patrian Iano had shot. He had not noticed that Kirk and Kalo had disappeared from the towers, but Spock was already out of his chair and running back toward the stairs leading to the basement. He had paused only long enough to tell Chekov to stay with McCoy, and then he was moving fast. He plunged down the stairs, unclipping his phaser from his belt as he pushed past one of the attendants and ran toward the entrance to the towers. Kirk was there, having his shoulder looked at by an attendant. Kalo was nowhere in sight.

"Captain!" Spock said with concern. "Are you all right?"

"I'm okay, Spock," Kirk replied. "I heard what sounded like a shot, and then the hatch opened up beneath me and I fell through. What happened?"

"Lieutenant Iano shot someone by the bar," Spock said. "Dr. McCoy is with him. What happened to Zor Kalo?"

"I don't know," Kirk said. "That was a pretty nasty shock. I couldn't see straight for a moment or two, and by the time I came around, Kalo was already gone. I'll be all right, but we'd better get back up there on the double."

They hurried back to the lounge area, where McCoy was crouching over the Patrian Iano had shot. He was putting away his medical kit. It was obvious that there was nothing he could do. The Patrian's chest was a mass of blood. Eyes bulging, McCoy got up and turned to Iano. "What did this man *do?*" McCoy demanded with disbelief.

"Take it easy, Bones," Kirk said, taking McCoy by the arm.

"Take it easy?" McCoy said. "Take it *easy?* He just

shot this man down in cold blood!" He glared at Iano. "What kind of police officer *are* you? This man didn't *do* anything!"

"He was thinking about it, Doctor," Iano replied flatly.

McCoy simply stared at him with amazement. *"What?"*

Kirk alone understood Iano's reply, but he could scarcely believe it. Turning to the Patrian lawman, he repeated Iano's words, as if uncertain he had heard them correctly. "He was *thinking* about it?"

"That's right, Captain," Iano said. "He was thinking about committing murder."

"Murder?" McCoy replied with astonishment. "How could you possibly know that?"

"Lieutenant Iano knew because he is a telepath," said Spock.

"What?" McCoy said.

Iano's gaze met Spock's. "Yes, that is correct, Mr. Spock," he said. "As you had already surmised some time ago."

"You *knew* this?" Kirk asked him with surprise.

"I was not completely certain, Captain," Spock replied, "but I had strongly suspected it."

"You mean . . . the Patrians are *all* telepaths?" Chekov asked with astonishment.

"No, Mr. Chekov," Iano replied. "Not all of us. Only a few."

"A few who comprise an elite force of telepathic law enforcement agents," Spock said.

"A deduction based on intuition, Mr. Spock?" Iano said.

"Merely a logical inference, Lieutenant," Spock replied. "I am correct, am I not?"

"Yes," Iano said. "You are correct."

"Telepathic law enforcement agents?" McCoy said. *"Thought police?"*

"Telepath or no telepath, that doesn't give you the right to act as judge, jury, and executioner," Kirk said grimly.

"Quite the contrary, Captain," Iano replied. "I have precisely that right. The law specifically grants me that authority."

McCoy stared at Iano with disbelief. "You mean to tell me the law here allows you to *execute* a man simply because of what he's *thinking?"*

"According to Patrian law," Iano said, "intent constitutes transgression." He looked down at the body. "This man intended to commit murder."

"Whose murder?" Kirk demanded.

"Mine," Iano replied as he bent over and removed a pistol similar to his from the corpse's body. "I believe this is what you would call 'acting in self-defense.' What happened to Zor Kalo?"

"I don't know," Kirk replied.

Iano merely stared at him for a moment, then he said, "No, I see you don't. I think that I had best take you back to the legation. There is nothing more we can accomplish here tonight."

"I'd like some answers," Kirk said.

"To what?" Iano asked. "To the ludicrous claims of a fanatic? They are not worth discussing. The rebels were more clever than we thought, Captain. They used you for a distraction while they made an attempt on my life. It was not the first, and it shall not be last. And if I had died, then rest assured, you would have been next."

Chapter Five

WHEN IANO DROPPED KIRK and his officers back at the legation, they found Secretary Wing and Ambassador Jordan waiting for them. Having completed their initial round of talks with the Patrian representatives, they had arrived shortly before Kirk and the others had returned. There were two other new arrivals as well. Scotty had beamed down Yeoman Jacob and Specialist Muir from the *Enterprise* to assist Kirk and his party. The two had already settled in and had started establishing working procedures with their Patrian police liaisons, officers Jalo and Inal.

Ambassador Jordan and Secretary Wing had waited for them in the central suite that had been set up as a conference room, anxious to learn how things had gone. Kirk quickly filled him in, but when he told them about what had happened at the Arena Club and

Iano being telepathic, they merely nodded, as if the information wasn't new to them at all.

"Yes, we rather were concerned about how you would respond if you discovered that," Jordan said.

"You mean to tell me you *knew* about this?" Kirk said with astonishment.

"How could you have known and not told us?" McCoy asked with disbelief.

"I don't appreciate being assigned to work with someone who can read my mind and not being told about it," Kirk said tensely.

"No doubt, Jim, that was the entire idea," Jordan replied. "We were only advised of it after the fact."

"After the fact?" Kirk repeated with a puzzled frown.

Secretary Wing sat down on the sofa and pulled her legs up beneath her. "In other words, Captain, it seems the Patrians purposely failed to inform us about the telepaths. We did not learn about them until only a short while ago, after you had already gone out with Lieutenant Iano. Otherwise, you would have been briefed, of course."

She had changed into a dark blue, embroidered silk lounging gown. It was simple and comfortable-looking, but at the same time, it draped very flatteringly on her figure and gave her a soft, attractively graceful, and very feminine look. When she sat down and drew her legs up, exposing them, Kirk caught himself staring. She had very lovely legs. He looked away for a moment and cleared his throat.

"Forgive me, I did not mean that remark to sound like an accusation," he said.

"Oh, I think you did, Jim, but that's all right,"

Jordan said. "I would have been equally upset if I were in your position. In fact, I'm not so sure I'm not."

Yeoman Jacob came in with a tray holding a steaming pot and several cups. "Your coffee, Ambassador," she said.

Jordan smiled. "Thank you, Yeoman. That smells delicious."

"They've got coffee?" McCoy asked, momentarily distracted.

"Oh, no, sir," Yeoman Jacob said. "Mr. Scott had us bring along a 'care package' from the *Enterprise* when we beamed down."

"Be sure to thank Mr. Scott for me," Jordan said. "That was very considerate of him."

Kirk made a mental note to thank Scotty for being on the ball. He should have thought of that himself, but his mind had been too preoccupied with other things to think about supplying the landing party with some creature comforts. And right now it would take a great deal more than a "care package" from the *Enterprise* to make him feel comfortable in his current situation.

"Please, gentlemen," Jordan said, "would you care for some coffee?"

"No, thanks," Kirk said, his thoughts turning back to the Patrian policeman.

"I could use a cup," McCoy said gratefully. "It's been one hell of a rough night."

Yeoman Jacob poured for McCoy and Chekov. Spock declined politely, and Secretary Wing shook her head and sighed.

"Actually, I could do with something a bit stronger," she said wistfully.

"We brought along some of that as well, ma'am," Specialist Muir said, coming in with a tray holding a carafe of Rigellian brandy and some glasses.

"Well done, crewman," she said with a smile. "I was afraid I was going to have to beg some of Anjor's whiskey from the captain."

Spock turned to Jordan with a thoughtful look. "A moment ago, Ambassador, you implied that you might be in the same position as we are. Do you have reason to suspect the Patrians have telepaths taking part in the negotiations?"

Jordan looked up at him over the rim of his coffee cup. "Under the circumstances, Mr. Spock, it would be rather naive of me not to consider that possibility, wouldn't you agree?"

"Indeed," Spock replied, raising an eyebrow.

"So you think the Patrians are reading your mind during the negotiations?" Kirk asked him.

"I've had no indications of it, but I think it's certainly possible," Jordan replied. "I have no way of knowing which of the Patrians are telepathic— apparently only a few of them are, at least judging by what I've been told—but put yourself in their place. If you had an advantage like that, wouldn't *you* use it?"

"Yes, I see your point," Kirk said.

"Well, one thing's for sure," McCoy said with a grimace. *"They* don't seem to have any reluctance to use it to their advantage. We saw Lieutenant Iano shoot a man down tonight as calmly as you please . . . because he was *thinking* about committing a crime!"

"He *did* have a weapon on him, Doctor," Spock pointed out.

"That's not the point," McCoy replied gruffly. "All right, maybe it was justified, I don't know, but the point is they actually have a law here that says *thinking* about committing a crime is tantamount to *committing* that crime!"

"It's called 'Transgression by Intent,'" Specialist Muir said.

Kirk turned around to face the young crewman. "That's right," he said. "What do you know about it, Mr. Muir?"

"I'm sorry, sir, I didn't mean to speak out of turn . . ."

"No, no, go on," Kirk prompted him.

"Well, we learned about it from our two liaisons, Jalo and Inal," Muir explained. "And I got the impression they're not exactly comfortable around the telepaths either. They like to keep their distance."

"You mean, they are not telepaths themselves?" Chekov asked.

"No, sir," Muir said. "Only special volunteers are selected for the Mindcrime Unit."

"*Mindcrime* Unit?" Kirk said.

"Yes, sir. That's what it's called," Muir went on. "It's a sort of elite police division."

"What do you mean, only 'special volunteers' are selected?" Kirk asked with a frown.

"Well, the telepaths are not born that way, sir," Muir replied. "They're surgically created."

"*What?*" McCoy said.

"Are you quite certain about this, Mr. Muir?" Jordan asked. "There's no chance that you misunderstood?"

"No, sir. I'm sorry, but I . . . I thought you knew all this," Muir said, looking a bit confused.

"Apparently, Mr. Muir, you and Yeoman Jacob have succeeded in learning a great deal more about this subject than any of us," Kirk said. "Perhaps you'd be so kind as to enlighten us further."

Muir glanced at Kirk, then at Yeoman Jacob. "Yes, sir, of course. Well, we sort of had some time on our hands after we beamed down . . ." he began. "I mean, we did have work to do, of course, but—"

"Andy . . . that is, Mr. Muir was able to figure out their computer systems fairly quickly," Yeoman Jacob said. "It really took him no time at all."

"Well . . . they're not really very complicated," Muir said with a shrug. "Their systems are fairly primitive compared to ours, and with Officer Jalo briefing me, it didn't take very long."

"He's being modest," Yeoman Jacob said.

Kirk caught the look that passed between Muir and the pretty, brunette yeoman and smiled to himself. "Get to the point," he said.

"Yes, sir," Muir said. "We really didn't have a lot to do after that other than stand by and wait for you to get back and issue further orders, so we started getting to know our liaisons a little better. Officers Jalo and Inal have been assigned to duty at the legation full-time, and they were just as interested in getting to know us."

"We talked about a lot of things," Yeoman Jacob said. "What it's like to serve in Starfleet, what it's like to work for the Patrian police . . . We wound up comparing our jobs and various aspects of our duties, and that's when we found out about the Mindcrime Unit."

"The way they explained it to us, the whole thing started out by accident," Muir said. "Their doctors had come up with some kind of new surgical procedure to treat certain types of brain damage caused by trauma. It turned out to be only partially successful, but a side effect was that the patients who'd had the surgery developed telepathic abilities."

"They continued doing research on it," Yeoman Jacob added, "and eventually someone came up with the idea of using the procedure to create an elite law enforcement unit that could deal with the increasing violence in their society."

"The members of the Mindcrime Unit have more official powers than the regular police," Muir said, "and more discretion in choosing how to use them. They've been given special authority to act on intelligence they pick up telepathically."

"Yes, tonight we saw a demonstration of just how that 'special authority' works," McCoy said grimly. "I still can't believe it. What kind of society would allow such a thing?"

"It's not up to us to answer questions like that, Doctor," Jordan said, "or ask them, for that matter."

"Well, exactly what is it that we're *doing* here, then?" McCoy replied. "I thought the whole purpose of this mission was to decide if the Patrians were going to join the Federation. Isn't that what these negotiations are all about? We're judging them and they're judging us. What kind of government allows a law like that? How do we deal with a society that permits its citizens to be found guilty of crimes simply because of what they *think?* Is this the kind of world we *want* in the Federation?"

Jordan gave him a pained look. "Doctor, whatever we may think as individuals about this law of Transgression by Intent, the fact is the Patrians are entitled to pass whatever legislation they wish. There are a number of planets in the Federation with laws that might strike us as repressive if they were passed in our society, but the point is that each society is different, and we cannot judge them all by our own standards. As a Starfleet officer, you should understand that. The Federation doesn't interfere with internal matters on its member worlds, and this is a Patrian *internal* matter. As such, it does not concern us."

"I don't disagree in principle," Kirk said, "but when somebody's reading *my* mind without my consent, it concerns me very much indeed."

"Amen to that!" McCoy said.

"I must say I agree," Chekov said. "There was, unfortunately, a time in my own country's history when a man could be found guilty for what he believed, but at least he had the freedom to think as he wished, whether he could act upon those thoughts or not."

"Precisely," McCoy said. "That's the core of the issue here, whether someone *acts* on their thoughts or not. How many times have you ever gotten mad at someone and thought you'd like to kill them? I'm sure it's happened to all of us at one time or another. You say or think something like that, it doesn't mean you're actually going to kill somebody, does it? It's just a way of coping, of venting anger and frustration. Only here, thinking something like that could get you tried, convicted, and executed . . . all by just one individual."

"So what is it you expect me to do, Doctor?" Jordan asked irately. "You want me to go to these people tomorrow and tell them their law is wrong and must be changed? Should we demand that they disband the Mindcrime Unit? Should we insist they discontinue the surgical procedures that create their telepaths?

Condemn their standards of morality and impose our *own* standards on them? Because that is what your argument amounts to, isn't it?"

"He's right, Bones," Kirk said, turning to McCoy. "We're all still keyed up over what happened tonight. Except for Spock here, who isn't troubled by emotional reactions. For a change, I envy him. I think we just need to cool down a bit."

Secretary Wing had listened to their exchange with interest. She turned to Spock. "Mr. Spock, you've voiced no opinion on this matter. Given the fact that Vulcans are capable of telepathy, how do *you* feel about working with someone who can read your mind?"

"If that were the case, then I must admit that I would have certain reservations," Spock said.

"If that were the case?" she said, leaning forward. "You mean . . . it doesn't work on you?"

"It's that incredible Vulcan mental discipline," McCoy said dryly. "He's shielding. So that's why Iano kept looking at him funny all night. He couldn't read him!"

"I think it is a new experience for him, and he does not seem to know what to make of the situation," Spock said with classic understatement. "I suspect that, as a result of not being able to read my mind, Lieutenant Iano does not trust me."

"It's probably driving him right up the wall," McCoy said with a grin.

"Much as Iano's telepathy seems to be affecting us," Kirk said wryly. "Obviously, with the exception of Mr. Spock, there's little if anything that we can do to conceal our thoughts from him. However, what we think is one thing. How we *act* is what matters."

"Maybe not here," McCoy said.

"If this duty is objectionable to you, Dr. McCoy, I could ask Captain Kirk to relieve you of this assignment," Jordan said.

"Then you'd have to relieve the whole damn landing party, with the exception of Spock here," McCoy replied irritably. "I'm not experiencing anything the rest of them aren't going through. No, thank you, Ambassador. As long as I'm here, I'll stick. I don't have to like it, though."

"Bones, take it easy," Kirk said, trying to calm him. McCoy was a dedicated physician, and he always took it hard when someone died and he could do nothing to prevent it. "I can understand how you feel. I don't like it very much myself. However, my own views—*or* yours—are not the issue here. The ambassador's right. This *is* a Patrian internal matter."

"And we must convince them to join the Federation because the alternative is even more immoral and reprehensible," Secretary Wing added. "We cannot turn our backs on the Patrians and leave them to the tender mercies of the Klingons merely because their sense of morality offends us."

"Precisely," Jordan said. "They do not yet fully understand what it would be mean to be conquered by the Klingons. We must try to make them understand. They must be brought into the Federation, for their own good."

"For their own good, or because it represents a feather in your cap as a Federation diplomat?" McCoy said.

"Bones! That's enough!" Kirk said, afraid that McCoy may have gone too far.

"Really, Dr. McCoy, you forget yourself," Jordan said.

"I think we all need to examine our thoughts and feelings here," Kirk said quickly, before McCoy could snap back at Jordan. "I think we need to consider them very carefully, because we're not going to be able to hide them from the Patrians. At least, not from the telepaths among them. We know Lieutenant Iano is a member of the Mindcrime Unit, but we have no way of knowing who else may be."

"Indeed," Jordan said uneasily. "I have to proceed on the assumption that there is at least one telepath taking part in the negotiations. And it's quite possible —even probable—there may be others with whom we shall come in contact on this mission who will not inform us up front as to who and what they are."

"My God, Scotty!" Kirk said suddenly. "He doesn't know anything about this! I've got to brief him on the situation. The *Enterprise* is going to be patrolling this sector for any vessels that might be smuggling Klingon ordnance. Our people are going to be working closely with Commander Anjor and his crew, as well as other ships in the Patrian fleet. If they're going to be boarding incoming vessels together to check on their cargo, they may well have a telepath or two among them."

"Yes, I'd be rather surprised if they didn't," Jordan replied, nodding in agreement.

"Just one thing, Captain," Secretary Wing said. "Make certain your people understand that if they encounter a Patrian telepath, chances are they probably won't know it, and unless they have the mental discipline of a Vulcan"—she glanced at Spock and smiled—"there's nothing they can do to prevent their thoughts from being read. They'll simply have to accept it. I know that's not going to be easy, but this situation is stressful enough as it is. We don't want to add to it by having everyone aboard the *Enterprise* trying to control what they're thinking all the time."

"Hell, if they all tried to do that, I'd have people piled up in sickbay with nervous breakdowns inside of a week," McCoy said.

"But the vast majority of the Patrians aren't telepaths, if I understand correctly," Kirk said. "I wonder how *they* cope with it?"

"Sir?" said the young communications specialist.

"Yes, Mr. Muir?"

"It just so happens that I asked Officer Jalo that same question earlier this evening."

"Really? And what did you find out?" Kirk asked, curious.

"Well, they don't, sir," Muir replied. "Cope with it, that is. At least, not very well, from what I understand. According to Jalo, the 'thought police,' as the people here refer to them, are very controversial. They're a relatively recent development."

"How recent?" Kirk asked.

"The translator rendered what he said as 'about ten years,' but then I'm not really sure how long a Patrian year is," Muir replied. "They only have their local dating system, and they're unfamiliar with the Federation Stardate Standard. In any case, Jalo's fairly young, and it all came about during his lifetime, so it's not as if several generations have grown up with the telepaths or with the law of Transgression by Intent. It's apparently caused a certain amount of culture shock. Most of the officers on the Mindcrime Unit go uniformed, like Lieutenant Iano, and they've got their own distinctive insignia, so they're pretty easy to spot. But if they're in civilian clothes, there's no way of telling who they are. They look just like anybody else. Jalo said it tends to make people a little paranoid."

"Just a *little?*" McCoy said.

"Well, that was how Jalo put it, sir," Yeoman Jacob replied. "As if he were purposely trying to downplay the whole thing. We sort of got the feeling that the more he talked about it, the more uncomfortable he became."

"Big Brother is watching," Chekov said.

"Yes, exactly," Kirk replied. "I can imagine how the average citizen must feel about the telepaths if even their fellow police officers aren't comfortable around them. It sounds to me as if these people have created a serious problem for themselves."

"It almost makes me wonder if our sympathies shouldn't lie with the rebels," McCoy said ironically.

"I wouldn't say that too loudly if I were you, Doctor," Ambassador Jordan cautioned him. "In fact, I wouldn't even *think* it."

"I want Scotty to know about this before anything else happens," Kirk said. "He doesn't like surprises, and for that matter, neither do I." He reached for his communicator.

Jordan got up and excused himself. "Well, it's getting late," he said, "and I could use some sleep. We've got a long day ahead of us tomorrow."

"I think we could all do with some rest," Kirk said, nodding to the others.

"I'm sure this whole thing will get sorted out," Jordan said. "You have my complete confidence, Jim. Good night."

The others also said good night and left for their

respective quarters. Outside in the corridor, Secretary Wing caught up to McCoy. "Can I have word with you, Doctor?" she said.

"Of course," McCoy said. "I'll walk you to your room."

"You really think we're wrong about this, don't you?" she said.

"Well, I don't know that I'd use the word 'wrong,' exactly," McCoy replied as they headed for the lift leading to her floor. "I just wonder if we're losing our perspective."

"What makes you think we are?" she asked.

"I didn't say I was sure," McCoy replied. He paused briefly, considering his words. "You see, I know something of your background, Secretary Wing—"

"Must we be so formal? My name is Kim."

McCoy smiled. "Leonard," he said.

"Yes, I know. You were saying, Leonard . . . about my background."

They got into the lift.

"Your father was one of the foremost advocates of human rights in his generation," McCoy said, "and your mother's record in fighting for equal rights under the law, regardless of race, creed, or species, is unsurpassed. I guess I just find it a little hard to believe that the daughter of Dr. Kam Sung Wing and Dr. Anna Stanford Anderson isn't absolutely outraged by what's happening here."

She sighed. "I didn't say I wasn't. But it's not my place to judge. We have to get the Patrian Republics into the Federation, so that we can extend our protection to them. They don't fully understand the threat they're facing. They've asked for our help, because they've been confronted with a type of weapon that's more advanced than anything they've ever seen before, but they're still being very cautious. Too cautious. They have absolutely no idea what the full might of the Klingon war machine can do. We have to make them see that joining us would be in their best interests. That's our mission, Leonard, and it *must* succeed. Everything else simply has to come in second."

"Well, you have your job to do," McCoy said as the lift stopped and they got off. "And it's our job to support you." He shook his head. "Lord knows, I'd be the last one to want to see these people conquered by the Klingons, but at the same time, sometimes I can't help but wonder if we don't take our policy of noninterference a bit too far. Would it be so terrible if we tried to exert a little beneficial influence? I don't know. Maybe it would be. I'm a doctor, not a diplomat. I suppose it doesn't really matter what I think."

"It matters to me," she said as they stopped in front of the door to her suite.

McCoy shrugged. "Why should it?"

"Don't sell yourself so short, Leonard," she replied. "You're an honest, intelligent, caring, and compassionate man who's not afraid to show his feelings or speak his mind. And there aren't many men like that around."

McCoy smiled. "You know, Kim, you really ought to be careful about saying things like that. If I didn't know better, I might be tempted to think you were making a pass at me."

She opened the door to her suite, then gazed directly into his eyes. "Be tempted," she said softly.

* * *

"Telepaths?" Scott said.

"That's not the half of it, Scotty," Kirk replied, speaking into his communicator. He quickly ran down the situation for his chief engineer.

"And we're supposed to be protecting these people from the Klingons?" Scott said when Kirk had brought him up to date.

Kirk grimaced wryly. "It does seem rather ironic, doesn't it? The Mindcrime Unit makes the Gestapo, the KGB, and the CIA look tame by comparison. And they're just getting started. They're on the way to building the ultimate police state, where even your thoughts are monitored."

"Did the ambassador know about this all along?" asked Scott.

"Apparently not," Kirk replied. "It seems to have been as much of a surprise to him as it was to us. However, this new development does not really alter the mission. Whatever we may think of the Patrian law of Transgression by Intent, and the manner in which they choose to enforce it, we still have to uphold the Prime Directive."

"Aye," Scotty said. "But I don't know that I could stand by and watch a man convicted just for thinking something."

"That's just what I wanted to talk to you about, Scotty," Kirk said heavily. "There's a good chance something like that might come up."

"I'm not sure I follow you, Cap'n."

"Look, Scotty, we've become caught up in this . . . this situation . . . where we've joined forces with the Patrians in an effort to stop the flow of Klingon weapons to their rebel terrorists. So far as that goes, we're just upholding the Prime Directive, trying to restore balance to an alien society that's been interfered with. But that's where things get a little sticky. We're in Patrian space, and we're technically under Patrian law. That means there's a chance you may be called upon to do something that under ordinary circumstances you would never consider doing."

"Just what is it that you're tellin' me, Cap'n?"

"I'm saying it's possible that you could be confronted with a situation where you may be called upon to make a response based not on actions you observe, but on *intent* reported to you by a Patrian telepath."

"Well now, how in the hell—beggin' your pardon, sir—am I supposed to do *that?*"

"With any luck, Scotty, you won't have to," Kirk replied. "But while I'm away from the ship, you may find yourself having to make just such a decision. Remember that under Patrian law, intent constitutes transgression. And information gained by telepathy constitutes hard evidence."

"With all due respect, Cap'n, that's about the craziest thing I've ever heard," Scott said.

Kirk took a deep breath and exhaled heavily. "I can't say I disagree with you, Mr. Scott. But on Patria it's the law. And so long as we're in Patrian territory, working on a joint mission, we're going to have to abide by it."

"Aye, sir," Scott said with resignation.

"Just do the best you can, Scotty," Kirk said. "We're all playing this by ear. Kirk out."

He closed his communicator and walked over to the large bay window looking out over the city. Thought crime. It was an unsettling concept. He thought about the rebel, Kalo. A champion, very highly visible. How had he avoided detection by Iano and the other members of the Mindcrime Unit? Was it the crowd he was surrounded by? But then, Iano had picked up thoughts of an attempt on his life in the middle of that crowd. Why hadn't he detected Kalo? Perhaps it was a question of proximity. What *was* the range of a Patrian telepath? And what about what Kalo had told him? Iano had dismissed his claims as "ludicrous." But were they?

This whole thing had started out as nothing more than a diplomatic support mission, Kirk thought, and now it had turned into a full-scale intervention, thanks to covert action by the Klingons. And Bob Jordan wasn't being much help at all. He was focused only on his negotiations, and Jordan seemed perfectly content to let him handle the problem of the disruptors, Iano, the rebels, all of it. Under ordinary circumstances, Kirk would have been the last one to complain about a Federation diplomat simply getting out of his way and letting him do what he did best. So why did he have this nasty feeling that his old Academy roommate was carefully setting him up as the fall guy in case anything went wrong?

"Captain Kirk!" Officer Inal said, rushing into the conference room, out of breath. "We have just received an urgent message from Lieutenant Iano. There is a rebel attack in progress. They are using disruptors. And this time, they have taken hostages."

Chapter Six

"STATUS REPORT, MR. CHEKOV," Kirk said, looking out over the city anxiously.

"Lieutenant Iano should be arriving momentarily, Captain," Chekov replied. "Officer Jalo is in communication with him, and Officer Inal is currently monitoring the reports of the situation in progress. It began approximately an hour ago, when rebels seized control of a government office building in the central section of the city. It has been confirmed that the rebels have taken hostages. It has also been confirmed that they are armed with disruptors."

"Where the hell's McCoy? And where are Muir and Jacob?" Kirk asked impatiently.

At the very moment Muir and Jacob both came racing out onto the roof pad. "Dr. McCoy's not in his room, sir," Muir said. "He's not in any of the other vacant suites either."

"Perhaps he went down to take a walk in the garden," Spock said. "He seemed a bit agitated earlier."

"Jalo said he'd have security look for him," Muir said.

"Here comes Iano," Kirk said as the police flier came in for a landing.

"What about Dr. McCoy?" Chekov asked.

"He should be safe enough on the building grounds," Kirk replied. "We can't waste any time looking for him now."

Iano's flier landed.

"All right, let's go," Kirk said.

They hurried out onto the landing pad, where Iano was waiting for them with his engines running. They piled into the vehicle and Iano took off immediately, swooping out away from the side of the building and gathering speed in a power dive, the police warning lights on the outside of the flier strobing brightly.

"My apologies, Captain Kirk," Iano said as he piloted the flier. "It seems you are not destined to get any sleep tonight."

"I've had sleepless nights before," Kirk replied. "What's the current situation?"

"A small assault force of rebels has seized the administrative offices of the Patrian Council," Iano said. "Fortunately, the Council was not in session. They had broken up a late meeting only a half hour earlier. The rebels must have hoped to strike while the Council was still meeting. Luckily, their timing was off. Unfortunately, there were administrative personnel still present in the building, working late preparing the reports and minutes of the meeting and performing various other duties. We do not yet know the exact number of hostages. It has been estimated at between twenty and thirty."

"As many as that!" Kirk said with concern.

"Some of the administrative personnel in the building apparently finished their work and left only moments before the assault took place," Iano said. "Most of them have not yet reached their homes, so they have no way of knowing what has happened, and we have no way of getting in touch with them as yet. Others managed to escape during the initial stages of the assault. That was when most of the deaths occurred. We have not yet had the time to sort out exactly who was killed. The rebels have their disruptors set to disintegrate, which means there are no bodies left to identify."

"Do you know how many people you're facing?" Kirk asked.

"At least ten or twelve," Iano said, "according to reports from eyewitnesses."

"And they're all armed with disruptors?" Kirk asked.

"It would seem so," Iano replied.

Kirk compressed his lips into a tight grimace. "That doesn't sound like a very promising situation. Have they made any demands yet?"

"No, not yet," Iano replied.

"And what steps have you taken so far?"

"We've taken whatever steps we could to contain the situation," Iano said. "Fortunately, there are no residential buildings in that area of the city. The building the rebels have occupied has been cordoned off, and all of the surrounding buildings have been evacuated. We have cleared the area around the site within a radius of one city block. Due to the lateness of the hour, there were not many people still working in the area, so fortunately, we were able to accomplish our task fairly quickly. At present we have armed police fliers circling the area and at least a dozen units on the ground, with more on their way. None of our weapons are any match for the disruptors, however. For the time being, we are merely trying to keep things from escalating."

"Is this a normal tactic for the rebels?" Spock asked.

Iano gave him a quick glance. "What do you mean?"

"From what you have told us before, Lieutenant," Spock said, "I was under the impression that the rebels have employed primarily explosives and guerrilla tactics, what is known as the 'hit-and-run assault.' However, this situation seems markedly different. Have the rebels ever been known to take hostages before?"

"No," Iano said. "This is the first time." He frowned. "Why? What inference do you draw from that?"

"When a pattern of observed behavior suddenly changes with no apparent explanation," Spock said, "it is often helpful to examine if any of the conditions present have changed as well. In this case, the most obvious change is our arrival on Patria One."

"You think they were expecting us, Spock?" Kirk asked.

"It would seem logical, under the circumstances," Spock replied. "They have taken hostages, but as yet have made no demands. In most similar cases, once hostages have been secured, demands follow almost immediately, as that was the entire purpose of taking hostages in the first place. However, if no demands have been made, and none seem to be forthcoming, then one must ask, what is the purpose of the hostages?"

"To use as pressure against us," Kirk said, following Spock's logical train of thought. "Of course. They don't know how well their new weapons will stack up against ours, so they're trying to find out. And at the same time, they're hedging their bets by taking hostages."

"So they can use the hostages to make us back off in the event our weapons prove superior," Chekov added.

"Precisely," Spock said.

"It fits," Kirk said, nodding in agreement. "It fits all too well." He took a deep breath and exhaled heavily. "Well, let's hope it doesn't come to that. Maybe we can make some headway in negotiating with them."

"That is not our policy," Iano said. "Our primary concern is to neutralize the threat they pose to others at this time. We do not negotiate with rebels. If taking hostages means they can force us into a position where we must negotiate, then it shall encourage them to continue doing so. We cannot allow that. If that means we must sacrifice the hostages, so be it."

"I'm not ready to accept that," Kirk replied. "There's got to be another way."

"There is only one way to deal with rebels," Iano said.

"Your superiors asked for our help and placed me in charge," Kirk said. "I have no intention of charging in there with phasers blasting and getting all of the hostages killed."

"Our primary concern—"

"Is to deal with the threat posed by the rebels, yes, yes, I know," Kirk said impatiently. "But *my* primary concern is not to get anyone else killed, if I can help it. If there's a chance that we can negotiate with these people—"

Iano gave a snorting bark. "You would be wasting your time. They are fanatics, prepared to die for their mad cause. They would agree to anything merely to bring you within range of their weapons, and then they would shoot you down without the slightest hesitation."

"Has anyone ever attempted to reason with them?" Spock said.

"If you wish to make the effort, Mr. Spock, then you can be my guest," Iano said. "I would not give great odds for your chances of survival, but if your life is of so little value to you, then who am I to dissuade you from throwing it away?"

"I did not mean to imply that I considered my life of little value," Spock said. "However, neither do I place little value on the lives of the hostages. The lives of the rebels also have value, if for no other reason than the fact that questioning them may produce information regarding how they are receiving their disruptors."

"I must admit that I am curious to see how Federation Starfleet officers would handle such a situation," Iano said. "However, if your efforts prove unsuccessful, then I see no alternative to an assault upon the building. And, assuming you have survived your failure, I will request that you participate in the assault with your phaser weapons."

"Fair enough," Kirk said.

The flier swooped down low over the streets, leveling off as it flew between the buildings. Within moments they could see the police blockades thrown up in the street and the crowds gathered behind them. Iano hit his forward thrusters and slowed, hovering low above the street, then set down where the police had set up a protected command post on a diagonal across the street from the occupied building.

The crowds were being kept well back, so that there were no civilians anywhere within line of sight from the windows of the occupied building. The police, however, were within range of the rebel's weapons, and every once in a while the rebels would open up with a disruptor blast or two aimed at the police positions.

Iano conferred quickly with several of his officers on the scene, then came back to the men of the *Enterprise*. "We've had more casualties," he said grimly.

"The hostages?" Kirk asked with concern.

"No, not so far as we know. But some of our officers have been killed by disruptor fire from the building. Apparently, they had underestimated the range of the weapons."

Even as Iano spoke, several more disruptor blasts came from the occupied building, aimed at police positions. One of the blasts struck a police flier and the vehicle exploded in a ball of fire, the fuel tanks igniting almost instantaneously, before the disruptor blast could disintegrate the vehicle. A number of officers on the Patrian suicide squads bravely swooped in toward the building on their rocket sleds in an attempt to get off some shots through the windows of the upper stories, but the rebels simply switched their disruptors to wide dispersal beam and vaporized them in mid-flight. Half a dozen of the sleds exploded into fireballs in seconds, and the remaining charred debris rained down onto the street.

"Get those people back now!" Kirk said. "If the rebels can see them, they can hit them. Is there any way we can communicate with the people on the inside?"

"There should be comscreens in the offices where they have taken up position," Iano said. "We can try calling them, but I do not know if they'll respond."

"Do it," Kirk said.

"Very well. I will have a portable comscreen brought up," Iano said. "But if you ask me, you're wasting your time."

"I didn't ask you," Kirk replied. "Mr. Muir . . ."

"Sir!"

"I want an in-line universal translator hookup to that comscreen. I don't want to waste time with interpreters. I want to be able to talk to these people directly."

"Yes, sir. I'll get on it right away."

Kirk flipped open his communicator. "Kirk to *Enterprise*. Come in, Scotty."

"Scott here, Cap'n."

"Mr. Scott, we've got a hostage situation here. I want you to get a fix on our position. There's a tall building directly to the northeast of where I'm standing, approximately sixty or seventy yards away. Have you got it?"

"I'm scanning a number of tall buildings in that immediate area, Cap'n," Scott replied. "Can you be a bit more specific?"

"This will be the only building within a one-city-block radius that will have any life-form readings inside it," Kirk replied. "All the other buildings in the area have been evacuated."

"Aye, sir, I've got it," Scott replied after a moment.

"How many life-forms are you reading, Mr. Scott?" Kirk asked.

"There's a bunch of 'em, sir . . . about forty or fifty maybe. . . . It's difficult to tell. There's a lot of 'em all clustered together. . . ."

"Those'll be the hostages," Kirk said. "What about the others?"

"I'm showing the rest spread out in the general area, all on the same floor, I'd say, judging by the elevation. No, wait . . . I'm reading six on the ground floor, near the building entrance."

"Those will be rebels, covering the entrance from the street," Kirk said. "Lock in those coordinates, Mr. Scott. We're going to beam those people out of there."

"Cap'n, most of 'em are pretty close," Scott said. "I don't think we can separate the hostages from the people holdin' 'em. The life-form readings are all similar."

"I know that, Scotty," Kirk said. "We're going to grab them all. Have two security teams assemble in the transporter room, phasers set on stun. They're to take out anyone who's holding a weapon. These people have never experienced transporter technology before. They're bound to be a bit disoriented when they're beamed up, but have security take no chances. I'd rather stun a hostage than risk losing anybody."

"Aye, sir. Stand by," Scott said.

"I'll have the comscreen hookup ready for you in a moment, Captain," Muir said.

"Very good, Mr. Muir," Kirk said. "Come on, Scotty . . ."

"Enterprise to Captain Kirk . . ."

"Go ahead, Scotty."

"Sir, we've got a problem," Scott said. "I canna' get the transporter to lock on."

"What do you mean? Why not?"

"Cap'n, I can scan the life-form readings, but I'm unable to lock onto them. There's something throwing off the transporter signals. Judging by the readings I'm picking, I'd say they've got an interference generator set up down there."

"Damn!" Kirk said through gritted teeth as he lowered his communicator.

"More Klingon technology, I take it?" Iano said.

"Need you ask?" Kirk said in a frustrated tone. "They expected us to try something like this. Somebody's briefed them on how transporters work, and given them an interference generator to prevent us from beaming out the hostages. I don't think we need any more proof about who's behind the rebels now. They've already demonstrated that the police are no match for their disruptors. Now they intend to prove that the Federation can't stop them either. But I'm not beat yet. Not by a long shot." He raised his communicator once again. "Scotty, keep that security team standing by. I'll need half a dozen portable deuterium blast shields and a deflector grid. You got that?"

"Aye, Cap'n, I've got it. Stand by . . ."

"I perceive what you're planning, Kirk," Iano said. "It's a bold plan, but it could be quite dangerous."

"If you can read my mind, Iano, then you already know I'm well aware of that," Kirk said dryly.

"You are offended that I can read your thoughts," Iano said.

"Not that you can, but that you do, and without my permission," Kirk said. "If you'd be so kind as to stay out of my head, Lieutenant, I would certainly appreciate it."

"I have a job to do, Captain," Iano said.

"So do I," Kirk replied. "And you're not making it any easier."

"What have you to fear from my knowing your thoughts, if you have nothing to hide?" Iano asked.

"That's a very old argument, Lieutenant," Kirk replied. "In the past, it's been used as a justification for every sort of abuse of power. If you're truly innocent, then what do you have to fear from an illegal search? If you have nothing to hide, then why object to being summarily detained and questioned? If you're not guilty, then why refuse to testify? It's the kind of crippled logic that leads to fascism and to . . ." He did not complete the sentence, but Iano got the thought.

"And to people like me," Iano said flatly. "That *is* what you were about to say, isn't it?"

"That's right, Iano," Kirk admitted. "I *thought* about saying it, but I *chose* not to. There is a difference."

"I'm curious, Kirk," Iano said. "If you had my ability, would *you* refrain from using it?"

"I'd like to think that if I had your ability, I wouldn't use it indiscriminately," Kirk replied. "I'd like to think that I would respect other people's rights, especially their right to privacy."

"I see," Iano said. "And who, I wonder, is to determine exactly what those rights are? The Federation council? Or perhaps the Patrian Council, determining the question of Patrian rights *for* Patrians?"

Before Kirk could respond, Scott came back on.

"I'm transporting those items you requested right now, Cap'n."

"Very good, Mr. Scott," Kirk said.

A moment later the blast shields and the portable deflector grid appeared on the street behind them.

"All right, we've got the shipment, Scotty," Kirk said. "Now listen carefully. That interference generator has to be portable for the rebels to have brought it in there. That means it's functioning off a power pack and can only generate a short range interference pattern. We can't transport the hostages out, but we *can* transport in."

"I don't like it, Kirk," Iano said. "Why don't we simply wait until they exhaust their power supply for that generator?"

"Hold on, Scotty," Kirk said. He turned to Iano. "That wouldn't do," he said. "Remember, they set this whole thing up with us in mind. I'm sure they're not stupid. They would have brought spare power packs. And the longer we wait, the more the situation favors them. So long as they have that interference generator, they can keep the hostages together and keep us from transporting them out. The minute they start running low on power, what's to prevent them from splitting up the hostages? We'd only be able to beam up one group at time, provided we could get a fix on them quickly enough. In the meantime, they could start killing people."

"I see," Iano said. "Very well. It's your decision. But as you humans would say, you're taking one hell of a risk."

"I know that," Kirk said. "Our only chance is to take them off balance." He spoke into his communicator again. "Scotty, I want you to compute transporter coordinates for the ground floor of that building, at a point just *behind* where you picked up those six life-form readings. I also want coordinates computed for the area directly *above* the one where you're picking up all the other readings. Find out how close you can get us in. Have you got that?"

"Aye, I should have that information for you in a moment, Cap'n," Scott replied.

"Go to it, Scotty. Kirk out." He snapped his communicator shut. "All right, Mr. Spock, Mr. Chekov, we're going to have to do this the hard way. We'll have to take out that generator before we can get the hostages out."

"I understand, Captain," Spock said.

"Let's hope we only have to do this as a last resort," Kirk said grimly. "Maybe there's still a chance we can negotiate."

"You think they will respond, Captain?" Chekov asked.

Kirk shrugged. "I don't know. It's worth a try. They've never talked to a human before. If they're opposed to Patrian involvement with the Federation, I'm sure they'll be interested to see just what it is that they're opposed to. I think they'll respond out of curiosity, if nothing else. At least, that's what I'm counting on. Meanwhile, we should be prepared to go in immediately if they won't negotiate. While I'm making contact with the rebels, you and Mr. Chekov are going to transport back up to the *Enterprise* and wait for my signal. If the rebels won't deal, then we'll have to move fast. On my signal, have Scotty beam you down inside that building, behind those six rebels stationed on the ground floor. I want you to take them out as quickly as possible, phasers on stun. Then I want you to beam back up at once and come back down again, on the floor directly *above* the rebel position, or as close to it as Scotty can get you. When I give the signal, make your move to secure those hostages and make it fast. If we're going to pull this off without getting anyone killed, speed will be our only chance."

"I understand," Spock said. Chekov nodded in agreement.

"All right, Iano—"

"I am already ahead of you, Kirk," Iano replied. "I have a police assault team standing by, ready to move in on your order."

"Damn it, Iano, I wish you'd stay out of my mind!" Kirk said angrily.

"I am merely trying to help expedite the situation," Iano said.

"I'm ready with that comscreen hookup, sir," Muir said.

Kirk had Yeoman Jacob brief the Patrian police assault team on the use of the deuterium blast shields. He then outlined what he wanted them to do.

"Enterprise to Cap'n Kirk."

Kirk flipped open his communicator. "Go ahead, Scotty."

"I can get you in on the ground floor no trouble, Cap'n," the chief engineer replied. "But that interference pattern won't let me get you on the floor above the rebels. The best I can do is bring you in two floors above the rebel position."

"All right, Scotty, that'll have to do," Kirk said. "Prepare to beam up Mr. Spock and Mr. Chekov on my signal. Stand by . . ." He turned to Spock and

Chekov. "Okay, if they won't negotiate, then we'll have to take out the people on the ground floor first. Then, while the police assault team moves in, Scotty will beam you back up and bring you in on the upper floors, as close as he can beyond the range of that generator. I want you to get down on the floor directly above the rebels as fast as you can, then on my signal, blast your way through, secure the hostages, and take out that generator. Remember, your only chance is speed. If you lose the element of surprise, you'll endanger both the hostages and yourselves."

"I understand, Captain," Spock said.

Kirk turned to Iano. "All right, let's make that call." The moment the rebels answered, Kirk held up his communicator close to his mouth and softly said, *"Now,* Mr. Scott."

As Spock and Chekov beamed back up to the *Enterprise,* Kirk stepped up to the comscreen. When the rebels learned that a Federation starship captain wanted to speak with them, they seemed highly interested and their leader immediately came to the screen. He had the look and manner of someone imbued with a sense of purpose, and on seeing him, Kirk had no doubt about what Iano had told him about these people being willing to die for their cause.

"I am Captain James T. Kirk, commander of the Federation starship *Enterprise,"* Kirk said. "Whom do I have the honor of addressing?"

"Honor?" the rebel said. He seemed amused. "It may be an honor for a humble freedom fighter to address the captain of a Federation starship, but are you quite certain that *you* regard this as an honor, Captain Kirk?"

"If you don't want to tell me your name, I understand," Kirk said. "I merely wanted to know how I should address you."

"My name is of no concern to you, Captain," the rebel leader replied. "What did you wish to say to me?"

"A moment ago you called yourself a freedom fighter," Kirk said. "Do freedom fighters threaten the lives of innocent people?"

"Freedom fighters do whatever they have to do to fight oppression," the rebel leader replied. "And those who serve the oppressors, such as the people we are holding here, can hardly be considered innocent. Besides, this is a Patrian internal matter, Captain. What possible concern is it of yours?"

"You've *made* it my concern," Kirk said, "by accepting weapons from the Klingons."

"I see," the rebel said. "And just what gives the Federation the right to decide with whom Patrians can trade?"

"Don't play games with me, mister," Kirk said. "You know *exactly* why we're here. By giving you disruptors, the Klingons are interfering with the cultural autonomy of the Patrian Republics. They're trying to destabilize your government and upset the treaty negotiations with the Federation, so they can come in and take over. You're not a freedom fighter. You're just an unwitting Klingon pawn."

"I would expect a Federation officer to denigrate the Klingons," the rebel leader replied, unruffled. "The fact remains that it was the Klingons, and not the Federation, who offered to aid us in our struggle against oppression. It is the Federation that seeks to ally itself with the oppressors."

"*If* that was our aim," Kirk said, "then we could

have simply supplied phaser weapons to the Patrian authorities, to counteract the disruptors that the Klingons have given you. But what would that have solved? It would have only served to escalate the violence, and violence has never been a solution to anything."

"Oh, come now, Captain," the rebel said with derision. "Are you seriously trying to tell me that *you,* a commander of a Starfleet battlecruiser, are a pacifist?"

"The *Enterprise* is not a battleship," Kirk protested. "It has the capability to fight, yes, but it is first and foremost a vessel of exploration. Our mission is to discover and contact other civilizations, and establish relations with them. We seek not to provoke war, but to promote peace. The weapons capabilities of Starfleet vessels are employed only as a last resort, when all other options have been exhausted. What I'm trying to do here is explore some of those other options with you, in the hope that further violence can be avoided."

"What do you propose, Captain?" the rebel leader asked.

Kirk shrugged. "I can propose nothing until I know what it is you want. *Why* are you doing this? What do you hope to accomplish?"

"We are doing this to draw attention to our cause, Captain," the rebel leader said. "And to demonstrate our will to fight against oppression."

"But what is it you *want?*" Kirk pressed him, wondering if Spock and Chekov were in position yet. "You have taken hostages. What will you accept for their release?"

"Accept?" the rebel leader said. "Why, we shall

accept nothing less than the resignation of the entire Patrian Council and the disbanding of the Mindcrime Unit. That will do . . . for a beginning."

"I told you they are mad," Iano said, coming up to stand beside Kirk. "You cannot reason with a fanatic."

Kirk waved him off. "What if *I* were to surrender myself to you in place of the hostages?"

"You?" the rebel leader said. "You want me to take you in trade for thirty people? You place no small value on yourself, Captain Kirk. Or is it that you think one human is worth thirty Patrians?"

"No, of course not, but I *am* a Federation Starfleet officer of command rank," Kirk said. "Your government is currently in negotiations with the Federation. Surely you must realize that, from a purely political standpoint, I would be a much more valuable hostage to you than a group of lower echelon administrative workers."

"Perhaps," the rebel leader said thoughtfully. "Your point is well-taken, Captain Kirk. I will consider it. Approach the building. And come alone."

"Release the hostages first," Kirk said.

"You are in no position to dictate terms, Captain Kirk," the rebel replied. "Surrender yourself first."

"And then you'll have both me and the hostages," Kirk said. "You'll have to do better than that."

"I have to do nothing, Captain," the rebel leader replied. "I have the hostages. And if our demands are not met, then they shall die. If you wish to discuss the matter further, then approach the building alone and unarmed. Otherwise, we have nothing more to talk about."

The screen went blank.

Kirk immediately flipped open his communicator. "Spock?"

"Standing by, Captain," his first officer replied from on board the *Enterprise.*

"Go!" Kirk said.

Spock and Chekov were immediately beamed down inside the building, materializing behind the six rebels who had taken up position on the ground floor. Three rebels armed with Klingon disruptors were guarding the front entrance, and three were watching the rear. Both entrances had been barricaded, but they had expected a frontal assault, not an attack from behind them.

As Spock and Chekov materialized, the surprised rebels turned to meet the threat, but they were not quick enough. Spock took the three at the front and Chekov took out the ones at the rear. Two quick blasts with their phasers on stun, set on wide dispersal beam, and the rebels were unconscious on the floor.

Not wasting any time, Spock and Chekov immediately transported back up to the ship and were once again beamed back down to the occupied building, arriving two floors above the rebel position. With their phasers held ready, they moved quickly toward the stairs. Within moments they had positioned themselves directly above the large conference room where the hostages were being kept.

Spock signaled Kirk on his communicator. "We are in position above the rebels, Captain."

"Stand by, Mr. Spock," Kirk said. "Scotty, three to beam up. Are you locked on?"

"Locked on and ready, Cap'n," Scott said.

Muir and Jacob both stood by with their phasers

ready beside the disassembled sections of the deflector grid.

"Okay, Spock . . . Scotty . . . simultaneously, on my word . . ." Kirk turned to Iano. "Deploy the assault team, Lieutenant."

Iano gave the order for the police assault team to move in. Holding the portable deuterium blast shields before them, the Patrian police team started to move out across the street, heading slowly but purposefully toward the occupied building. With the blast shields held before them, they moved directly out into the open, spreading out as they came in toward the building at a steady pace.

They drew disruptor fire from the building, but when the rebels saw that no fire was being directed against the advancing police unit from the ground floor, they realized that something had gone wrong down there. Precisely what Kirk had been counting on.

Holding his communicator down by his side, Kirk watched intently as the police assault team advanced slowly. "Come *on,*" he said to himse'f, thinking of the rebel leader. "Don't let me down. . . ."

He waited, counting off the seconds. He figured maybe ten, maybe twenty seconds for the rebel leader to realize that something had gone wrong on the ground floor, and then possibly another ten or fifteen seconds for him to dispatch a portion of his force down to the ground floor to see what happened, thereby weakening his position where the hostages were being held.

Moments later Kirk saw disruptor fire being directed at the advancing police unit from the front entrance of the building. He brought up his communicator. "Spock, Scotty—*now!*"

Simultaneously, Kirk, Muir, and Jacob were beamed up to the *Enterprise,* while Spock and Chekov used their phasers to blast their way through the floor above the rebels. As Spock and Chekov blasted their way through the floor, Kirk and the two *Enterprise* crewmen materialized in the transporter room. Scott was at the transporter controls himself, unwilling to delegate the responsibility for an operation that required such crucial timing to anybody else.

"Scotty, get me down there! Muir, Jacob, stand by for my signal! The moment that generator's out, get in there, fast!" Kirk said. "Energize, Mr. Scott!"

"Aye, Cap'n," Scott said, activating the transporter.

Kirk materialized on the same coordinates where Spock and Chekov had arrived. He could hear the sounds of phasers as Spock and Chekov made their move, and he started sprinting hard toward the stairs to get to them.

As Spock dropped through the hole in the ceiling, the rebels firing at the advancing police assault team turned from the windows, alerted by the sound of the phasers. Spock fired, aiming at anyone he saw holding a weapon. Four phaser blasts, in quick succession, and four rebels fell, unconscious.

Chekov dropped down and immediately crouched, firing as he landed. A moment later three rebels guarding the hostages all lay senseless on the floor, but there were still others outside in the corridor. As they came running in, altered by the sound of phaser fire, Spock was taking out the last of the rebels in the room, firing rapidly and methodically, his quick Vulcan reactions giving him an edge over the surprised rebels. A disruptor shot coming from behind him slammed into the opposite wall, missing him by inches. He dropped to the floor and rolled, but even as he came up, Kirk came flying through the hole in the ceiling, like a diver, and his body slammed into the rebels as they came running into the room.

They all went down, and as Kirk came up, he came up fighting. He punched one rebel hard in his scaly stomach, then chopped him to the ground with blow to the back of his neck. He pivoted quickly and lashed out with a roundhouse at the jaw of another rebel. The second rebel crumpled to the floor, unconscious, as a third rebel grabbed Kirk from behind. Kirk flipped him over his back, directly into another rebel, who was bringing up his disruptor. As they went down in a tangle, Kirk drew his phaser and fired, stunning them. He turned quickly, crouching low and scanning the room with a quick gaze, his phaser held ready before him. He spotted the interference generator, quickly changed settings on his phaser, and took it out with one quick blast.

"Quick, cover the door!" Kirk said, reaching for his communicator and flipping it open. "Kirk to *Enterprise*. Lock on my coordinates, Scotty, and energize!"

Seconds later the shimmering forms of Muir and Jacob appeared.

"All right, quickly!" Kirk said, taking charge. "We haven't got much time! Move!"

Muir and Jacob immediately started to assemble the sections of the deflector grid that had been transported into the room with them. As they did so, Spock and Chekov took up their positions by the door, covering them. Kirk turned quickly to the frightened hostages.

"My name is Captain James T. Kirk, of the Federation starship *Enterprise*," he told them. "Don't be alarmed. We're going to get you out of here. Just remain calm and follow instructions." He glanced up toward the door. "How are we doing, Spock?" he asked.

Spock glanced over his shoulder as he held his phaser ready, set on stun. "I believe we are about to have company, Captain."

"They're coming up the stairs," Chekov said.

"I need that grid operational, Mr. Muir!" Kirk said tensely.

"Just about ready, sir," Muir said, snapping the last section in place. "There, that's got it!"

"Spock! Chekov! Get back here!" Kirk called.

"One moment, Captain," Spock said as he and Chekov both fired their phasers down toward the landing at the advancing rebels. There were yells as the ones stunned by the blast fell back down the stairs upon their comrades.

"That should hold them for a minute or two," Chekov said confidently.

They retreated behind the deflector grid.

"Okay, Yeoman," Kirk said to Jacob. "Activate the grid."

As Yeoman Jacob threw the remote control switch, Kirk flipped open his communicator. "Kirk to *Enterprise* . . ."

"Scott here, Captain."

"Scotty, start transporting the hostages. *Now!*"

"Aye aye, sir."

As a portion of the group of hostages were transported up to the *Enterprise,* several disruptor blasts came through the doorway from the stairs below.

"Here they come," Chekov said tensely, holding his phaser ready.

Slightly less than one-third of the hostages had been beamed up to the *Enterprise,* but as Scotty brought up the second group, the rebels burst through the doorway, firing their disruptors as they came. The interconnected strips of the deflector grid laid out on the floor, however, set up a short-range field of energy that functioned on a principle similar to that of the ship's deflector shields. As the disruptor blasts struck the field projected by the grid, they were deflected and the rebels suddenly found themselves standing in a room where their own shots were being deflected right back at them. In the moment or two it took them to realize what was happening, several of them were killed by their own shots. The others, confused, quickly retreated to regroup.

Scotty was beaming up the last of the hostages. Only Kirk and the crew members of the *Enterprise* were left. Spock checked his tricorder, taking a reading on the grid.

"Grid shield still holding, Captain," he said.

Kirk spoke into his communicator. "Scotty, have you got all the hostages up safely?"

"Safe and sound, sir, if a mite confused," the chief engineer replied.

Yes, well, they certainly would be, Kirk thought, having never experienced anything even remotely like being teleported by a transporter before. However, at least they were all alive and well. We've pulled it off, he thought. We got them all out in one piece. Federation officers save thirty hostages, without any losses.

Simon Hawke

That should make Bob Jordan very pleased. It would certainly help in his ongoing negotiations.

"Energize, Mr. Scott," Kirk said.

When the rebels came back up the stairs for their second try, more cautiously this time, they found an empty room, with only the glowing deflector grid laid out on the floor.

Chapter Seven

"WHAT DO YOU MEAN, they got away?" Kirk asked, staring at Iano with disbelief. "How could they possibly get away? You had the entire building surrounded and the roof covered from the air!"

Before beaming back down to the planet surface themselves, Kirk and his crew had seen to it that the hostages were all transported safely down to the planet surface, where the police could question them. However, when they followed the hostages back down, they discovered that the rebels had made good their escape.

"When they saw that they had lost their hostages, they must have panicked," Iano said. "As we were moving in, they took the lift down to the basement level and blasted their way through into one of the underground conduit tunnels that conducts sewage underneath the city to the treatment plants. It had not occurred to us that they might choose such a method of escape."

Kirk grimaced and shrugged. "Frankly, it would not have occurred to me either."

"I know," Iano said.

Kirk took a deep breath and gave the Patrian cop a hard stare, but said nothing.

"In any event, they all managed to escape," Iano said. "Pity. I had hoped that we could take some of them alive for questioning."

"What about the six that were left unconscious on the ground floor?" asked Spock.

Iano shook his head. "There was no sign of them. They must have recovered and made good their escape with the others."

Spock frowned. "It is virtually impossible that they could have recovered from a phaser stun so quickly," he said. "Even allowing for biological variables in the Patrian constitution, they should have remained unconscious for at least another three to four hours, and they would have continued to feel some aftereffects for at least the next six to twelve hours."

"Well, then I suppose their friends must have carried them away," Iano said. "We held back until we were reasonably sure that you were out of there, because we didn't want to take a chance on hitting you or getting caught in a cross fire. However, when we did go in, there was no sign of the rebels you had stunned. We merely saw the blast marks on the floor."

"Blast marks?" Kirk said with a frown. *"What* blast marks? A phaser on stun doesn't leave any blast marks."

"I will show you, if you like," Iano said.

He led them back inside the building. They entered through the doors on the ground floor and went into the building lobby. Iano pointed out the large, discolored blast marks on the floor where three of the men had been positioned by the front doors, and three more at the back.

Spock glanced at Kirk significantly. "Captain, these discolorations are blast burns from a disruptor," he said.

"Well, that explains what happened to them," Kirk said grimly. "They were killed by their own people. Rather than encumber themselves with six unconscious rebels, the others simply disintegrated them where they lay. They probably did the same thing with the others."

"As I told you, Kirk," Iano said. "These people are fanatics. They simply will not allow themselves to be taken alive."

"Because they know the Mindcrime Unit could squeeze their brains dry," Kirk said. "They may be fanatics, Iano, but it's because you've given them no other choice."

"Sympathy, Kirk?" Iano said. "For terrorists?"

"I didn't say that I felt sympathy for them," Kirk replied. "I'm merely trying to understand them. Understanding the opposition is often half the battle."

"A very astute observation," Iano said.

"Just something I've learned from experience."

"Well, your experience has served you very well tonight," Iano said. "You managed to rescue all of the hostages without incurring any losses. I must admit, I am impressed. And I believe my superiors will be equally impressed. You've done much for your cause tonight, Captain."

"Perhaps," Kirk said, "but my primary concern was making sure those hostages weren't hurt. I'm grateful that we were able to help."

"And I, in turn, am grateful for that help," Iano said. "Now, I am sure you and your people must be tired. I must remain here and complete my investigation for my report, but I will arrange for a police flier to take you back to the legation."

McCoy was waiting for them in the conference room when they arrived back at the legation. He was anxiously pacing back and forth, and the moment they walked in, he came rushing over to them.

"I heard about what happened," he said. "Inal told me about the rebels seizing the hostages. Is everything all right?"

"Yes, everything's fine, Bones," Kirk replied. "I'm afraid some of the rebels managed to make good their escape, but at least we were able to get all the hostages out safely."

"Well, thank God for that!" McCoy said, looking greatly relieved. "And I'm pleased that everyone's all right. When I found out you'd gone off with Iano and that I'd been left behind, I was afraid that . . . well, I'm just glad you're all right, that's all."

"I appreciate your concern," Kirk said. "By the way, Bones, where the devil were you?"

"I . . . I was in my room. I guess I must have fallen asleep. . . ."

Muir and Jacob exchanged glances, but neither one of them wanted to openly contradict a senior officer. Spock, on the other hand, had no such problem.

"Forgive me, Doctor, but it is my understanding that Mr. Muir had sought you there without success."

"That is true," Chekov added. "We could not find you anywhere."

"Yes, so where *were* you?" Kirk asked.

"I . . . well . . . if I wasn't in my room, then . . . uh, I guess I must have been . . ." McCoy's voice trailed off as he floundered helplessly, searching for a reply.

Spock raised an eyebrow, gazing at him with a questioning look.

McCoy swallowed uneasily and moistened his lips nervously. "I was . . . well, that is, I . . ."

"Yes?" Kirk said, prompting him. It wasn't like McCoy to fabricate excuses, yet that was clearly what he was trying to do, though without very much success.

"He was with me, in my quarters," Secretary Wing said from the doorway.

They turned to see her standing there, dressed in a robe and barefoot, her long black hair cascading down her back and shoulders. Kirk simply stared at her. Chekov's jaw dropped. Even Spock cocked his head and raised an appreciative eyebrow. Muir saw Yeoman Jacob catch him staring, and he quickly looked down at the floor.

"He was with *you?*" Kirk said with astonishment. He turned to McCoy. "You were with *her?*"

"Secretary Wing wasn't feeling very well," McCoy began, "and I went up to see if there was anything that I could—"

"There was nothing wrong with me at all," she said, contradicting flatly as she entered the room. "Dr.

McCoy is trying to be gallant, and a gentleman. I appreciate that, but it's entirely unnecessary. I have nothing of which to be ashamed, and we are all adults here, are we not?"

"Indeed," Spock said, inclining his head slightly. His expression, as usual, was entirely unreadable.

Chekov closed his mouth, then opened it again, then closed it and cleared his throat. "Absolutely," he finally managed to get out.

Kirk gaped at her, then turned to McCoy with amazement and repeated, "You were with *her?*"

"I think we've established that already, Captain," she said, before McCoy could reply. "The ambassador's asleep, and I didn't want to disturb him, but I'm sure he'll want a complete report from me as soon as he wakes up in the morning. So, Captain, if you don't mind?"

"Ah," Kirk said, glancing from her to McCoy and back again. "Yes . . . of course. A report . . . Uh . . . Mr. Spock?"

Spock quickly filled her in on the events of that night. As he was doing so, Ambassador Jordan arrived, dressed in a robe and slippers. Spock started over, and when he completed his report, Jordan merely pursed his lips thoughtfully and nodded. "It appears I've missed a good bit of excitement this evening," he said.

"More than you know," Kirk said.

"What was that, Jim?" Jordan asked.

"Nothing," Kirk said quickly. "Just thinking out loud. It's getting late. I think we'd all better turn in. Some of us need to get our rest," he added with an arch look at McCoy.

"You did very well tonight, Jim," Jordan said.

"You all did very well," Secretary Wing added as they passed her on their way out and said good night.

She was referring, of course, to the rescue of the hostages, but it was a straight line that Kirk wasn't going to touch with a ten-foot pole.

"What you did tonight should do a great deal to increase our standing around here," Jordan said after the others had gone, leaving him alone with Kirk, McCoy, and Spock. "But our first priority must be to find out how those disruptors are getting through to the terrorists, stop the shipments, and confiscate the ones they already have."

"That last one's not going to be so easy," Kirk said.

"I realize that," Jordan replied. "I don't necessarily expect you to perform miracles, Jim. But I do expect you to *try*. I don't really want to be forced into a position where I'll have to agree to supplying the Patrian authorities with phaser weapons."

"Are they putting pressure on you about that?" Kirk asked.

"Yes," Jordan replied wearily. "And they're being rather insistent about it. It isn't really being presented as a demand, but it practically amounts to one, to all intents and purposes. The way they see it, if we agree to supply them with phasers, with no strings attached, we're merely demonstrating our goodwill and creating a comfortable atmosphere in which the negotiations can proceed. But if I remind them that sharing weapons technology with nonmember planets is against our current policy and something I cannot agree to without express authorization from the Federation council, then they make it seem as if I'm taking refuge behind policy in an attempt to strengthen my negotiating position and extort concessions from them. We get absolutely nowhere, so we go on to something else, but it always comes back to the same thing again. It's simply maddening."

"I guess you can't really blame them, Bob," Kirk said. "They're frightened. They're not only facing weapons more advanced than anything they've got, but the situation only serves to remind them that there are cultures out there with technologies vastly superior to theirs. And it's bound to be making them nervous."

"He's got a point," McCoy said. "It's got to be a sobering experience. One moment you're the dominant species in your system, master of all you survey. And then the next thing you know, you find out there are other intelligent beings out there, and they've got bigger clubs than you."

"The problem is, we simply cannot share weapons technology with a nonmember planet," Wing said. "When we've done it in the past, it's always caused problems."

"Yes, I know," Kirk said, thinking back to his old friend, Tyree. Back then, he had done what he felt he had to do, but he'd never forget what happened as a result.

"On the other hand, our reluctance makes it look as if we're trying to take advantage of the situation to force the Patrians into the Federation," Jordan said.

"I can appreciate your problem," Kirk said sympathetically.

"Which is why I'm counting on you, Jim," Jordan replied. "What you did tonight in rescuing the hostages will certainly help matters a great deal, but I'm afraid it's not enough. I think we're going to have to help the Patrians break the back of the rebellion."

"What?" McCoy said.

"Are you serious?" Kirk asked, taken aback by his suggestion.

"With all due respect, Ambassador," Spock said, "I feel I must point out that becoming directly involved in the internal political conflicts of the Patrians is completely outside our province. It would be a clear violation of the Prime Directive."

"Perhaps," Jordan said. "But I think there's a gray area here. If the Federation became directly involved in their internal political conflicts, then that would certainly be the case. However, that's not really what we're doing here. We are attempting, at the request of the Patrians, to compensate for cultural interference in their society effected by the Klingons, and we are confining our activities to dealing with the source of that interference."

"Come again?" McCoy said with a frown.

"I think I see what he's getting at, Bones," Kirk said. "Stopping the flow of illegal, off-world weapons to the Patrian rebels is within our authority, so long as the request has been made officially by the Patrian government. It's a matter of trying to stop cultural interference from outside. Dealing with the source of that interference would ordinarily imply the Klingons, but then one could make the argument that the disruptors themselves are the actual, *direct* source of the interference, while the Klingons, who supply them, are only *indirectly* responsible."

"Precisely," Jordan replied, looking relieved.

"And since the rebels are the ones who actually *have* the disruptors, then going after the rebels themselves could be interpreted as going after the source of the interference," Kirk finished.

"Excellent," Jordan said. "I see we're thinking along the same lines, Jim."

"Good Lord!" McCoy said. "Talk about splitting hairs! Isn't that pushing things a little far?"

"Maybe," Jordan replied, "but if we pull this off, nobody's going to be asking any questions."

"There will have to be reports," Spock reminded him.

"True, Mr. Spock," Jordan replied. "I admit that we *are* on rather delicate ground as pertains to our interpretation of policy in this situation."

"But the fact remains that the rebels are in possession of an unknown quantity of Klingon disruptors," Kirk said, "and even if we can prevent any more weapons from reaching them, that still leaves us with the problem of the ones already in their hands. Short of helping the Patrian authorities break the back of the rebellion and apprehend the leaders, thereby enabling us to recover those weapons, there doesn't seem to be any other way to deal with this problem. It's either that or supply the Patrians with phasers and then keep our noses out of it."

"I'm afraid that's not a decision I'm in a position to make," Jordan said. "Not without authorization from the Federation council. And who knows how long that would take?"

Kirk shrugged. "Well, then I guess our course is clear."

"Good," Jordan said. "I'm glad to see you're on top of the situation. I knew I could count on you, Jim. I'm sure you've made the right decision. Well, I'll say good night, gentlemen. I've got a long day ahead of me tomorrow."

He turned and left the room. Secretary Wing said good night and followed him out.

Kirk glanced at McCoy and grinned. "Why, you old dog, you. I didn't know you had it in you."

"Frankly, neither did I," McCoy replied wryly.

"She's really quite a woman," Kirk said.

"She's unlike anyone I've ever met before," McCoy replied.

"Bones . . . this isn't serious, is it?"

"Oh, I very much doubt that," McCoy said. "For one thing, I'm really much too old for her."

"A lot of women like older men," Kirk said.

"And she's much too young for me," McCoy said with a grimace.

"Chronologically, perhaps, but she's a mature young woman, and highly intelligent too," Kirk said. "Besides, age is really just a state of mind. It didn't seem as if it bothered her at all."

"Look, just because you exert your fatal charm on every nubile female between Earth and Rigel Seven doesn't mean that *I* have to start acting like I'm having a second adolescence!" McCoy replied gruffly.

"Now . . . let me get this straight," Kirk said. "Somehow, God only knows how or why, you've managed to get a beautiful, intelligent woman romantically interested in you—which only goes to show there's no accounting for taste, I suppose—and you're actually *complaining* about it?"

"Don't be ridiculous," McCoy snapped. "Of course I'm not complaining. I feel unbelievably lucky. But . . ."

"But?"

"Well, it's just too good to be true, that's all. I'm not

161

going to start reading anything into this. It was a one-time thing, that's all."

"What makes you so sure?" Kirk asked.

"Kim's been under a lot of stress," McCoy said. "She's a long way from home and she's in a very high-pressure situation. And Jordan's been depending on her quite a lot, apparently. I got the impression that she has to carry the ball much of time. I guess it was just . . . just one of those things, that's all."

"One of those crazy, wonderful things," Kirk said, quoting the old song lyric with a perfectly straight face.

"Well, if we are quite finished discussing matters of substance, gentlemen, then *I* am going to bed," Spock said.

"Good night, Mr. Spock," Kirk said with mock gravity.

"Good night, Captain. Doctor . . ."

McCoy merely grunted.

"Hell, don't worry it to death, Bones," Kirk said. "Why not just accept it for what it is?"

McCoy simply grunted again.

"Well, it *has* been a long day," Kirk said. "I'm going to go check in with Scotty and then I'll be turning in myself. Good night, Bones. Sleep well."

Kirk left, leaving McCoy alone in the large conference room. He went over to the bar and poured himself a drink of "Scott's Whiskey."

"Well, it was fun while it lasted," McCoy said wistfully, though there was no one in the room to hear him. He raised the glass in a silent toast.

He tossed back the drink, set the empty glass down on the bar, and headed back down the corridor to his room. He closed the door and started to pull off his uniform when he heard a soft, rustling movement behind him and turned, quickly. In the moonlight coming in through the window he could make out a slim, curvaceous figure outlined underneath the covers.

"What kept you?" she said softly.

"Sir, long-range scanners are picking up an unidentified vessel entering Patrian space," Sulu said.

"Can you identify it, Mr. Sulu?" Scott asked.

"Not at this distance, sir. She's still too far away, even for maximum magnification."

"We'd better let the Patrians know about it and see if they're expecting any visitors," Scott said.

Lieutenant Uhura broadcast the message to the Patrians. A moment later she received a reply. "Mr. Scott, I am picking up a message from Commander Anjor aboard the *Komarah*," she reported, swiveling her comchair toward the command console on the bridge.

"Put it on the screen, Lieutenant," Scotty replied.

A moment later the image of the Patrian commander appeared on the main viewer.

"This is Lieutenant Commander Scott, acting captain of the *Enterprise*," the chief engineer said, acknowledging the call. "We are receiving you, Commander."

"Greetings, Mr. Scott," Anjor replied. "Our long-range sensors have also picked up the unknown vessel now entering Patrian space. We have hailed the vessel repeatedly, but it is refusing to respond. We are currently on an intercept course."

"What is your present location, sir?" Scotty asked.

"I will have my navigator transmit our current

heading and coordinates," Anjor replied. He turned and spoke briefly to someone off screen.

"Heading and coordinates coming in now, Mr. Scott," Uhura said.

"Put them through to Mr. Sulu please, Lieutenant," Scotty said.

"Aye aye, sir."

"*Komarah*'s heading and coordinates received and locked in, Mr. Scott," Sulu said. "We should be able to reach them in less than five minutes."

"All right," Scott said. "We're on our way, Commander. *Enterprise* out."

Scott gave the commands to the helmsman filling in for Chekov, then ordered Mr. Sulu to get a long-range scanner fix on that unknown vessel as they approached the *Komarah*'s location coordinates.

As he settled back in the captain's chair, Scott could not repress a smile. He didn't often have the chance to fill in for Captain Kirk, but each time he received the opportunity, he reveled in it. It was not that he enjoyed being in a position of superiority, for he didn't really care about that. He was not interested in having his own command and never had been. He was an engineer, first and foremost, and would always be. What he enjoyed on such occasions was the opportunity to put the *Enterprise* through her paces and watch how she performed under his capable hands.

He loved this ship. Perhaps even more than the captain did. He had not only his heart and soul in it, but his sweat and toil too. He knew every inch of her, each engine bay and Jeffries tube, each thruster and deflector grid and phaser bank. He had barked his knuckles on the wiring access hatch of every single console in the ship, and there wasn't a square inch of it that he did not know like the back of his own hand. He viewed the performance of the *Enterprise* with pride, because it was his hard work and skill that kept the ship running tight. At times like this he felt almost like a proud parent watching a child flawlessly execute some complicated performance. It was a feeling that no one except another engineer would ever truly understand.

"We should be within visual range in a moment or two, Mr. Scott," Sulu said.

"Put it up on the screen as soon as you've got her, Mr. Sulu," Scott said.

"Aye aye, sir."

A moment later the *Enterprise's* long-range scanners were able to detect the ship and Sulu put the visual display up on the main viewer. In the foreground the *Komarah* appeared, filling up much of the viewscreen, but in the far background there was the small shape of a distant ship, too small to make out any of its details.

"Maximum magnification please, Mr. Sulu," Scotty said.

"Aye aye, sir."

The image on the screen seemed to jump, and the *Komarah* disappeared from view as the visual display was magnified to focus on the small ship in the distance. Now, on the screen, it appeared much larger and they could make out its configuration.

"It's an Orion ship, Mr. Scott," Sulu said with surprise.

"Give them a hail, Lieutenant Uhura," Scott said.

"Aye aye, sir," Uhura said, and spoke into her mike. "Ahoy, Orion vessel. This is the Federation starship *Enterprise*. Please acknowledge." A moment later she repeated the hail, then turned and said, "They're not responding, Mr. Scott."

"Try them again," Scotty said, a little tensely.

Uhura tried again and shook her head. "Still no response, sir. The Orions are capable of receiving all standard Federation hailing frequencies. They just aren't responding."

"Perhaps they have some sort of a malfunction on board," Scott said. "Or, quite possibly, they're carrying something in their cargo holds they shouldn't be."

"Freebooters?" Sulu said.

"Aye, could be, Mr. Sulu," Scott said. "The Orions have no great love for the Klingons, and the Klingons like the Orions even less, but politics and greed often make for some mighty strange bedfellows."

"You think Orion freebooters might have made a deal with the Klingons to smuggle disruptors to the Patrian rebels?" Sulu asked.

"I wouldn't put it past them," Scott said, watching the viewscreen as they rapidly closed the distance between their ship and the Orion vessel.

"I wouldn't think the Klingons would trust the Orions to deliver the disruptors," Sulu said. "Once the freebooters took the shipment on board, what would prevent them from simply turning around and selling the cargo to the highest bidder?"

"Probably nothing at all," Scott said, "and you can be sure the Klingons would know that. However, if I was a clever Klingon looking to destabilize the Patrian government, I'd simply *give* the Orion freebooters the disruptors and then pay them to deliver the weapons to the Patrians, knowing they'd only sell them to the rebels for as much as they could get. That's a deal no freebooter would be able to refuse. It's one hundred percent pure profit. Despite the risks, they'd deliver every shipment and hurry back for more."

Sulu nodded. "It makes sense. It would be worth it to the Klingons, having the freebooters take all the risks, and the Orions would accept the risks because they stood to make a significant profit on both ends. So everybody gets exactly what they want."

"Except for the Patrian government," Uhura reminded them.

"Aye," Scott said. "But we still don't know that's what we've got here, though I must admit their failure to respond does not bode well."

"They haven't turned to run, and surely they must be scanning us by now," Sulu said.

"Aye, but they'd never outrun this ship," Scotty said confidently, "and what's more, they know it too."

"You think they'll try to brazen it out?" Sulu asked.'

"I think they're going to do just that, Mr. Sulu," Scott replied. "They know we've got no call to challenge them outside Federation space, and they'll try to stand on that, but I don't think that will cut any ice with our friend Anjor."

"Sir, I'm getting a message from the *Komarah*," Uhura said.

"Put it up on the main viewer please, Lieutenant," Scotty said.

Anjor's face appeared on the viewscreen. "We monitored your attempt to hail the vessel, Mr. Scott," he said. "You called them Orions?"

"Aye," Scott said with a grimace.

"We know nothing of this race," Anjor said.

"They're a violent people, capable of giving even the Klingons a good run for their money," Scott said. "The Orions are not part of the Federation, and Orion freebooters have little respect for the Federation Accords. They're a bunch of devious smugglers and black marketeers who'd strike a deal with the devil himself if there was a profit in it for them."

"I very much resent that characterization," said a new voice, breaking into their conversation.

The visual display on the main viewer changed abruptly as Uhura switched over to the new transmission, revealing the face of the Orion commander. He had the emerald-green skin and thick, almost manelike black hair that were the chief distinguishing features of the Orions, and he was wearing a glossy, black, lizard-hide tunic over a dark red shirt. The lower part of his humanoid face was narrow, aquiline, and thin-lipped, and his chin was pointed. Scotty was very open-minded and not one to generalize broadly about other races, but with the Orions, he always felt privately that there was something cruel and repellent about their appearance.

"So, if you can monitor our transmissions, then you were able to receive us when we hailed you," Scott said. "Why didn't you respond?"

"We are not obliged to respond to every ship that hails us," the Orion replied arrogantly. "Besides, we were having some trouble with our communications system and were unable to transmit at the time."

Trust an Orion to be defiant and to cover his backside at the same time, Scotty thought. And in the same sentence too!

"Well, you are certainly capable of responding now," said Scotty said. "My name is Lieutenant Commander Montgomery Scott of the *U.S.S. Enterprise*. What is your business here?"

"I fail to see what concern that is of yours," the Orion replied unpleasantly, refusing by omission to identify himself. "This is not Federation space. You have no authority here."

"This is Commander Anjor, of the Patrian space cruiser, *Komarah,*" Anjor broke in, "and you have entered Patrian space. The *Enterprise* is currently functioning under Patrian authority. I repeat Lieutenant Commander Scott's question: What is your business here?"

"We had merely wandered off course," the Orion replied evasively. "As I have said before, we have been having some minor difficulties with our communications system, and the problem affected our navigational computers as well. It was not our intention to violate your space, Commander. However, now that we have those difficulties resolved, we shall be on our way."

"I think not, Captain," Scott replied. "Stand by to be boarded for inspection."

The Orion bristled. "I shall do no such thing! You have no right to detain me or to board my ship!"

"You are in Patrian space," Anjor repeated. "And we have reason to believe that you may be smuggling contraband weapons to Patrian rebels. If you resist, you shall be fired upon."

Scotty shook his head. This was not the way to handle this sort of thing, he thought. Anjor was throwing his weight around unnecessarily and was backing the Orion into a corner. He was forcing a fight, a fight that Scotty didn't want. The Orion captain realized that he had blundered into a bad situation and would probably be willing to cut his losses after putting up some face-saving protests, but Anjor was pushing him into a situation where his only choice would be to surrender his ship or fight. Anjor was giving the Orion no other options.

"Firing on our vessel would be unwarranted and most unwise, Commander," the Orion captain cautioned. "We have merely strayed off course. We have done nothing to cause you to commence hostilities against us. If we are fired upon, we shall defend ourselves."

"Let's not be too hasty now," Scotty said, speaking to both Anjor and the Orion captain. He had to think of a way to defuse this situation, and he would have to do it quickly. He quickly signaled to Uhura to cut transmission. "Mr. Sulu, shields up, go to impulse power and position the *Enterprise* between the *Komarah* and the Orion vessel."

"Aye aye, sir," Sulu said.

"You want me to try to raise the captain, Mr. Scott?" Uhura asked.

"No," Scott said. "This is my responsibility, Lieutenant. The captain left me in charge. But I think perhaps we'd best clarify our position, as far as diplomacy is concerned. See if you can raise Ambassador Jordan."

"Aye aye, sir."

A moment later, as the *Enterprise* positioned itself between the Patrian vessel and the Orion ship, Uhura turned to Scott. "Mr. Scott, we're being hailed by the *Komarah.*"

"Just as I expected," Scott said tensely. "Have you got Ambassador Jordan yet?"

"No, sir. I'll keep trying."

"Very well, put the *Komarah*'s call up on the screen," Scott said. "We'll have to buy some time here, if we can."

Anjor's face appeared on the main viewer. "Lieutenant Commander Scott, the *Enterprise* has moved into position between our batteries and the Orion ship. I would like an explanation of your actions, sir."

"I'm just trying to let cooler heads prevail, Commander," Scott replied. "We don't want to go rushing into anything, do we?"

"Mr. Scott, I remind you that, as per Captain Kirk's agreement with Ambassador Jordan and my government's representatives, the *Enterprise* is functioning under Patrian authority in this joint effort. You will kindly withdraw your ship, sir."

"Mr. Scott," Uhura said, "I've gotten through to the ambassador at the legation."

"One moment, Commander, I have another message coming in," Scott said. He signaled to Uhura to cut off the transmission. "Put the ambassador on scrambler frequency, Lieutenant," he said.

"Aye aye, sir. Go ahead."

Jordan's face appeared on the screen. He looked as if he had just been woken up. "What is it, Mr. Scott?" he said impatiently. "I was preparing for the morning's meeting with the Patrian Council. This had better be important."

"Sir, we've got a bit of a ticklish situation here," Scott said. "We've intercepted an Orion vessel entering Patrian space, and they are refusing to be boarded."

"So what do you expect *me* to do, Mr. Scott?" Jordan asked irately.

"Sir, the *Komarah* is present on the scene as well. We're trying to get this resolved peacefully, but Commander Anjor seems determined to force the issue. I merely wanted a clarification of our position in this situation, sir."

"Mr. Scott, are you or are you not in acting command of the *Enterprise?*" Jordan asked.

"I am, sir, but—"

"Am I supposed to hold your hand everytime something comes up you're not sure of?" Jordan demanded. "Frankly, Mr. Scott, I don't have the time. I have more important things to do."

"I understand that, Ambassador," Scott replied, "but I'm merely seeking a clarification of our status in this joint mission, sir, as pertains to your agreement with the Patrian Council. If we're supposed to be under Patrian authority in this joint effort, then does that imply that—"

"Mr. Scott," Jordan interrupted, "I have a very busy and stressful day ahead of me tomorrow. Captain Kirk left you in charge aboard the *Enterprise.* If you're incapable of carrying out your duties, then I suggest you contact Captain Kirk and request to be relieved. And now, if you don't mind, Mr. Scott, I have important duties to attend to."

The screen went blank.

"Well, how do you like that?" Scott said.

"Sounds as if we've just been told to sink or swim," Sulu said.

"Mr. Scott, I'm picking up another hail from the *Komarah,*" Uhura said.

"I shouldn't be surprised," Scott said with a grimace. "What's the Orion doing, Mr. Sulu?"

"Holding steady, Mr. Scott," Sulu replied.

"Waiting to see how this pans out," Scott said grimly. "All right, Lieutenant, put the *Komarah* through."

Anjor's face appeared on the main viewer once again. "Mr. Scott, if you do not immediately withdraw the *Enterprise* and back me up in this operation, then I will go around you, sir, and you will leave me with no choice but to file a formal protest with the Patrian Council."

Scott stood there, tight-lipped, considering the situation. "Commander," he said, "with all due respect for Patrian authority, I strongly urge you to reconsider—"

The screen suddenly went blank.

"The *Komarah* has broken off the transmission, Mr. Scott," Uhura said.

"Mr. Scott, the *Komarah* is changing position to get in line with the Orion ship and powering up her weapons," Sulu said. "The Orion vessel has raised shields in response."

"Damn," Scotty swore. "Anjor's biting off a lot more than he can chew. The Orion has him hopelessly outgunned."

"I think he probably knows that, Mr. Scott," Sulu said. "He's counting on us to even out the odds."

"To save his bacon for him, you mean," Scott said through clenched teeth. "Lieutenant Uhura, open a channel to the *Komarah,* quickly!"

"Too late, sir," Sulu said. "The *Komarah's* firing."

"What? Bloody hell!" Scott swore.

The shots fired by the *Komarah* struck the Orion vessel's shields without any apparent effect.

"The Orion vessel is preparing to return fire, Mr. Scott," Sulu said, watching his scanner screens intently.

"She'll blow the *Komarah* straight to kingdom come," Scotty said, gritting his teeth. "Lock in phasers!"

"Locked in and standing by," the weapons officer said, having already anticipated the command.

"The Orion ship is firing!" Sulu said.

The Orion's plasma blasts struck the *Komarah* squarely amidships, sending debris raining out from it into space.

"Fire all phaser banks!" Scott said.

The *Enterprise* fired its phaser banks, but the commander of the Orion vessel had anticipated their response. Immediately after firing on the *Komarah*, he had engaged his engines. The *Enterprise*'s phasers narrowly missed the Orion vessel as the small and highly maneuverable ship darted out of the way.

"Clean miss," the weapons officer reported tersely.

"He's coming in for a run underneath us!" Sulu said.

"Full power to aft, lower maneuvering thrusters!" Scott commanded.

"Full power to aft lower thrusters," Sulu repeated the command, by rote. "Engaging now . . ."

As the Orion ship closed in rapidly for a run beneath the *Enterprise*'s hull, Sulu engaged the maneuvering thrusters located on the lower hull of the ship. Designed for short burst, minor attitude adjustments during docking procedures, the aft lower hull thrusters were never intended for combat use, but under full power they pivoted the *Enterprise* around its own axis, like a clock hand going from a quarter of twelve to midnight. The aft end of the ship rose as the *Enterprise* started an end-over-end revolution to bring the ship's saucer section around in a vertical plane, with its phaser banks bearing directly on the Orion ship as it was making its pass.

"Stand by phasers!" Scotty ordered.

"Standing by, sir."

As the Orion ship came in fast, its commander was suddenly confronted with a completely different and unexpected situation. Intending to run underneath the *Enterprise* and rake it from below, he instead found himself running directly into the path of the *Enterprise*'s phaser banks. Committed, he had no choice but to follow through. His only options were to fire or increase power in an attempt to outrun the phasers. He chose both.

"Orion ship is firing, Mr. Scott," Sulu said.

"Steady on," Scott said. "Continuous fire on my command . . ."

As the *Enterprise* continued to revolve, the blast from the Orion vessel narrowly missed them, the Orion ship's commander failing to compensate for the Federation starship's continued momentum.

"Fire!" Scotty said.

As the Orion ship passed the saucer section of the *Enterprise,* accelerating to the maximum output of its engines, the phaser banks fired and kept on firing as the *Enterprise* continued its end-over-end revolution. The result was that as the Orion ship went by them, the *Enterprise* kept turning in a vertical plane, maintaining the Orion vessel in its line of fire as the smaller ship streaked past.

The phaser blast struck the Orion ship's engine nacelles, and the viewscreen was filled with blinding light as the Orion ship exploded silently in the vast vacuum of space. When the light from the explosion faded, there was nothing left of the Orion ship but some scattered, floating debris.

"Direct hit!" the weapons officer said, unnecessarily. "A brilliant maneuver, sir!"

It was, indeed, a most unorthodox maneuver, Sulu thought, as he shook his head in admiration of Scott's quick thinking. Certainly one for the books. However, if he knew Scott, that would be the last thing on his mind right now. And, a second later, Scott proved him right as he pounded his fist furiously on the arm of the captain's chair.

"Damn it to hell!" the chief engineer swore. "This wasn't necessary!"

"Mr. Scott, the *Komarah*'s in trouble," Lieutenant Uhura said. "I'm picking up a distress signal. Her hull has been breached and there are fires aboard. There have been casualties. Commander Anjor has given the order to abandon ship and he requests assistance."

"The rash fool!" Scott said angrily. "Have all transporter rooms stand by to beam the crew of the *Komarah* aboard. As soon as they've all been safely transported, we'll take the *Komarah* in tow." He clenched his teeth and shook his head. "Och, there'll be the devil to pay for this, I'll warrant! None of this should have happened. What a bloody, awful waste! Lieutenant Uhura, send word to the transporter rooms and have them ask Commander Anjor to join me on the bridge as soon as he comes aboard."

"Aye aye, sir," Uhura replied.

A short while later, the crew of the *Komarah* had all been beamed safely aboard and Commander Anjor came onto the bridge of the *Enterprise*. He was absolutely furious.

"Why did you wait?" he demanded, storming up to Scott. "Why did you not fire on the Orion when we did? *Look at my ship!* This is all your fault! Why did you hesitate and give them a chance to strike?"

"You are on board the *Enterprise* now, Commander, not the *Komarah,"* Scott reminded him evenly, keeping his temper in check with an effort. He was careful to keep his voice level, though the tension in it was apparent to all who could hear him. "I may only be acting captain, but I *am* in command here."

Anjor stared at him angrily, his chest rising and falling heavily, but he restrained himself from another outburst. "Yes, of course," he said after a moment. "My apologies, Mr. Scott. However, my ship has been severely damaged, and that would never have happened had you supported me with your weapons!"

"I had no just cause to fire on the Orion!" Scott replied. "Nor, for that matter, had you! Aye, his ship may have violated Patrian space, but that's no cause to open fire! We had no proof that he was smuggling weapons to your rebels! You forced a fight when there was no need for one!"

"I disagree," said a voice from behind them. Scott turned to see another Patrian officer coming out of the turbolift and onto the bridge. "Commander Anjor fired on the Orion ship because *I* ordered it."

"And who might *you* be?" Scott asked with a frown.

"My name is Captain Lovik," the officer said.

"But I thought that *you* were in command of the *Komarah,"* Scott said, turning to Anjor with a puzzled expression.

"Indeed, he is," Lovik replied before Anjor could answer. "However, it is *I* who am in command of this mission."

"I don't understand," Scott said.

"Captain Lovik is deputy commander of the Mindcrime Unit of the Patrian police," Anjor explained. "As any case pertaining to the rebels falls under his jurisdiction, he is technically in charge of this mission."

"And *you* ordered him to fire on the Orion?" Scott asked, angrily turning toward Lovik.

"I did," Lovik replied. "And before you continue, Lieutenant Commander Scott, allow me to anticipate you, for I have already perceived what you were about to say. You were thinking that the attack on the Orion ship was unprovoked and therefore inexcusable. You were going to protest that by firing first, we had drawn you into the conflict when, in fact, there was no legal justification for your actions. Allow me to assure you that nothing could be further from the truth."

"What do you mean?" Scott asked, taken aback at having his thoughts read by the Patrian.

"The Orion was smuggling weapons to the rebels," Lovik said. "He had Klingon disruptors packed in the cargo holds aboard his ship, enough to equip a small army. Allowing those weapons to reach the rebels would have had disastrous consequences for our government and for our entire society. They had to be destroyed."

"Now, wait just one minute," Scott said. "Are you telling me that you were capable of reading the Orion's mind over a *comm link?* How can that be possible?"

"I hardly need justify myself to you, Lieutenant

Commander Scott," Lovik replied, "but the fact is that face-to-face, or within a reasonably close distance, I can read your thoughts as easily as you can hear my voice. At a distance, I could not do so unless you spoke or I had some visual cues from which I could infer your thought patterns."

"Infer?" Scott said with disbelief. "You had Commander Anjor open fire on the Orion ship because you *inferred* that they were smuggling weapons?"

"The Orion's actions spoke for themselves," Lovik replied. "His physical attitude and movements all indicated duplicity, and by hearing his voice, I could clearly tell that he was lying. And before you take umbrage, as I see you are about to, let me assure you that it was much more than simply guesswork on my part. The Orion's vocal patterns gave me indirect access to his thoughts, and it is within my purview to enforce Patrian law and execute judgment in such cases, in Patrian space as well as on Patrian soil."

"Well, that may be all well and good for you," Scott said angrily, "but *I'm* no telepath and I canna' simply take it upon myself to *infer* any such—"

"If I may anticipate you once again," Lovik interrupted, "you are not *required* to take anything upon yourself, Lieutenant Commander Scott. In its current mission, the *Enterprise* is functioning under Patrian authority. Both Captain Kirk and the special Federation envoy, Ambassador Jordan, gave assurances to the Patrian Council that the *Enterprise* would support the Patrian fleet in its efforts to patrol this sector and prevent disruptor weapons from reaching our rebels. We were assured of your cooperation in this matter. Today, you have failed in that task, and your failure has brought about extensive and possibly irreparable damage to the *Komarah,* along with the deaths of at least a dozen of her crew. There will be an accounting for this, I can assure you."

"Now, hold on just one minute—" Scott began, turning red in the face, but Lovik did not give him a chance to continue.

"I do not wish to hear any of your excuses, Lieutenant Commander Scott. Captain Kirk and Ambassador Jordan shall hear of this, and the final disposition of this matter shall rest with the Patrian Council. It would be pointless to discuss this matter any further."

Lovik beckoned to Commander Anjor and they left the bridge together. Scott simply stood there, staring after them, sputtering with outrage. "How do you like the *nerve* of that guy?" he said. "He provokes an attack upon his own ship from a superior vessel and then turns around and blames *us* when he gets his bloody backside shot off!"

"Even if we'd tried to add our fire to theirs, there was no way we could have done it before the Orion opened up on the *Komarah,*" Sulu said. "The Patrians never communicated their intent to us. They simply opened fire on the Orion."

"Based on nothing more than the word of a supposed mind-reader," Scott said, clearly disgusted. "He *inferred* that they were carrying disruptors! Aye, but the only trouble is, there isn't any *proof.* We just blew a ship out of the sky for doing nothing more than encroaching on Patrian space! How are we supposed to explain that?"

Sulu and the other members of the bridge crew simply exchanged glances. They were all thinking exactly the same thing. Scott was absolutely right. There *was* no way to explain it. Regardless of what

Patrian law said, the Federation Accords governing interplanetary commerce and relations did not recognize "telepathic inference" as proof of anything. Even those cultures that were not signatories to the Federation Accords, such as the Orions, understood that there were certain unwritten rules and unstated agreements governing how interplanetary relations functioned. One did not attack another vessel based upon an intuition, telepathic or otherwise. Not unless one wished to provoke a war.

If the vessel they had just destroyed was an Orion freebooter—as it had appeared to be and probably was—then chances were that Orion would not lodge any formal protests or complaints. If they had been freebooters, then Orion wouldn't even know about the vessel and its cargo, or its destination. Still, that didn't change the fact that the *Enterprise* had fired on and destroyed an Orion vessel without adequate provocation in the eyes of Federation law.

From a purely pragmatic and a moral standpoint, they could have done nothing else. The Orion had been clearly in the wrong, and if they hadn't fired, the *Komarah* would have been totally destroyed, along with all her crew. They could not have simply stood by and done nothing. But from another standpoint, they had participated in an unprovoked attack upon an Orion ship. And they had destroyed it. Scott was not looking forward to explaining *that* to Captain Kirk.

Chapter Eight

HALF ALSEEP, Kirk heard his communicator beep, and flipped it open.

"Enterprise to Captain Kirk . . ."

Kirk came fully awake to the sound of Uhura's voice speaking in the darkness of his bedroom.

"Enterprise to Captain Kirk . . . Come in, sir . . ."

Kirk brought the communicator to his face. "Kirk here. Go ahead, Lieutenant . . ."

Scotty's voice came on. "Sir, there's been some trouble. . . . We have had an engagement. We were forced to fire upon an Orion vessel. The Orion ship has been destroyed. The *Komarah* has been crippled and we have it in tow."

Kirk came fully awake instantly, sitting bolt upright in bed. "Casualties, Mr. Scott?" he said, his first concern for his crew.

"Negative for the *Enterprise,* sir," Scotty replied. "However, the *Komarah* has sustained a dozen killed and twenty-five wounded."

Kirk was out of bed now and pulling on his uniform. "I want a complete report, Mr. Scott!" he said, tossing the communicator down on the bed as he got dressed.

By the time Scotty finished briefing him, Kirk was fully dressed. He picked up the communicator. "What kind of shape are the Patrian wounded in?" he asked.

"I haven't got all the particulars, sir," Scotty replied, "but some of them are in pretty bad shape, and I'm not sure if they can be moved or not. We could use Dr. McCoy up here as soon as possible. The *Komarah's* surgeon is not familiar with the equipment in our sickbay."

"Stand by, we'll be beaming up momentarily," Kirk said.

"Aye, sir, I'll have the transporter room standing by," Scott replied.

Kirk ran out of his room and down the corridor. "Spock! Chekov! Wake up!" he shouted as he ran past their rooms. He reached McCoy's room at the far end of the hall and punched the signal on the door. "Bones! Wake up! The *Komarah's* been hit!"

From inside the room he heard a sudden flurry of movement, and a few choice McCoy expletives. "Uh, Jim," McCoy's voice rang out, "could you give us—I mean me, a few minutes?"

Kirk had been caught "en flagrante" enough times to understand exactly what was going on. "Uh, sure, Bones," Kirk said. "Catch up as fast as you can."

"Is something wrong, Captain?" Spock said, coming out of his bedroom. He was already fully dressed. "Is Dr. McCoy all right?"

Chekov was right on Spock's heels, pulling on his uniform blouse as he came out running out into the hall. Muir and Jacob were right behind him.

"Uh . . . no . . . that is, yes. Dr. McCoy . . ." Kirk fumbled for words. "We'll . . . uh, wait for him in the conference room."

Spock raised his eyebrow in a puzzled fashion but did not press Kirk for details, much to Kirk's relief. They went down the hall to the conference room. A few moments later McCoy entered, followed closely by Secretary Wing. McCoy had a somewhat sheepish expression on his face, but Wing looked perfectly calm and composed. Kirk quickly told them all what happened.

"Dr. McCoy and I are beaming back up to the ship at once," he said. "Mr. Spock, you'll be in charge while we're away. If Iano arrives before we return, please fill him in on what's happened."

"Yes, Captain," Spock said.

"Where's the ambassador?" Kirk asked.

"He's probably asleep or preparing for the morning's meeting," Wing replied. "They'll undoubtedly know all about this by tomorrow morning, so he'll want a complete report. I'll be back to give it to him as soon as I've seen things for myself. We'll want to have all the details firsthand when we meet with the Patrian Council tomorrow."

Kirk noticed that McCoy was purposely avoiding his gaze. Wing was simply acting as if nothing at all had happened. He flipped open his communicator. Scotty came on.

"Three to beam up, Mr. Scott," Kirk said. "Secretary Wing will accompany us."

"Aye, sir," Scotty said.

A moment later they materialized in the transporter room aboard the *Enterprise*. Scotty was waiting for them. They immediately made their way to sickbay.

"Where's Commander Anjor?" Kirk asked as they walked.

"He's in sickbay, seeing to his wounded," Scott replied tensely. His face was drawn and the strain on him was obvious. "Captain, I feel just terrible about this. If there was any way we could have avoided this—"

"You did what you had to do, Mr. Scott," Kirk said, cutting him off. "There's no point in blaming yourself. From what you've told me, the *Komarah* opened fire on the Orion and they shot back before you had a chance to do anything."

"I should have anticipated the possibility—"

"You followed procedure, Mr. Scott," Kirk said, cutting him off again. He did not want Scotty punishing himself for something he couldn't have helped. "The Patrians brought this on themselves. According to the facts you gave me, their attack was completely unwarranted."

"I'm afraid that's not the way they see it, Cap'n," Scotty replied with a tight grimace.

"Frankly, I don't care *how* they see it," Kirk said curtly. "And I'm not going to stand still for their holding my crew responsible for their actions. You are not at fault here, Mr. Scott. Understand?"

"Aye, sir," Scotty said with a sigh. "But I fear this is gonna play havoc with the negotiations," he added, with an uneasy glance at Secretary Wing.

"That can't be our concern right now," Kirk said.

"The captain's right, Mr. Scott," Wing added. "We shall deal with the political fallout of this situation at the appropriate time. Right now, we have to make sure the wounded are taken care of."

They came into sickbay and McCoy was immediately all business. "Nurse Chapel, I want a quick report on what we've got here."

"Dr. McCoy . . ." Anjor came up to him before Nurse Chapel could reply. "I want you to make certain that—"

"Not now, Commander," McCoy said, cutting him off abruptly. "The best thing you can do right now is stay out of my way. Your people will get the best possible care."

"We've got nine Patrians in critical condition, Doctor," Nurse Chapel said. "I'd classify a dozen as serious, and the rest are either borderline or superficial."

"Where's the *Komarah*'s surgeon?" McCoy asked.

"Over there, seeing to the critical cases," she replied, pointing the Patrian doctor out. "I've been assisting him to the best of my abilities, but I'm not really familiar with Patrian biology and we're spread pretty thin here."

"Anything I can do, Bones?" Kirk asked with concern. All around them the sickbay was crowded with Patrian wounded, some unconscious, some moaning and gasping in pain.

"Yes, get me every corpsman-rated crewman we've got aboard," McCoy said. "Anyone who's had any EMT or medical training. We're going to have our hands full."

"Scotty?" Kirk said.

"I'm already on it, Cap'n," Scott replied. "I made the announcement over the ship's intercom just before you came aboard."

"Good man," Kirk said.

The doors opened behind them and several male and female crew members came in. "We came in response to the announcement, sir," one of them said. "There's more coming right behind us."

"Good. Nurse, find out the level of their training and assign them accordingly," McCoy said quickly. As Nurse Chapel moved to comply, McCoy hurried over to the Patrian surgeon. "I'm Dr. Leonard McCoy, ship's surgeon," he said, introducing himself to the *Komarah*'s doctor. "These are your people, Doctor. As of right now, you're in charge here. What can I do to help?"

"Thank you, Doctor," the *Komarah*'s surgeon replied, obviously relieved to have some assistance. "I am Dr. Javik. Nine of the patients are very seriously injured. I need help in stemming their internal bleeding and I am not familiar with your instruments. . . ."

"Let's get out of their way," Kirk said to the others as McCoy and Javik went to work. He led the others out into the corridor.

"Captain Kirk," Anjor said, "I want you to understand—"

"Yes, I *want* to understand," Kirk said, interrupting

him angrily. "I want to understand why *one* Orion vessel, a ship that had taken *no* hostile actions and was confronted by an armed Patrian cruiser *and* a Federation starship, presented enough of a threat that an unprovoked and unilateral attack was deemed necessary!"

"Captain . . ." Secretary Wing cautioned him, "perhaps this is not the best time to get into such matters."

"With all due respect—" Kirk began, but he didn't get the chance to finish.

"Commander Anjor fired on the Orion vessel on *my* orders, Captain," Lovik said, approaching them. "Orders that neither Commander Anjor nor myself are required to justify to any diplomat *or* Federation officer."

"You must be Captain Lovik," Kirk said.

"I am. And I intend to lodge a formal protest with my government concerning the *Enterprise*'s actions and the conduct of Lieutenant Commander Scott."

"Lieutenant Commander Scott was acting on my orders," Kirk said, "and as captain, *I* am solely answerable for the actions of my ship and the conduct of my officers."

"Then you shall answer for them, Captain Kirk," Lovik said.

"Gentlemen, this is neither the time nor the place for such discussions," Secretary Wing said, stepping between them. "Captain Lovik, you may register your formal protest with the Patrian Council at your convenience. If you are unwilling to wait until you can transport down to the surface, I am sure that

Captain Kirk would gladly extend you the use of this ship's communication facilities for that purpose."

"And if you're in a hurry, feel free to use our transporter facilities to beam down to the surface," Kirk added. "I can have one of my officers escort you there now, if you wish."

"Am I to take it that you are *ordering* me off this ship, Captain?" Lovik asked.

"In the spirit of our cooperative venture, I am merely offering you the use of our ship's facilities, Captain Lovik," Kirk said in a clipped tone. "However, you may take that any way you wish. I am accountable to my superiors at Starfleet only for my words and deeds, not for my thoughts."

"In that case, Captain, would you be so kind as to have me escorted to your transporter room?" Lovik asked coldly.

"Mr. Scott?" Kirk said.

"Aye, Captain," Scott replied. "This way, sir."

Lovik gave Kirk a hard look, then stiffly accompanied Scotty to the transporter room.

"I can see that diplomacy is not exactly your strong suit, Captain," Secretary Wing observed dryly.

"I don't have much patience with bureaucrats," Kirk replied with a grimace.

"Including Federation diplomats?"

"I didn't say that," Kirk replied. "However, as long as you brought it up, I would appreciate a word with you in private, if I may."

"Of course," she said.

"In my quarters?"

"After you, Captain."

When they reached his quarters, Kirk stood aside to let her enter first, then came in after her. As the door slid shut behind them, he beckoned her to the table. "Please, sit down. May I offer you a drink?"

"Thank you. Black coffee, please."

Kirk punched the request into the synthesizer in the bulkhead of his quarters, and a moment later brought two steaming cups of black coffee over to the table. He sat down across from her.

"I'm sorry if I didn't handle that situation very well just now—" he began.

She made a dismissive motion with her hand. "Never mind that," she said. "What was it you wanted to speak to me about?"

"I realize that this is hardly the best time for this," he said, "but . . . I wanted to talk to you about Dr. McCoy," Kirk said.

She raised her eyebrows. "I see," she said. Then, with a smile, she added, "Are you going to ask me my intentions, Captain?"

Kirk did not return her smile. "As a matter of fact, yes."

"My God, you're serious, aren't you?" she said, surprised.

"If I may speak candidly . . ." Kirk said.

"Well, if we're going to be candid with each other about such personal matters, then perhaps you should call me by first name," she said.

"All right, Kim," Kirk said. He took a deep breath, then plunged ahead. "Leonard McCoy is more than merely my ship's surgeon. He's also one of my closest friends."

"Meaning no offense, Jim," she said quietly, "but before you continue on this tack . . . are you sure that this is any of your business?"

"Perhaps not," Kirk admitted. "On one hand, your personal relationships are really none of my concern. But looking at it another way, anything that affects the morale of my officers and crew also affects their performance and the performance of this ship. From that standpoint, it is very much my concern. The last thing I need right now is to have McCoy distracted or upset."

"All right, I will concede your point," she replied with a nod. "Go on."

"I trust that we may speak in confidence."

"Of course."

"This . . . thing . . . with you and McCoy . . ." he began, somewhat awkwardly. He took a deep breath. "I don't know how much you know about McCoy's personal life . . ."

"I know that he was married once," she said, "and that it ended in divorce. He didn't seem to want to talk about the details."

"That doesn't surprise me," Kirk said, nodding. "It happened before he joined Starfleet. In fact, it was the reason for his joining Starfleet."

"He never mentioned that."

"No, he wouldn't," Kirk said. "I don't think he's ever really gotten over it."

"I had a feeling there was something . . ." she said. "What happened?"

"It's not really my place to discuss the details with you," Kirk said. "He *is* my friend, and if he wanted you to know, he would have told you. My point is that in all the years since, McCoy has never been seriously involved with anybody else. He tends to affect a somewhat gruff exterior, but he's really a very gentle man. He can be quite vulnerable when it comes to . . . certain things. He's capable of very deep feelings."

"I think I understand," she said. "You're concerned that I might be selfishly toying with his affections, that I might be using him?"

"Don't get me wrong, I'm not trying to read anything into your motives," Kirk said.

"But you *are* concerned," she said. And then she smiled. "I think Leonard's very fortunate to have a friend like you, Jim."

"I consider myself very fortunate to have a friend like McCoy," Kirk replied. "I just don't want to see him hurt."

She nodded and stared down into her coffee cup as she gathered her thoughts. After a moment she said, "I've devoted most of my life to my career, Jim," she said. "I haven't had much time for personal involvements. The way I look, I've never suffered from a shortage of male attention. Most of the time, I've found it merely annoying and distracting. That was a part of my life I had simply shut down. Some men may find that hard to understand, but I channeled all that energy into other directions. I fell in love with my career, with my calling, my duty. . . ."

"Some men don't find that difficult to understand at all," Kirk said sympathetically.

"Yes," she said, meeting his gaze. "I can see that. I've seen the way you care about your ship and crew.

What we're talking about is a perfect example. In some ways, we have a lot in common. With both of us, our careers have always come first. *Duty* always comes first. And responsibility."

Kirk nodded.

"You've asked me some rather personal questions, Jim. Now it's my turn to ask you. Have you ever found yourself in a situation . . . with someone . . ." She paused and moistened her lips. ". . . someone very special . . . where you found yourself thinking how things might have been different?"

Kirk pursed his lips thoughtfully and looked down at the table. "Yes . . . once or twice."

"Then maybe you can understand how I feel about McCoy," she said. "He's a very special man, Jim. I saw that from the very start. He's touched something in me, awakened feelings I haven't felt in a very long time. This morning, when you . . . disturbed us—"

Kirk cleared his throat uneasily. "Yes, well . . . I'm very sorry about that . . ."

"I'm not a prudish woman, Jim," she said, casually dismissing the matter. "I am not easily shocked or embarrassed. That wasn't my point. What I was going to say was that we'd been talking most of the night. We had both realized that this was more than something casual, but at the same time, we also realized that any sort of serious commitment was simply out of the question. We had both been thinking about that, but in fact Leonard was the one who brought it up." She smiled. "He was concerned that *I* might be hurt."

Kirk smiled. "Yes, that would be just like him."

"He has his duties and responsibilities," she said,

"just as I have mine. And those duties and responsibilities will take our lives in different directions. We both know it won't last. But for a while—even if it's only a short while—we intend to make the most of it."

Kirk smiled. "I appreciate your frankness. And I think McCoy's a very lucky man."

"Thank you. And now that we've got that out of the way, we'd better discuss just what I'm going to tell Ambassador Jordan about the engagement with the Orion, and what we're going to put in our report to Federation Headquarters."

Spock sat before the computer terminal in the meeting room of the legation, scanning the Patrian police files on the rebel terrorists with a thoughtful expression. There was something illogical about it all, and he wasn't quite sure what it was.

Across from him, at the table, Chekov was at another terminal, going over arrest reports and transcripts of witness interrogations conducted by the Patrian police. Specialist Muir and Yeoman Jacob were with their counterparts, officers Jalo and Inal, interviewing various rank-and-file Patrian police officers in an effort to assemble a complete profile on what the Patrian authorities had done in dealing with the crisis. Spock was trying to cover all the bases, but he still felt that something was missing.

"I still don't know exactly what it is we're looking for, Mr. Spock," Chekov said, leaning back in his chair wearily. "We have been at these files for hours now, and we still don't seem to know much more than when we started."

"That, Mr. Chekov, is part of the problem," Spock replied. "We seem to have a surfeit of data, but precious little in the way of useful information. Doesn't that strike you as rather incongruous?"

Chekov looked perplexed. "All that tells me is that the Patrian authorities have had very little success in gathering information about the organization of the rebel movement," he said. "Whoever their leaders may be, they have managed to remain underground and undiscovered."

"Precisely," Spock said. "They have been most secretive. And that, in itself, would seem incongruous when one considers the length of time the rebels have been active and how long the Patrian authorities have been pursuing them."

Chekov frowned. "I'm afraid I do not understand."

"Any organized underground movement, no matter how well-disciplined and tightly structured, is bound to have its share of leaks, breakdowns, and defections," Spock replied. "No organization, no matter how efficient, can be immune to the effects of random chance. Simply put, Mr. Chekov, things go wrong. And yet, despite all efforts by the Patrian authorities, they have never succeeded in penetrating the resistance movement, either through the agency of spies or informants, or making any truly significant arrests. The rebel leaders are as unknown now as they were at the beginning of this crisis. And that seems particularly puzzling when one considers that the Patrian authorities employ telepathic law enforcement agents in addition to their regular police."

Chekov frowned. "That does seem difficult to comprehend," he said. "How could anyone conceal information from a telepath?"

"Unless one possesses the mental discipline of a Vulcan, one could not," Spock replied. "Therefore, the possible conclusions are as follows: either the rebel leaders and their immediate subordinates who can identify them have found some means to block or outwit the telepaths, or else they have devised some foolproof method for avoiding them."

"But how could they possibly do that?" Chekov asked.

Spock frowned. "I do not know, Mr. Chekov. At least, not yet."

However, a suspicion had arisen in his mind, based on the evidence he was confronted with. What if the Patrian authorities—or at least the Mindcrime Unit —were not really *trying* to break the back of the rebellion? If that was true, then it suggested that they had a vested interest in its continuation. If so, then there had to be some reason for it, and for the present, Spock was at a loss to imagine what that reason might be.

"Are you on to something, Mr. Spock?" Chekov said. "Have you discovered something in the records?"

"Not exactly, Mr. Chekov. There is nothing in the files themselves that would seem to lead to any definitive conclusion. However, there *is* an implication there, between the lines, so to speak."

Spock had the ability to scan computer files much more quickly than a human could, and so far he had absorbed much more information than had Chekov and the others. Eventually, a curious pattern had begun to emerge, a pattern he had not discovered until he went back and examined the records dealing with the Patrian rebellion that predated the current crisis.

"Each police report I have so far examined clearly gives the specifics of each incident, as well as the names and designations of the officers involved," Spock said. "After going over several dozen of these reports, I seem to have observed a pattern emerging. And each time, it has been consistent."

"What sort of pattern?" Chekov asked, curious.

"In every arrest made by the regular Patrian police force," Spock replied, "and in every documented interrogation of witnesses, the information produced was either inconclusive or else those arrested were strictly lower echelon foot soldiers in the rebellion who knew nothing of any consequence. In all those cases, when I have followed up on the eventual disposition, the guilty parties were subsequently convicted and jailed. Arrests were made, convictions were secured, and there is every appearance that the Patrian police have diligently been doing their job."

"But you see something else?" Chekov asked. "What have I missed?"

"Perhaps nothing, Mr. Chekov," Spock replied. "At least, nothing that becomes apparent on a straightforward examination of the files. However, you may recall Lieutenant Iano told us that the rebels were fanatics who generally did not allow themselves to be taken alive."

"Yes, I remember," Chekov said. And suddenly a look of comprehension dawned. "But clearly this has not been the case. At least, not according to these records. You think perhaps the police files have been falsified?"

"Perhaps. But let us proceed, for the moment, on the assumption that they have not," Spock said. "The majority of those rebels arrested by the regular Patrian police did *not* take their own lives, nor were any such attempts recorded in the files. On the other hand, the ones who *had* committed suicide were always those who had been taken into custody by the Mindcrime Unit."

"But if a rebel captive possessed information that could damage the resistance or expose its leaders, the telepaths could obviously detect it during an interrogation, correct?" Chekov said.

"Correct, Mr. Chekov," Spock replied. "And by committing suicide, a rebel could ensure that he would take that information with him to his grave. On the surface, it all seems to make perfect sense. However, why is it that only those rebels who were arrested by the Mindcrime Unit killed themselves? What was to prevent telepaths from interrogating those rebels who had been captured by the regular police?"

Chekov shook his head. "Nothing," he replied. "In fact, according to the reports I have been checking, that was exactly what happened. Following each arrest made by the regular police, there was always an interrogation, and an officer of the Mindcrime Unit was always present as part of the interrogating team. It appears to have been standard operating procedure, and it makes sense. With a telepath present, it made no difference whether the perpetrator was cooperative or not. However, because of the tight cell structure of the rebel underground, nothing significant emerged from those interrogations that would disclose the rebel leaders."

"Yet, in virtually every case where the Mindcrime Unit made an arrest," said Spock, "or even *attempted* to take rebels into custody, those rebels invariably committed suicide. What logical conclusion can be drawn from this?"

Chekov frowned. "I suppose one possible answer is that the only arrests made by the regular Patrian police were insignificant arrests, as appears to have been the case, while the only arrests that *could* produce useful information were made by the Mindcrime Unit."

"Perhaps," Spock said thoughtfully. "On one hand, it could be inferred that the Mindcrime Unit, possessing the marked advantage of telepathy, invariably made more significant arrests, but then that suggests that they simply didn't bother arresting those rebels who could be regarded as insignificant."

"Well, that's possible," Chekov said. "Once a lower echelon rebel was detected by the Mindcrime Unit, it's possible they simply marked that individual for surveillance, in the hope that he would lead them to bigger game. Law enforcement agencies throughout the universe often follow similar procedures."

"However, to follow that line of thought through to its logical conclusion," Spock said, "that seems to imply that the regular Patrian police had never succeeded in making even *one* truly significant arrest that was capable of damaging the rebel underground. Even if they were hopelessly inefficient, the odds would seem to argue against that. Random chance alone should have resulted in at least one, if not more, arrests that would produce some significant information capable of damaging the rebel underground. And yet, Mr. Chekov, according to these files, that has never happened. Not even once."

Chekov frowned. "It does seem highly improbable," he said.

"It certainly does seem to defy the odds," Spock replied. "And there is yet a further incongruity. If the rebels captured by the Mindcrime Unit invariably committed suicide, rather than be forced to divulge any information, one would certainly think that greater precautions would have been taken to prevent that. Indeed, if a prisoner was contemplating suicide, surely a telepath would be capable of detecting that intent."

"And yet, most of them still succeeded in killing themselves somehow," Chekov said thoughtfully. "But how? The files do not specify the details."

"That, too, seems rather unusual," Spock said. "One would think the details of the suicides would be reported. However, the suicides are simply reported as a fact, without any details as to how the prisoners managed to kill themselves. And there seems to be no logical explanation for that omission . . . unless they were not suicides."

"You think the Mindcrime Unit was simply *executing* rebels who fell into their hands?" Chekov asked. He shook his head. "But even if that is what they were doing, why bother to cover it up? Under the Patrian law of Transgression by Intent, they had that authority."

"Indeed," Spock said. "And we have seen Lieutenant Iano exercise it. Leaving aside questions of morality, under Patrian law, it is not illegal for an officer of the Mindcrime Unit to summarily execute a criminal. However, if that is what they were doing with the rebels who fell into their hands, then why not simply say so? And why execute only those rebels they arrested, while allowing those arrested by the regular police to live?"

Chekov simply shook his head. If Spock was on to something, whatever it was, he couldn't see it.

Spock quit the files and cleared the computer display as Iano came into the conference room. He felt the Patrian attempt to probe him and turned toward him, raising an eyebrow.

"If you persist in trying to accomplish that which you know you cannot do, Lieutenant," Spock said, "your efforts will only meet with repeated frustration."

"Your pardon, Mr. Spock," Iano replied. "Merely force of habit."

"Indeed?" Spock said. "You did not think your probe might be successful if you caught me off guard?"

Chekov watched silently and listened to the exchange with interest. He had marked the tension that had developed between Spock and Iano, and he wondered how it would resolve itself.

Iano stared at him for a moment. "Perhaps you are a bit of a telepath yourself, Mr. Spock?"

"Among my people, there is a technique known as the Vulcan mind meld," Spock replied. "It is not telepathy as you know it, rather, it is a temporary union of two minds, a blending of consciousness in which two can become one. If you like, I would be happy to demonstrate."

Iano shook his head. "I think not. I prefer my thoughts to remain my own."

"I rather suspected you would say that," Spock replied.

"You trouble me, Mr. Spock," Iano said. "I do not feel very comfortable with someone whose thoughts are hidden from me. Especially someone who conceals his thoughts on purpose."

"I, too, prefer my thoughts to remain my own," Spock replied, throwing Iano's own words back at him.

"You don't like me very much, do you, Spock?" Iano said.

Spock raised an eyebrow. "Your question is irrelevant, Lieutenant. To like or dislike someone requires an emotional response. I am Vulcan, and as such, I am not a creature of emotion."

"Indeed? Then your response to all individuals is the same?"

"No, that would mean that I lacked discrimination. My responses to different individuals are based purely on logic."

"I see. And what is your 'logical' response to me, I wonder?" Iano asked sarcastically.

"That you *are* a creature of emotion," Spock replied. "One who does not trust easily or often, and one who is not comfortable unless he can control or otherwise manipulate those who surround him."

"Well," Iano said, "that would, of course, be a logical description of a law enforcement officer, would it not?" He quickly changed the subject. "Has there been any word from Captain Kirk aboard the *Enterprise?*"

"Not since he beamed back up with Undersecretary Wing and Dr. McCoy," Spock replied. "If necessary, I could contact the ship and—"

"No, never mind," Iano said. "I'm sure he has his hands full right now. The story about what happened to the *Komarah* is just now being reported in our media. I'm afraid it's engendering some strong criticism of the Federation. I am not sure how it's going to affect the ongoing negotiations."

"That is not really our concern," Spock said. "Ambassador Jordan will undoubtedly take up that question with the Council this morning. I am more concerned with the matter of the disruptors in the possession of your rebels."

"And what progress have you made in your investigation?" Iano asked.

"So far, none of any consequence," Spock replied. It was, strictly speaking, the truth. What he had discovered would remain of little consequence until he found some hard facts to back up his suspicions.

"That does not surprise me," Iano said. "You will not learn anything new by going over old police reports. These cases are solved out in the streets. That is where you will find the rebels, Mr. Spock. Not there," he added, indicating the computer terminal. Then he suddenly winced and brought his hands up to his temples.

"Is something wrong, Lieutenant?" Chekov asked.

"Merely a headache, Mr. Chekov," Iano replied irritably. "It has been growing steadily worse ever since this case began. And so far, the Federation has done little to bring it to a speedier conclusion."

"We remain at your disposal, Lieutenant," Spock replied. "We are more than willing to assist you in any way we can."

"Then I suggest you join me on patrol," Iano said, rubbing his temples. "Our last encounter with the rebels did not prove very fruitful. Let us see if we cannot provoke another."

Chapter Nine

THE DOOR TO SICKBAY opened and Kirk came in. He spotted McCoy sitting at his desk, intent on the display screen of his terminal. "How's it going, Bones?" he said. "You look tired."

"I *am* tired," McCoy replied, leaning back in his chair with a sigh. "I sent Dr. Javik down with the last of the wounded that we transferred to the planet surface. We managed to get most of them stabilized, but I'm afraid we lost one."

"I'm sorry to hear that," Kirk said. "Under the circumstances, I'd say you did extremely well. Maybe you should go and get some rest."

"I just couldn't figure out why we lost him," McCoy said.

"I'm sure you did the best you could, Bones," Kirk said, trying to reassure him.

"No, you don't understand," McCoy said. "He

wasn't even one of the critical cases. He wasn't that seriously injured. Jim, I want you to see something." He punched up a display on the screen as Kirk looked over his shoulder. "This is a scanner image of a normal Patrian brain, taken from one of the other patients." Then he punched up another image. "And this is from the one we lost."

Kirk stared at the screen, uncomprehending. He shook his head. "I don't get it. What am I looking for?"

"Try it this way," McCoy said, punching up a split screen display that directly compared the two separate brain scans.

Kirk stared at the display for a moment, then nodded. "This one's different," he said, pointing to the one on the left.

"That's right," McCoy said. "This cranial lobe has been artificially enlarged." He pointed to the screen. "And this organ over here, which seems to serve some of the same functions as our pituitary gland, has been surgically altered. What's more, the chemical composition of this brain is markedly different from this normal one, indicating chemically forced growth. Jim . . . this is how they create their telepaths."

"You mean this man was a member of the Mindcrime Unit?"

"Placed in with the crew," McCoy said. "And his wounds were not what killed him."

"What did?"

"It was the procedure that made him telepathic."

Kirk stared at him. "Are you *sure?*"

"There can be no doubt about it," McCoy replied. "They altered his brain chemistry through surgery and chemical treatments, inducing growth and a corresponding increase in brain function. The only trouble was, the procedure triggered off a chemical chain reaction. In essence, Jim, his brain simply self-destructed."

"What about the other telepaths?" Kirk asked. "Could this same thing happen to them?"

"It's practically inevitable," McCoy said. "Each individual's brain chemistry is different to some degree, but sooner or later the treatment will trigger off a vicious cycle of malignant growth that is absolutely lethal. The effect is similar to that of a virus that could remain dormant in the system for years and then suddenly become active. And once it starts, it proceeds so rapidly that there's just no stopping it. It could be all over in a matter of days, or even hours. Jim, each of the Patrian telepaths who's had this operation is a walking time bomb."

"How long?" Kirk asked with concern.

McCoy shook his head. "There's no predicting it. I can't tell at this point what other factors could be involved. My best guess is that someone who's had this operation could remain normal for years, and then suddenly, without warning, the cycle will be triggered. The length of time could depend on health and general level of fitness, the amount of stress an individual's exposed to . . . hell, a mild case of the flu could be all it takes to set this thing off."

"What would be the symptoms?" Kirk asked.

"It would depend on how quickly the disease progressed," McCoy replied. "It could strike so quickly that it could cause a massive brain hemorrhage, and the victim would simply drop dead before he noticed anything was wrong. Or there could be a gradual onset. The initial symptoms would probably be migraine headaches, increasing in severity at a rate that would correspond with the speed of the malignant growth cycle. If death did not occur soon afterward, the victim would probably start to behave erratically, experience personality changes, perhaps even go insane. Schizophrenia, delusions of persecution . . ." He shrugged. "There would be bleeding at the final stages, but by that point it would be only a matter of minutes or even seconds until it was all over."

"My God," Kirk said. "Can anything be done? Can the procedure be reversed?"

"That's what I've been trying to figure out," McCoy said. "I'll need to check my findings with Dr. Javik to be absolutely certain, but I think it's possible . . . *if* we can get to these people in time, before the disease is triggered off. Once it starts . . ." He shook his head. "Maybe, if it can be caught in its early stages, it still might not be too late. But right now, Jim, I just don't know."

"We'll have to get back down to the planet surface right away, Bones," Kirk said. "Iano's got to know about this."

"I just can't believe they haven't figured this out for themselves," McCoy said. "I mean, I suppose it's possible that this could have been the first case, but that would seem highly unlikely. Surely there must have been other cases among the Mindcrime Unit by this time."

"Perhaps there have been," Kirk said, "and they've been covering it up."

"But . . . *why?*"

"For the same reasons cover-ups always occur," Kirk replied. "Either somebody's got something to gain, or else they've got something to lose. And one way or the other," he added grimly, "I intend to find out."

Night was falling on the city. Iano's police flier wound its way through the airborne traffic lanes about sixty feet above the ground. Spock sat beside him and Chekov sat in the rear. Muir and Jacob were still back at the legation, conducting interviews along with Jalo and Inal. Iano thought that it was all a waste of time.

"I don't see what you hope to gain from questioning police officers," he said irritably. "Anything they might have learned about the rebel underground from incidents in which they were involved was filed in their reports. You've been studying those. It's merely a wasteful duplication of effort."

"On the contrary, Lieutenant," Spock said. "It is never wasteful to be thorough and methodical. I have frequently seen official records that were accurate in terms of their content, yet incomplete in terms of reporting all the details of an event. Official reports are, by their very nature, merely a summary of events. Rarely will they contain a detailed account of what actually occurred."

"And you hope to discover some small detail that might somehow have been overlooked?" Iano said dubiously.

"Small details can often add up to important findings," Spock replied. "It is often the small detail that can make all the difference in a complex investigation."

"If you ask me, the only thing that would make any useful difference would be a supply of your phaser weapons for our officers," Iano replied.

"Undoubtedly, that would make a difference,"

Spock conceded. "However, that is a question that will have to be taken up by those in higher positions of authority than ourselves."

"In other words, we join your Federation and accept your rules, and then we *might* get what we need, is that it?" Iano asked scornfully.

"The Federation does not resort to using pressure to induce people to join, Lieutenant," Chekov said stiffly. "The Federation's chief concern is to avoid interference with other cultures, not exercise control over them."

"I suppose you really believe that," Iano said.

"It is something that we all believe and live by," Spock said quickly, before Chekov could reply with an angry rejoinder. He gave the young helmsman a warning glance. Iano's behavior was becoming increasingly confrontational for some reason. Probably it was the stress of the investigation, Spock thought. They didn't seem to be making any significant progress, and Iano was undoubtedly getting pressure from his superiors. To Iano's way of thinking, they were outsiders who were only in the way. Antagonizing him would certainly not help the situation.

"We have been in this area before," Spock said, recognizing some familiar details of the neighborhood.

"We are going back to the Arena Club," Iano said.

"You have reason to suspect a rebel presence there?" Spock asked.

"I am still seeking the suspect named Rak Jolo," Iano replied. "I have reason to believe that he frequents the Arena Club. What's more, the last time we were there, I picked up a telepathic impression, but it was only fleeting and I was unable to focus on it in the crowd. And then I became distracted."

"Yes, I seem to remember," Chekov said flatly.

Spock shot him another warning glance, but Iano ignored the comment and whatever Chekov must have been thinking.

"I suspect that the Arena Club may be a gathering place for rebels," Iano said. "It is dark, noisy, and always crowded. It would make an ideal contact point for them."

He brought the flier in for a landing outside the club. It was still early and the place was closed. However, the staff had already arrived and were at work inside. Iano used his police credentials to get them in, where he demanded to see the manager. The nervous employee who admitted them told them that the manager had not yet arrived, and Iano was apparently satisfied it was the truth and that the worker knew nothing that would be of any use to them.

"I intend to search the premises," he told the worker. "When the manager arrives, I wish to see him at once, you understand?"

"Yes, Officer, certainly," the anxious employee replied. "We don't want any trouble."

Spock could see that the employee was clearly afraid of Iano. He saw the same reactions among the other employees of the club as they began to search the place. Their search, Spock realized, was really nothing more than an excuse for Iano to go through the club and use his telepathic ability on the employees. They realized it, too, for their reactions were all quite similar. When they saw him, they stopped whatever they were doing and simply froze, staring at

Iano with fear and apprehension. They knew that if they tried to rush off and avoid him, they would appear guilty, but at the same time the idea of having their thoughts ransacked by a telepath was obviously frightening to them. Nor could Spock blame them for the way they must have felt.

As they entered the kitchens of the club, one worker suddenly saw Iano, dropped the tray of dishes he was carrying, and took off running toward the back. Iano shouted for him to stop, drew his weapon and immediately gave pursuit.

Spock and Chekov followed him past the stunned kitchen workers, who simply stood there immobile as they rushed past. The fleeing suspect had a head start on them as he bolted down a corridor at the back of the kitchen and down a dark flight of stairs. They could hear his running footsteps ahead of them as they plunged down the stairs after him, with Iano leading. When they reached the bottom, they turned and came into the darkened basement. Iano found a light panel and turned it on.

A series of lights came on in the ceiling, one after the other, revealing a cavernous chamber containing large pipes and boilers and a row of generators. Spock had been here before, though he had come down another set of stairs last time. Ahead of them they could see the large, monolithic towers that rose up through the floor of the club. Part of the basement was divided into rooms where the weapons for the game were stored and where the arena players could change and shower. There were a lot of places for someone to hide.

"Spread out and draw your weapons," Iano told

them. "I want Jolo alive, if possible, but don't take any chances. The rebel won't hesitate to shoot."

"Phaser on stun, Mr. Chekov," Spock said.

"Aye, sir."

"And take care that you don't shoot me while you're at it," Iano added dryly.

Chekov looked as if he were about to give a smart rejoinder, but he kept silent at a glance from Spock, who realized that it was all probably pointless. Iano could undoubtedly tell what the young ensign was thinking. They spread out slightly, keeping one another in sight, and moved slowly and cautiously through the basement, listening for the slightest sound. The only thing they heard was the hum of the machinery.

They came to the large arena towers and split up to go around them. Spock beckoned Chekov one way while he went the other. Iano was a bit ahead of them, but still in sight. Spock listened intently for the sound of movement, but with the noise from the machinery, it was difficult to tell if their quarry was nearby or not. Spock did not relish the thought of a disruptor being fired among all these pipes and boilers. In this situation, the suspect had the advantage. As an employee, he was undoubtedly familiar with this place.

Iano cautiously moved into the players' changing rooms, with Chekov going in behind him to provide cover. Spock remained outside to watch the door, in case anyone came in behind them. Suddenly, he heard a soft footstep right behind him. He turned quickly, bringing up his phaser, and then felt a sharp blow to his head.

He staggered, dropping his phaser, and through blurred vision, managed to catch a quick glimpse of someone raising a metal object. He cried out a warning to the others as he brought his arm up to parry the blow, and felt the shock of it travel through his arm as the metal pipe made contact. He struck out with his fist and heard the rebel cry out as his blow connected, then someone was leaping on him from behind.

He hurled the attacker off, throwing him a distance of about fifteen feet, then two more were on him. As he broke away from one attacker and hurled another aside, tossing him through the air as if he weighed nothing, Spock heard the sound of a door slamming, then he heard Chekov's phaser cycling. Four more attackers piled on him. As Spock struggled to break free, throwing one off and knocking down another, he felt another sharp blow to his head, followed by another, even harder, and then everything went black.

"Where is everybody?" Kirk asked as soon as he arrived back at the legation. He came into the meeting room with McCoy and Wing, where Muir and Jacob were busy compiling their reports.

"I don't know, Captain, we only just got back a little while ago," Yeoman Jacob said. "Mr. Spock and Mr. Chekov may be out with Lieutenant Iano. We've been downstairs, conducting witness interviews with officers Jalo and Inal."

"Ambassador Jordan returned from his meeting with the Patrian Council about half an hour ago, Captain," Muir added. "They're supposed to meet again this evening. He said he wanted to be notified as soon as you returned, sir. He looked rather anxious."

"I can imagine," Kirk replied. "Let him know we're back, Mr. Muir."

"Aye, sir."

As Muir got up to go get Jordan, Yeoman Jacob glanced up a Kirk. "Captain?"

"Yes, Yeoman, what is it?"

"Sir, we've been going over the notes of the interviews we've been conducting with various Patrian police officers who have been involved in rebel incidents," she said. "A couple of interesting things have come up, but we're not quite sure what to make of them."

"We've come up with something pretty interesting ourselves," Kirk said. "Go ahead, Yeoman, but make it quick."

"In most of the cases where the police had gone up against the rebels, where there were no Mindcrime Unit officers present on the scene, if there were any rebels killed, they left their dead behind. However, anytime the confrontation involved officers of the Mindcrime Unit, the rebels who escaped either took their dead with them or else disintegrated their bodies using disruptors. It raises a puzzling question, sir. What could the telepaths learn from the dead? And if the rebels were so anxious to prevent the bodies from being identified, then why remove or destroy them in some instances and not in others?"

"That's a very good question, Yeoman," Kirk said with a frown.

"There also seem to be two distinctly different patterns to the rebels' activities, sir," she continued. "In the past, most incidents centered around attacks on the police and the destruction of government property. In each of those cases, the rebels seemed to have taken special pains to avoid harming civilians. Whenever a bomb was planted in a building, it was always set off when the building was empty, or else a warning was issued to ensure that the building would be evacuated. And in past armed confrontations with police, civilians were never fired upon. If there was any danger of civilians being hit by stray fire, the rebels always immediately withdrew. The consensus of opinion among most of the officers we interviewed was that the rebels were targeting only the police and scrupulously avoiding injuring the general populace."

"But that doesn't fit the pattern we've observed," Kirk said.

"No, sir, it doesn't," she replied. "Since the disruptors have appeared, there has been a change in that pattern. While incidents of rebel attacks where only police or government property was targeted have continued, there have also been incidents in which civilians have been harmed, sometimes as the result of an explosion, sometimes as a result of being directly targeted, as in the recent hostage situation. And it seems that civilians have been harmed only in those incidents involving the use of the disruptors."

"I see," Kirk said. "And what do you and Mr. Muir infer from this, Yeoman?"

She shook her head, looking puzzled. "We're not sure, sir," she replied, "but we've considered two possible explanations. One is that the rebels have not yet gained sufficient skill in the use of the disruptors, and cannot control them to the extent of making sure that there are no civilian casualties."

"They seemed to have gained sufficient skill according to my observations," Kirk said dryly. "And the other explanation?"

"At this point, sir, it's really only a theory," she replied cautiously, "but the evidence would seem to suggest the possibility of *two* separate rebel groups, one more indiscriminately violent than the other, each with their own separate organization, only one of which is armed with the disruptors."

"Yes, I suppose it's possible," Kirk said thoughtfully. "Such groups often have splinter factions, in which there is a division of opinion as to their methods. There are always those who are more militant, who don't think the others are going far enough. However, if that is in fact the case, then I'm afraid that's not going to make our job any easier. And right now, we've got a much more pressing problem."

He flipped open his communicator. "Kirk to Spock, come in."

There was no answer.

"Kirk to Spock, are you receiving me?"

"Ensign Chekov here, Captain."

"What's happening, Mr. Chekov? Where's Spock?"

There was a brief pause. "They've got him, sir."

"What? *Who's* got him?"

"The rebels, sir."

"Good God," McCoy said.

"Quiet, Bones," Kirk said. "I want a full report, Mr. Chekov."

"We were accompanying Lieutenant Iano on a search of the premises of the Arena Club, Captain," Chekov said. "While we were there, one of the employees of the establishment bolted when he saw us, and we gave pursuit. It was a suspect Lieutenant Iano had been seeking. We followed the suspect into the basement of the club, where we lost him. We had gone in to search the area set aside for the players to change, and Mr. Spock remained behind, watching the door. While we were inside, somebody bolted the door on us from the outside and barricaded it. By the time we broke out, Mr. Spock was gone. We searched the entire place, Captain, but there was no sign of him. We found some blood on the floor, and a piece of metal pipe with blood on it, but that was all. It was Vulcan blood, sir. I'm very sorry——"

"Get ahold of yourself, Mr. Chekov," Kirk said, though he suddenly felt as if the bottom had dropped out of his stomach. "Where are you now? Where's Iano?"

"He's directing a police search of the area, Captain," Chekov replied. "There must have been a hidden way out of the basement, because none of the people in the club saw anything. What are your orders, sir?"

"Get back here as soon as you can," Kirk said. "If Iano can't bring you back, have him get someone to drop you off at the legation. There's not much more that you can do there now. Leave it to the police. If there's any word, I'm sure they'll let us know."

"Aye aye, sir."

"Kirk out."

He snapped shut his communicator, his lips compressed into a tight grimace. For a moment no one spoke. Then Kirk broke the silence himself.

"Chances are he's still alive," he said. "If they wanted him dead, they would have simply shot him, not clubbed him with a metal pipe. He'd be worth a lot more to them alive than dead."

"What are we going to do, Jim?" McCoy asked.

"For the moment, there seems to be nothing we *can* do, except wait," Kirk said. "And I'm not very good at waiting," he added grimly.

"Jim," Jordan said, coming into the meeting room,

followed by Muir, "we've got a major problem on our hands."

"If you don't mind, Bob," Kirk said, holding up his hand, "I've got problems of my own right now."

"Well, whatever they are, they're simply going to have to wait," Jordan said. "The actions of Chief Engineer Scott, whom *you* had left in command of the *Enterprise* in your absence, have resulted in a major diplomatic incident. Our negotiations have just about collapsed. I'm holding you personally responsible. It was all I could do to—"

"*Damn* your negotiations, Jordan!" Kirk said, grabbing the startled man by his lapels. "They've got my executive officer!"

"Jim . . ." McCoy said, putting his hand on Kirk's shoulder gently, but firmly. "Take it easy. There's no way he could have known."

"Take your hands off me," Jordan said stiffly. "You've just gone way over the line."

Kirk released his old friend with a grimace of disgust.

"Ambassador, we've just learned that Captain Kirk's first officer has been abducted by the rebels," Secretary Wing said. "And that's not even the half of it. There's a lot you don't know. We're all under a strain. Fighting amongst ourselves is not going to help Mr. Spock."

"I see," Jordan said. "Well, I'm sorry to hear about Mr. Spock, Jim, but our first priority has to be the successful completion of our negotiations for Patrian membership in the Federation. I don't need to tell you what's at stake, not only for ourselves, but for the Patrians as well. Mr. Spock is a Federation officer. He knew what the risks were when he enlisted."

"So we're just supposed to write him off, is that it?" McCoy said angrily.

"Over my dead body," Kirk said.

"Leonard, Jim . . . please," Secretary Wing said. She turned back to Jordan. "Ambassador, we're all supposed to be a team on this."

"That was my general impression," Jordan said, glancing from her to the others. "But you seem to have chosen sides."

"Oh, don't be childish," she snapped back, losing her temper. "So you've taken a small blow to your ego. So what? As you yourself just pointed out, there are a lot more important things at stake here. Aside from the news about Mr. Spock, Dr. McCoy has just discovered that the procedure used to create telepaths for the Mindcrime Unit is lethal. Every one of them stands in danger of losing his life at any time."

"Don't you think that's rather melodramatic?" Jordan replied. "The Mindcrime Unit has been in existence for over a decade."

"And the clock's been ticking all this time," McCoy said. "Besides, we don't know how many fatalities there may have been in all this time. It's possible that any deaths were covered up."

"If, indeed, that is the case, Dr. McCoy," Jordan replied, "then it is nevertheless none of our concern."

"None of our concern?" McCoy said, shocked. "My God, you can't be serious!"

"I assure you that I am quite serious," Jordan replied. "Such a situation would be strictly an internal matter that would concern the Patrian authorities. If you have documented medical findings capable of proving your assertions, then you can report them through me to the Patrian Council. What they do with that information is entirely up to them, Doctor. We are not here to investigate any cover-ups, whether real or imagined. We are here to successfully conclude these negotiations. That, and *only* that, Dr. McCoy, is our responsibility."

"What about the rebels and their disruptors?" Kirk said tersely. "Or have you forgotten about that?"

"I have not forgotten," Jordan replied, "but neither have I lost my sense of perspective. Our involvement in that investigation is purely a courtesy to the Patrian authorities, a gesture of goodwill intended to further the negotiations. Your efforts in that regard, Jim, are of purely secondary importance."

"I see," Kirk said, barely restraining his temper. "Well, your 'gesture of goodwill' just may get my first officer killed."

"If that should come to pass, then it would certainly be regrettable," Jordan said, "but it must not deter us from our mission."

"Our mission?" McCoy said. "I don't think it's the mission you really care about, Ambassador. All you're concerned about is your career!"

Jordan looked as if he had been slapped. "I've given you a lot of latitude, McCoy, for the sake of my old friendship with the captain," he said stiffly, "but you've been a disruptive influence ever since the start of this mission. I've just about run out of—"

"All right, that's enough," Kirk interrupted impatiently. "This isn't getting us anywhere. I didn't want to say this, Bob, but you've changed. The Bob Jordan I used to know was a very different man. I don't know what the hell happened to him. Somewhere along the line, he became just another feather-bedding bureaucrat, taking refuge behind policy and regulations and playing it safe every chance he gets, never making any tough decisions for fear they might bounce back on him. I don't know who you are anymore, Bob. But I don't like what I see."

"I don't know what you're talking about, Jim, but—"

"Don't you? I spoke to Mr. Scott when I went back aboard the *Enterprise*. You're so quick to condemn and put all the blame on him, but the fact is that he *called* you when they intercepted the Orion ship, but you avoided making a decision. You put all the responsibility right back on his shoulders, and when he did the only thing he could have done, you decided to cover your own ass at his expense. Well, I'm not about to let you hang one of my officers out to dry just because you didn't have the backbone to make a tough decision! As of right now, I'm taking charge of this mission."

"You?" Jordan said with outrage. *"On what authority?"*

"Starfleet General Order 29, paragraph B, subsection 3," Kirk said. "I know it's been a while since you served on active duty, so I'll refresh your memory. Quote: in the event of any hostile, life-threatening actions against a Federation starship or Starfleet personnel during a diplomatic support mission, it shall be up to the discretion of the ranking Starfleet officer to assume command and either abort said mission or take whatever actions he deems necessary to neutralize the threat. Unquote. The lives of my officers are being threatened, and I hereby exercise my authority under General Order 29 to assume command of this mission."

Jordan stared at him coldly, then turned to Wing.

222

"I'll be in my quarters, composing my report to Starfleet and Federation Headquarters. I would greatly appreciate it if you could join me there for a conference at your earliest convenience."

With that, he turned on his heel and stalked out of the room.

"You shouldn't have done that," she said to Kirk. "I think you're making a very serious mistake."

"You're entitled to that opinion," Kirk said flatly.

"I just hope you know what you're doing," she said. "I'm concerned about Mr. Spock as well, but I'm also concerned about this mission. I have to be. You had better be very sure of your ground, Captain."

She turned and followed Jordan out of the room.

"That was a handy thing, your remembering that regulation," McCoy said. "Your quoting it that way shut Jordan's act right down."

"I hate to admit it, Captain," Yeoman Jacob said, looking perplexed, "but I've never even heard of General Order 29."

"That's because there isn't one, Yeoman," Kirk said. "I made it up."

She stared at him with disbelief, as if she wasn't sure she had heard him correctly. *"You made it up?"* Belatedly, she added, "Sir?"

"That's right, Yeoman," Kirk said. He smiled wryly. "You see, unlike you, no diplomat in my experience has ever had the guts to admit being ignorant of anything."

"But . . . what if they check, sir?" she said.

"It was a calculated risk," Kirk replied. "When you bluff, bluff big."

"Do *not* play poker with this man," McCoy said to her with a grin.

"But, sir," Muir said with a stricken expression, "how can you possibly hope to get away with this? You could be court-martialed!"

"I'll cross that bridge when I come to it, Mr. Muir," Kirk replied. "Meanwhile, we've bought ourselves—and Mr. Spock—some time. And right now, that's all that matters."

"All right, so what's our next move?" McCoy asked.

"To a large extent, that depends on what Jordan does," Kirk said. "Right now, he's probably fit to be tied. Eventually, one of two things is going to happen. Either he'll send a message to Starfleet, hoping to get them to override my decision, or else he'll start racking his brain to come up with a way to circumvent General Order 29."

"But there *is* no General Order 29!" Muir said.

"Exactly, Mr. Muir," Kirk said, "but then he doesn't know that. And he won't know it unless he beams back up to the ship and uses the computer to consult Starfleet regulations."

"But, sir, what's to prevent him from doing that?" Yeoman Jacob asked.

"This," Kirk said, flipping open his communicator. "Kirk to *Enterprise.*"

"Scott here, Cap'n."

"Mr. Scott, the *Enterprise* appears to be having a transporter malfunction."

"There must be some mistake, Cap'n," Scott replied. "There's nothing wrong with the transporters!"

"I'll say again, Mr. Scott, there *appears* to be a transporter malfunction. Do you get my drift?"

"Aye . . . I think I understand, sir," Scott replied. "Exactly how *long* do you think this . . . appearance may persist?"

"Until I tell you otherwise, Mr. Scott. Mr. Spock has been captured by the rebels, and if we're going to get him back, we'll have to stall for time. For the present, this apparent malfunction will, unfortunately, prevent either Secretary Wing or Ambassador Jordan from beaming aboard the ship. In the event they request to beam back up, you will, needless to say, assure them that everything possible is being done to remedy the situation."

"Aye, Cap'n. I get your drift."

"I thought you would, Mr. Scott. Meanwhile, I want you to start a scanner sweep of the city and see if you can locate Spock. There's only one Vulcan on the planet surface. Program the ship's scanners to search for his life-form reading and filter out all Patrian life-forms."

"Aye, but in an area that size, and so densely populated, that could days, Cap'n!" Scott replied.

"Make it hours, Mr. Scott. Kirk out."

"That was very sneaky, sir," Yeoman Jacob said with a grin.

"I prefer to call it 'creative,' Yeoman," Kirk replied with a straight face.

"What happens now, Captain?" Muir asked.

"We wait, Mr. Muir," Kirk replied. "Maybe we'll get lucky with those scanner sweeps. But if not, and if I'm reading this situation correctly, we still won't have to wait very long. I think we could all use some coffee."

"I'll get it, sir," Yeoman Jacob said.

Ten minutes later Chekov arrived. However, he didn't have much new information to report.

"The police are searching the entire area where Mr. Spock had disappeared, Captain," he said, "but so far they have discovered nothing. Lieutenant Iano asked me to inform you that he was personally taking charge of the search and would not rest until Mr. Spock was found. He also asked me to tell you that he believes the rebels will keep Mr. Spock alive, and that they will most likely use him as a hostage to make certain demands."

"I'm counting on that, Mr. Chekov," Kirk said. "I'm counting on that very much indeed."

His communicator signal sounded and he quickly raised it and flipped it open. "Kirk here," he said.

"Spock here, Captain."

"Spock! Are you all right? Where are you?" He quickly gestured to Chekov and pointed at his communicator. Chekov immediately realized what he meant, flipped open his own communicator, moved to a far corner of the room and called the ship.

Suddenly, a new, unfamiliar voice came over Kirk's communicator. "He is quite well, Captain Kirk, with the exception of some bruises and several cuts on his head. Vulcans seem to be a tough species."

"Who *is* this?" Kirk demanded. The voice sounded vaguely familiar, somehow, but he couldn't place it.

"Never mind who this is," the voice replied. "If you want to see your first officer alive again, you will listen very carefully and do *exactly* as I say. You will leave your present location and proceed alone and on foot to the Central Plaza square. You will have *precisely* twenty minutes to reach that location, so you had best not waste any time. Once you reach the square, you will be contacted again. You will be watched. If there is anyone following you, the Vulcan dies. If you attempt to communicate with anyone, the Vulcan dies. And if I even smell the faintest hint of any trickery, the Vulcan dies. Understood?"

"Understood," Kirk replied. "Let me speak with Spock again."

The contact was abruptly broken.

"Surely you're not thinking of doing as they say?" McCoy said.

"I have absolutely no intention of doing as they say," Kirk replied. He changed the channel on his communicator and punched in the scrambler frequency. "Kirk to *Enterprise*. Come in, Scotty."

A moment later the reply came. "Scott here, sir. Sorry for the delay, Cap'n, but it took a moment to switch to scrambler frequency."

"Have you got him, Scotty?"

"Aye, Cap'n, I've got him."

Chekov grinned. The moment Kirk signaled him, he had called the *Enterprise* and had Scott home in on Spock's communicator signal. And unless the rebels knew the code for switching to scrambler frequency, they could not use Spock's communicator to monitor their transmissions.

"Lock in transporter coordinates, Mr. Scott," Kirk said, "and have a full complement of Security standing by in the transporter room, phasers on stun. As soon as they're in position, beam up everyone at those coordinates. Let me know as soon as you've got them all aboard. Kirk out."

"Nicely done, sir," Muir said with admiration, perceiving what Kirk intended.

"That's going to be one very surprised group of rebels," McCoy said.

"Let's just hope like hell they haven't got one of

those interference generators set up wherever they are," Kirk replied. "If they do, we're in a lot of trouble."

They waited tensely for several moments, then Scotty called back.

"Enterprise to Cap'n Kirk."

"Have you got them, Scotty?"

"Aye, sir, we've got 'em! And a mighty angry bunch they are too!"

"How's Spock? Is he all right?"

"He's got a bloody bandage on his head, Cap'n, but otherwise he appears none the worse for wear."

"All right, Scotty, stand by to beam me up," Kirk said. "Once I'm back aboard, our transporter will start having those problems once again."

"Aye, Cap'n. Standing by."

Kirk turned to the others. "I want a chance to talk to those rebels," he said, "but as soon as Iano finds out we've got them in custody, he'll want us to turn them over. Legally, we have to comply, and there's no way we'll be able to keep him from finding out. He'll know immediately. So we'll have to stall. Bones, you're in charge until I return. Get ahold of Iano and let him know the danger he's facing, along with all the other members of the Mindcrime Unit. The Patrians have got to be convinced of it. Do whatever it takes. The rest of you remain here until you hear from me."

They all replied in the affirmative.

"All right," Kirk said. "Good luck, Bones. Scotty . . . energize!"

Chapter Ten

SPOCK WAS WAITING FOR HIM in the transporter room. "Spock, are you all right?" Kirk asked with concern as he stepped off the transporter pad.

"I'm fine, Captain," Spock replied. "Merely a lacerated scalp and a slight concussion, nothing more. Nurse Chapel applied sealer to the wound."

"How did they treat you?"

"I was not mistreated, Captain, save for the blows on the head that rendered me initially unconscious. In fact, the rebels were quite concerned about my welfare. I was restrained while in their hands, but nothing more."

"I'm glad to hear that," Kirk said. They left the transporter room and took the turbolift, en route to the brig. "I want a few words with those rebels," he said grimly.

"They want a word with you, sir," Spock replied. "In fact, they have been most anxious to make contact with you."

"Have they indeed?"

"I think you will find what they have to say most illuminating, Captain. I certainly did."

"What do you mean?" Kirk asked, gazing at Spock curiously.

"I think that you had best hear it from them, sir," Spock replied. "I'll be most curious to witness your reaction."

They stepped out of the turbolift and walked down the corridor leading to the brig. Inside, six rebels were being held in custody, guarded by a squad of armed Security personnel. They looked up sullenly as Kirk came in with Spock.

"I am Captain James T. Kirk, commanding the *Starship Enterprise,*" Kirk said to them in a firm tone that brooked no nonsense. "Which one of you is the spokesman for your group?"

A familiar voice said, "That would be me."

It was the rebel whose voice Kirk had heard over his communicator. As he stood inside the cell, Kirk suddenly realized why his voice had sounded familiar.

"My compliments, Captain Kirk, for the way that you outwitted us. It seems we have greatly underestimated your technological capabilities. I would be curious to know how you managed it."

"We traced your location through the signal transmitted by Mr. Spock's communicator," Kirk explained. "We've met before."

"Yes, at the Arena Club, Captain."

"Zor Kalo," Kirk said.

The rebel inclined his head slightly. "I am flattered

that you remember, Captain. I am one of the leaders of the rebel underground, and the money I had won in the Arena helped to finance our movement. Of course, my competing days are over now that my association with the underground has been revealed through my match with you."

"But how were you able to keep it secret for so long?" Kirk asked. "You were right out in the open, at the center of attention during all the games. How were you able to keep the Mindcrime Unit from discovering who you were?"

"It is difficult for one telepath to read another," Kalo replied. "I was able to shield myself."

"You?" Kirk said, frowning. "But that would imply—"

"That I was once a member of the Mindcrime Unit," Kalo said. "You are quite correct, Captain. I had volunteered for the procedure, as did my brother before me. And I watched him die from it, as no doubt I shall before too long."

"Then . . . you know?" Kirk said.

Kalo nodded. "That the procedure is fatal? Yes, of course I know. We have always known."

"I don't understand," Kirk said with a frown. "You mean to tell me you all *knew* that you were going to die? From the beginning? And you *still* volunteered?"

"Yes," Kalo said simply. "We were patriots, Captain, and we were more than willing to give up our lives in the service of the republic. Each one of us had been carefully selected from the rank and file of the police force. Each of us had seen the violence that was tearing apart our society firsthand, and each of us had lost close family members to it. My brother and I had lost our parents."

"It would appear, Captain," Spock said, "that they specifically selected those officers whose exposure to violence, resulting in significant personal loss, had left them traumatized."

"They picked cops who had a death wish," Kirk said grimly. "And then they used that to condition and train them."

"A death wish," Kalo repeated. "Yes, I suppose that would be a good way of putting it. We did not know when we would die, exactly, but we were all told what to expect. We knew we would have ten, maybe twelve years, but during that time we could truly make a difference and make what was left of our lives count for something. And in the meantime, we would have the best of everything for our reward. Power, wealth, position . . . They knew it would have been pointless trying to keep it secret from us. We would have known anyway, immediately after the procedure. How do you keep secrets from telepaths?"

"So then the Council knows all about the effects of the procedure?" Kirk said with astonishment.

"In a sense, they do not really *want* to know," Kalo replied. "They choose not to confront it. The people have never been told, of course. The Mindcrime Unit is controversial enough as it is. If it was known to the general public that we were all going to die, and knew it, and had nothing left to lose, then there would be an outcry such as the government has never seen. Especially if it became known that toward the end we begin to lose our minds. That was the one thing they did not tell us, Captain, for they did not know themselves. Now, of course, they do, and the doctors who perform the procedure carefully avoid any contact with telepaths afterward, to prevent them from discovering the truth. We in the underground have tried to make the truth known to the people, but the government discounts it as lies and rebel propaganda aimed at frightening the populace." Kalo shook his head sadly. "Nobody believes us, Captain. We try to tell the truth, but the people do not wish to hear it."

"Indeed, why should they," Kirk said, "when it comes from terrorists who kill innocent civilians?"

"We have never killed civilians, Captain," Kalo replied. "Police officers, yes, and members of the Mindcrime Unit. I will freely confess to that. We are fighting a war, and they are the oppressors, the soldiers of the opposition. And it was *they* who began the killing, not us. But we have never harmed civilians. We have gone to extraordinary lengths to avoid doing so, often at the cost of our own lives."

"You forget, we were there when your people took civilian hostages," Kirk said, "and when you threatened their lives with your Klingon disruptors."

"No, Captain," Kalo said, shaking his head. "That was not us. I do not know how to make you believe me, but the rebel underground does not make war on Patrian civilians. We are battling to win their hearts and minds, not to destroy them. What is more, we do not possess any of these disruptor weapons of which you speak. Ask your own people. Ask them if they found any such weapons among us when we were brought aboard this vessel and taken into custody."

Kirk glanced at the senior Security officer present. "Lieutenant?" he said.

"He's right, sir," the Security man replied. "They were carrying these." He held out a small hand weapon, similar to the pistol Iano carried. "Simple projectile weapons. Crude and very primitive in comparison to energy weapons such as phasers or disruptors, sir."

"Then there is more than just one rebel group," Kirk said, feeling his spirits sinking. He had thought, perhaps, that they might have made a breakthrough in the case.

"No, Captain, there is not," Kalo said. "There is the rebel underground . . . and then there is the Mindcrime Unit."

Kirk stared at him. "Are you suggesting that the Mindcrime Unit is *staging* these incidents? That they're the ones with the disruptors?"

"I am not suggesting it, Captain, I am stating it as a fact."

"What *proof* do you have of this?" Kirk asked with astonishment.

"None that you would accept, I fear," Kalo replied. "I joined the Mindcrime Unit well after my brother did, at a time when the rebellion had already been under way for some years. In the beginning I had no sympathy with the rebels. I regarded them as criminals, and my motives for joining the Mindcrime Unit and undergoing the operation you already know. Unlike my brother, however, I was recruited into a special clandestine operations group *within* the Mindcrime Unit. Initially, the stated goal of this secret group, known only to a handful of superiors at the very top, was to infiltrate the rebel underground and destroy it from within."

"And that's how you got into the underground?" Kirk asked.

"At first, yes," Kalo replied. "I infiltrated them as a police spy, and over time I gained their trust. It was necessary for me to break the law in order to accomplish that, in more ways than I care to enumerate. However, my superiors had no difficulty with that. The end, they felt, justified the means. However, the more deeply involved with the underground I became, the more I came to understand them and their grievances against the government. And the longer I worked for the clandestine operations group, the more I came to see just why they had those grievances."

"And you became converted to the rebel cause," Kirk said.

"No, not even then," Kalo said, "though I began to suffer serious doubts about what I was doing. I had joined Mindcrime to fight criminals, and instead I had become one. Yet, at the same time, I was beginning to understand those so-called criminals. I was living with them, struggling with them, accepted by them as one of their own. They had become my family, Captain, and they seemed to show more concern for me than my own superiors did."

"So that's what finally brought about your conversion?" Kirk asked.

"What happened to my brother was what finally made me see the truth," Kalo said. "The truth that all of us were being used. I had kept in contact with him, though strictly speaking, that violated regulations. Each of us in the undercover group were supposed to function completely on our own, reporting only to our superiors, and never was there any direct contact. That way, the odds of our covers being broken were dramatically reduced. We did not know who the other undercover agents were, and the organizational structure of the rebel movement practically ensured that those of us who had successfully infiltrated one cell or another would not come in contact with each other.

And those agents of Mindcrime who were not actively a part of our undercover group did not even know that it existed."

"So then Lieutenant Iano wouldn't know about this group?" Kirk asked.

"Not unless he was a part of it himself," Kalo said. "And if he was, then he would not be functioning openly as a Mindcrime agent. Those of us who were undercover worked alone and tried to remain shielded at all times. It can be quite a strain, Captain. Sometimes, we have been known to slip. I slipped once, briefly, in Iano's presence."

"Lieutenant Iano mentioned that he had picked up a stray thought impression the first time he came to the Arena Club, Captain," Spock said. "It was what alerted him to the rebel named Rak Jolo." He nodded toward one of the rebels in the cell.

Kalo nodded. "Yes, that was a close call," he said to Kirk. "And later, during our match, I knew that contacting you would mean exposure, because you could not shield yourself from Iano. However, I felt that it was worth the risk. Our only chance was to get the truth to the Federation. That was why we had abducted Mr. Spock. We were trying to get to you, Captain. Not only did we have to try and make you see the truth, but we had to warn you of the danger you were facing."

"What danger?" Kirk asked.

"Iano," Kalo said. "He had undergone the procedure at the same time as my brother, and he is running out of time. That means he has become dangerous and unpredictable. The same thing that happened to my brother is doubtless happening to him, even as we speak. Toward the end, my brother started to complain of severe headaches, which grew steadily worse. After a while these headaches started to interfere with his telepathic ability."

"In what way?" asked Kirk.

"It became erratic and undependable," Kalo said. "At times, he was unable to pick up any impressions at all, and these 'blank periods,' as he called them, had started to occur more and more frequently. He had avoided getting any medical attention because he was afraid of being relieved of duty. It was much more than just a job to him, as it was to all of us. It was a way of life. Mindcrime agents do not have much success with personal relationships, as you might imagine. Their short-lived careers are all they have. Nevertheless, I convinced him to see a department physician, and in doing so, I killed him."

Kalo paused to compose himself. It was obviously still an acutely painful memory.

"How?" Kirk asked, prompting him gently. "How could *you* have been responsible?"

"Because the moment his condition became known, it signed his death warrant," Kalo said with difficulty. "We had kept in contact by an arrangement where messages were passed between us, and in his last message, he sounded full of hope and excitement. He had been told that his condition was merely temporary, the result of stress, and would soon pass. He was not dealing directly with anyone who knew the truth, so he had no way of knowing what was really happening. And since his telepathic ability had become undependable, chances were he couldn't have known regardless. He was returned to duty and given a special assignment. They had received a report, he said, of a high-level rebel cell that was headquartered in a certain building, and he had been assigned to a unit that was going to raid it. In his excitement, he had carelessly told me where the building was and when the raid would occur. It just happened to be in our area of operation. I knew that there was no such cell present in that building, and was concerned that innocent people might be hurt. However, there was no time to send a message back to him, so I risked breaking cover and tried to reach him at the scene."

Kalo paused again and took a deep breath to settle himself. "I was too late," he continued. "My brother's unit was supposed to gain entrance to the building posing as maintenance workers, so they were not in uniform, of course. It turned out to be an ambush. They were all killed. There was nothing I could do to stop it. And the next day, it was reported that the so-called raid my brother had participated in was a rebel terrorist attack foiled by the police."

"So you're saying the whole thing was a setup," Kirk said.

"Yes," Kalo replied. "Those whose orders created the Mindcrime Unit to begin with kill their own people when they start to become unstable, merely to protect themselves. And at the same time, they blame it on the rebel underground. There have been many such incidents, Captain, especially since the disruptors have appeared. More and more Mindcrime agents are reaching their terminal date. And they are becoming a liability."

"Like putting down an attack dog that can no longer be controlled," Kirk said nodding.

"Despite what you have been told, Captain, we are *not* against the Federation," Kalo said. "We would *welcome* Federation membership, and Federation help to arbitrate our problems with our oppressive, autocratic government. Those who are hoping to upset the negotiations are the same ones who have the most to lose if our government becomes more democratic. They are the members of the Council under whose authority the Mindcrime Unit is administered, those who surround themselves with secretaries and assistants and bodyguards to ensure that no telepath ever gets near them, because then the truth would be discovered. If you want to know who is smuggling disruptor weapons, Captain, look to them, not us."

"Your argument sounds quite compelling," Kirk said. "Unfortunately, there is no proof. We have only your word."

"Perhaps not, Captain," Spock said. And he told him of the suspicions he had formulated earlier, which confirmed at least some of what Kalo had told them. "Aside from which," he concluded, "evidence produced as a result of the Vulcan mind meld *is* accepted as evidence in Federation courts. I could easily confirm the truth of what Kalo has told us."

"For our own purposes, Mr. Spock, I agree," Kirk said. "But I'm afraid it's not a Federation court that we'll have to convince."

"In that case," Spock said, "why not bring Lieutenant Iano aboard and let him ascertain the truth for himself?"

"Of course," Kirk said. "That would be the obvious solution."

"Allow a Mindcrime agent to probe my thoughts

and discover all he needs to know about the rebel underground?" Kalo said scornfully. "I cannot allow that. I would die first."

"Somebody's got to start trusting someone, somewhere," Kirk said with exasperation. "How else can you hope to convince anyone of the truth?"

"They are not interested in the truth," Kalo said. "Lieutenant Iano will merely convince himself that I *believe* it to be the truth because I have been brainwashed by my compatriots. In his eyes, I will be nothing but a traitor who had been suborned to the rebel cause. I know how these people think, Captain. They have been conditioned well. Remember, I was one of them myself."

"But you managed to break through the conditioning and accept the truth," Kirk said. "Damn it, Kalo, we're not going to get anywhere unless you're at least willing to *try!* We have medical records that can *prove* the procedure to create the telepaths is lethal, and that it affects their minds as the disease progresses. We're willing to use all of our resources to get the truth out into the open, but you've *got* to meet us halfway!"

"Only on one condition," Kalo said after thinking it over for a moment. "You must agree to keep us in your custody, and not turn us over to the Patrian authorities."

"I'm afraid I don't have the authority to do that," Kirk replied. "I can try to stall things off as long as possible, but legally, I'll have to surrender custody of your group sooner or later."

"Perhaps not, Captain," Spock said. "Admittedly, it would be stretching the truth slightly, since Mr. Kalo and his group were not brought aboard the *Enterprise* voluntarily, but if he were to request political asylum for himself and his compatriots, it would be within your perogative to grant it, pending an official inquiry and determination of their status by a Federation court."

"Yes . . ." Kirk said as he considered the suggestion, "yes, that could work, Spock."

"Captain, I hereby officially request political asylum for myself and my comrades," Kalo said immediately.

Kirk nodded. "Granted, Mr. Kalo. Subject to your agreement to cooperate."

"Agreed," Kalo said. "Our fate is entirely in your hands, Captain. As you said, somebody has to start trusting someone, somewhere."

"What do you mean, the transporters are inoperative?" Jordan demanded angrily. "They were in perfect working order just a short while ago!"

"Don't look at me, Ambassador," McCoy said. "I'm a doctor, not an engineer. All I know is what I was told."

"Where is Captain Kirk? I demand to see him immediately."

"The captain went back on board the *Enterprise*," McCoy replied.

"Oh, I see. And the transporter was working perfectly for him, is that it?" Jordan said, his voice laced with sarcasm. "What kind of a fool do you take me for, McCoy?"

"I don't know," McCoy replied smoothly. "What kind are you?"

"I'll have you cashiered from Starfleet, McCoy!" Jordan said furiously. "By the time I'm through with you, you'll be a lowly corporal washing out bedpans!"

"Not if I'm cashiered from Starfleet, I won't be," McCoy said. "You can't have it both ways, Ambassador."

"Are you going to sit still for this?" Jordan said, turning to Secretary Wing in exasperation.

"If you'll only calm down, Ambassador, I'll do my best to try and sort this out," she said. "Let me have a word with Dr. McCoy in private, please."

"As you wish," Jordan said stiffly, turning and leaving the room.

"Would the rest of you give us a moment alone, please?" she said, speaking to Chekov, Muir, and Jacob. McCoy simply nodded, and they left.

She pursed her lips thoughtfully and stared at McCoy for a moment, then leaned back against the table and folded her arms across her chest. "All right, Leonard, what's going on?"

"Just what I've told you, Kim," he said. "Jim went back aboard the *Enterprise* as soon as they rescued Spock, to make sure he was all right and to interrogate the rebels. And apparently, some sort of minor transporter malfunction has developed since then and—"

"Do you really expect me to believe that?" she said.

"It's what I've been told," McCoy replied evasively.

"Are you sure you don't mean it's what you've been *ordered* to tell me?" she countered. "Before you answer that, I want you to think about this very carefully, Leonard, because I don't want to see you get hurt."

"Who's going to hurt me, Kim? You?" McCoy asked.

"Not willingly," she replied, shaking her head. "I care about you very deeply, Leonard. And I know you care about me. We shouldn't let this come between us."

"I can't believe you'd throw that in my face," McCoy said. "What we've got between us has nothing to do with this, Kim."

"Doesn't it? I have my job to do, Leonard, just as Jordan has his. You know how much is riding on this mission. It's much more than just our careers. Whatever you may think of Jordan, he *is* trying to do his job. You and Kirk may not like the way he's going about it, but that's not the issue here. I've never heard of General Order 29. Granted, I'm not really up on Starfleet regulations, but it just seems a little too convenient that the transporters have broken down right when we want to go back up to the ship to check the data banks."

"If that's how you want to interpret it—" McCoy began, but she interrupted him angrily.

"For God's sake, Leonard! Stop it! If you don't care anything about me or the mission, at least think of yourself! If Kirk's done what I think he has, he's just flushed his career right down the toilet! Do you want to go down with him? Is he *that* important to you?"

"Jim Kirk is not only my captain, he's my friend, Kim," McCoy said.

"And what am *I?* Just a passing fancy?"

"You know that isn't true," McCoy said softly. "You're very special to me, Kim. But don't force me to choose between you and my duty to my captain and my friend."

She stared at him, her face expressionless. "I'm going to ask you one last time, Leonard," she said.

"Will you call the *Enterprise* and ask them to beam us up?"

"I'm sorry," McCoy said flatly, "but I'm afraid there's a malfunction with the transporter."

"And I'm afraid that you, Dr. McCoy, are lying," Lieutenant Iano said from the doorway.

McCoy glanced sharply in his direction. "How long have you been standing there?"

"Long enough," Iano said.

"It's bad enough invading people's thoughts," McCoy said, "must you eavesdrop as well?"

"Your personal relationships are no concern of mine, Dr. McCoy. I'm pleased to learn that Mr. Spock's release has been secured. But you are holding rebel prisoners aboard your ship and I want them."

"You'll have to take that up with the captain," McCoy said.

"Who is conveniently absent," Iano said. "Perhaps you would be good enough to use your communicator to call him."

"I'd be glad to," McCoy said, "but first you're going to listen to me. You need medical help, Iano. And if you don't get it soon, you're going to die. The procedure that gave you telepathic powers is killing you."

"Please, Doctor, spare me the melodramatics," Iano said. "You are not telling me anything that I don't already know. We all knew when we volunteered for it. We all understood the risks. And we were all well-compensated for our choice, I can assure you. We knew we'd have maybe ten, twelve years of life, but in that time we could accomplish something that could help bring about an end to the violence and unrest in our society. A short life, Doctor, but a glorious and meaningful one, and then a quick death from a brain hemorrhage. It seemed a small enough price to pay, especially to those who did not have much reason to continue living in the first place."

"It's not that simple," McCoy said, suddenly realizing that Iano did not seem to understand the full implications. "There's no guarantee that death will be quick. It's possible, yes, if the disease progresses rapidly enough, but it's much more likely to be slow and agonizing. The odds favor a gradual, painful deterioration, accompanied by bouts of erratic behavior leading to eventual insanity. They didn't tell you *that,* did they?"

Iano brought his hands up and rubbed his temples with his fingers. "I don't have time for this right now, McCoy. Call your captain. I want to speak with him at once."

McCoy simply stared at him, then suddenly comprehension dawned. "If you don't believe me, Iano, why don't you read my mind? You *can't,* can you?"

"Don't be ridiculous," Iano said. "How else would I have known that you were lying about your transporter malfunction?"

"Your head hurts, doesn't it?" McCoy said. "It came upon you suddenly, just now. A splitting migraine headache. And when it happens, you blank out. You can't read anything! It comes and goes, but the frequency's increasing. How long has this been happening?"

"If you think you can alarm me with this pathetic ploy—"

"*If* I think? Why don't you *tell* me what I'm thinking, Iano? You're the telepath! You're the one who's so infallible! Damn it, man, can't you see? The truth is staring you right in the face!"

245

Iano drew his weapon suddenly and aimed it McCoy. "Enough!" he shouted. "I want those rebels! And I want them *now,* do you hear?"

"What are you going to do, Iano?" McCoy said, facing him squarely. "Shoot me? *Kill* me? Can't you see you're starting to lose control? For God's sake, let me *help* you!"

"I'm warning you, McCoy! Call Kirk! *Now!*"

"That won't be necessary, Lieutenant," Kirk said from behind him.

Iano began to spin around with his weapon, but even as he started to react, Spock applied the Vulcan nerve pinch and Iano collapsed, senseless, to the floor.

"We've got to get him back up to the ship at once," McCoy said, rushing forward and bending over him with his medical scanner.

Kirk flipped open his communicator. "Kirk to *Enterprise.*"

"Scott here, Captain."

"Prepare to beam up the landing party, Mr. Scott."

"Everybody, sir?"

"That's right, Mr. Scott. And Lieutenant Iano's coming with us. Get a fix on everyone and lock in the coordinates. Prepare to transport on my signal."

"Aye, sir."

"I see the transporter seems to be working now," Secretary Wing said dryly.

"I'll save you the trouble of consulting Starfleet Regulations," Kirk said. "There is no General Order 29."

"I had suspected as much," she replied. "You realize what this means, don't you?"

246

"You and the ambassador can have me court-martialed later," Kirk replied. "Right now, I've got bigger things to worry about. Scotty, are you ready to transport?"

"Aye, sir. Locked in and standing by."

"Energize," Kirk said.

Chapter Eleven

IANO CAME TO in the sickbay of the *Enterprise,* stretched out on one of the tables. Nurse Chapel was bending over him. He immediately pushed her away, sat up, jumped off the table and snatched up an instrument from a nearby tray. Before the startled nurse could do more than cry out with surprise, he had seized her from behind and pressed the instrument up against her throat.

"And just what do you intend to do with that?" McCoy asked.

"Don't come any closer!" Iano said.

"Or you'll do what, apply wound sealer to her throat?" McCoy asked dryly. "You can't hurt anyone with that, Lieutenant."

Iano moistened his lips nervously, then tossed the instrument aside. "I'll break her neck!" he said, shifting his grip quickly.

"Yes, I have no doubt you could," McCoy said, "but whatever else you may be, Iano, you *are* a police officer, after all. You may have the authority to execute criminals on your world, but Nurse Chapel's not a criminal, and I think even you would draw the line at cold-blooded murder."

Iano took a deep breath, exhaled heavily and released her. "You're right," he said. He brought his hands up to his head and pressed in hard at the temples, wincing. "Forgive me," he said to her. "The pain is maddening. I don't know what's wrong with me. I . . . I just . . . cannot seem to think straight."

McCoy bent down and picked up the instrument Iano had tossed aside. "It's a good thing you can't read minds when you've got a headache," he said, "otherwise you'd have known this was a laser scalpel. All you all right, Christine?"

"Yes, Doctor, I'm—I'm fine," she said, glancing at Iano uneasily.

Iano gave a snort. "I should have remembered how you lied about the transporter," he said.

"Nobody's perfect," McCoy said, replacing the instrument in a locked cabinet. "How do you feel?"

"The pain seems to be fading now," Iano said. He gazed intently at McCoy for a moment. "You were telling the truth," he said. "I can see that now."

"You could have saved us all a lot of trouble if you weren't such a stubborn, obstinate bastard," McCoy said.

The door to sickbay opened and Kirk came in with Spock. "How is he, Bones?"

"He's almost as difficult a patient as you are," McCoy said gruffly.

"That bad?" Kirk said, raising his eyebrows. He turned to Iano. "How do you feel, Lieutenant?"

"I'm well enough, at present," Iano replied.

"Not for long, if you don't get back on that table," McCoy said.

"I'm sorry, Doctor, but I'm afraid I must refuse," Iano replied.

"What do you mean you *refuse?*" McCoy said angrily. "Don't be a fool! Don't you understand what's happening to you?"

"Perhaps I do," Iano said, "but I cannot afford to become what you humans call a 'guinea pig' for a procedure you have never even attempted before. You are not familiar with Patrian biology, and I have too much to do right now to take that kind of chance."

"I'll admit, this is an untried procedure," McCoy said, "but damn it, you've got no other choice! And I'm not entirely ignorant. I've already treated Patrians after the *Komarah* incident, and what's more, I've got a call in to Dr. Javik. He's going to come up and assist me in the procedure."

"That will take time, Doctor," Iano said. "And right now, time is something I simply do not have."

"You're absolutely right," McCoy said. "You can't afford to put this off any longer."

"I can't afford not to," Iano replied. "I *must* interrogate the rebels, Doctor, before my government officially demands that you surrender custody of them. I am your best and only chance for corroborative testimony. If what you and Captain Kirk believe is true, then I assure you that the rebels you're now holding will never live to tell their story to anyone."

"Not if they remain aboard the *Enterprise,*" Kirk said. "They've asked for—"

"Political asylum, yes, I know," Iano said.

"I don't know why I even bother speaking out loud around you," Kirk said wryly.

"Forgive me, Captain, but I don't have time to waste with unnecessary explanations," Iano replied. "If you grant the rebels political asylum and refuse to surrender custody to my government, the negotiations will undoubtedly collapse. And if what you suspect is true, then that's exactly what certain individuals in our government desire. It would give them the perfect excuse to break off the negotiations, and everything you've done will have been for nothing."

"He does have a point, Captain," Spock said.

"All right. What do you propose?" Kirk asked.

"First, I must see the rebels," Iano said. "I can only testify after I have interrogated them personally. I have no doubt in my mind that *you* believe what they have told you to be true, but that is simply not enough. It would not constitute proof in a Patrian court of law, whereas my telepathic impressions would. Secondly, if what they've told you is the truth, then we must find a way to convince the Council of it."

"Won't your testimony do that?" Kirk asked.

"*If* I am allowed to testify," Iano said. "We are dealing with the complexities of political intrigue, Captain. If there are certain people on the Council who wish to see these negotiations fail, then they will find ways to prevent my testimony, such as insisting that the matter of the surrender of the rebels be resolved first, before any other issues can be dealt with. There are any number of ways in which we could be blocked from presenting our case. Delay will work against us."

"In more ways than one," McCoy said. "You've

already started to experience the first symptoms. There's no telling how much time you may have left."

"Which is why we cannot afford to waste it, Doctor," Iano said. "Even if you are successful in reversing my condition—and your own findings indicate that once it's started, it may already be too late—then my usefulness in this matter will have ended. I cannot present testimony as a Mindcrime agent when I am no longer telepathic."

"You realize the chance you're taking?" McCoy said.

"I do, Dr. McCoy. I also realize that I have no other choice. You need me, and aside from that, I want to find out the truth as much as you do."

"All right," Kirk said. "Let's go see the rebels."

"Jim . . ." McCoy said anxiously. "He may die at any time if we don't operate right now!"

"He understands his options, Bones. I can't force him."

"I can't go along with this," McCoy said.

"I understand," Kirk replied. "But you can't operate against his will either."

"I can't simply stand by and watch him die!" McCoy said with exasperation.

"I appreciate your concern, Doctor," Iano said, putting a hand on McCoy's shoulder. "Believe me, I have no wish to die. Not now. But I also have no wish to see my government controlled by a corrupt element. I swore an oath to serve my people and my government, and that is what I must do. And if it means I lose my life, then at least I will have died for something I believe in."

McCoy watched helplessly as they left sickbay.

"You did what you could, Doctor," Nurse Chapel said, coming up beside him. "Maybe there's still time."

McCoy shook his head. "The progression of the disease has already begun," he said. "Even if we operated now, I still don't know if we could stop it."

Kalo got up to his feet in his cell when Kirk and Spock came in with Iano. For a moment the two Patrians simply stood and stared at one another through the force field.

"Cancel the force field, Lieutenant," Kirk said to the Security officer in charge.

Several of the officers took up position with their phasers, covering the prisoners as the force field was canceled. Kalo stepped forward out of the cell and approached Iano.

"Zor Kalo," Iano said, facing him. "Or should I say, Kar Janik? We meet at last."

"Kar Janik?" Kirk said, glancing at Kalo with a frown.

"It was my name when I was an agent of the Mindcrime Unit, Captain," Kalo said. "But that was another lifetime. I left that life behind."

"He has changed his name and had reconstructive surgery to alter his appearance," Iano said, "but we have known about him for some time. The renegade Mindcrime agent who turned traitor and joined the rebel cause. We have been looking for him for a long time, and meanwhile he has been right out in the open, competing in the games. Congratulations, Janik. Very clever. You have made fools of all of us."

"You know who I am only because I allowed you to

know it," Kalo said. "I am not now nor have I ever been a traitor, Iano. At least, not to the Patrian people. And if your mind remains open as you read mine, then you will see that too."

Kirk watched as Iano stared at Kalo for a long moment, trying to read his thoughts. Perspiration stood out on Iano's forehead and he started to breathe heavily.

"It's coming back, isn't it?" Kirk said with concern.

"I will be all right, Captain," Iano said, taking a deep breath.

Kalo shook his head. "It is no use," he said. "He cannot read my thoughts. It is the same thing that happened to my brother and that will happen to all of us sooner or later."

"Iano," Kirk said, coming up beside him and taking him by the arm, "you've *got* to try!"

Iano shook his head. "I *am* trying, Kirk. But the pain . . . I cannot concentrate with the pain. . . ."

Spock came up to stand before him. "Perhaps I can help, Lieutenant. If you will allow me . . ."

He raised his right hand, his fingers spread wide, and gently placed his fingertips against Iano's face. He closed his eyes and concentrated as he began the Vulcan mind meld. "Your thoughts are my thoughts," he said. "Our minds are one. . . ."

Iano stiffened slightly as Spock's mind made contact with his own.

"Your pain . . . is my pain," Spock said.

Kirk and Kalo both watched intently as Iano's breathing grew more shallow and he seemed to relax. Spock stiffened as the pain Iano was experiencing flowed into him. He groaned, then broke off the contact.

"Now, Lieutenant . . ." he said, his voice ragged. "Quickly . . ."

Iano turned toward Kalo and concentrated as he probed the rebel's mind. Kalo simply stood there, leaving his mind unshielded, allowing Iano to read his thoughts. After a moment Iano broke the contact and nodded.

"It's all true," he said, taking a deep breath. "They do not possess any disruptors." He shook his head wearily. "We have all been used," he said.

"Spock . . ." Kirk said, approaching his first officer anxiously. "Spock . . . are you all right?"

Spock nodded. "The pain is beginning to fade now, Captain," he said. "I will be all right in a moment."

"Thank you," Iano said to him. "It has passed for now."

Spock merely nodded.

"What do we do now?" Kirk asked Iano.

"We must convince the Council of the truth," Iano replied. "But that will not be easy. There are members of the government who are behind all this, and they will want the negotiations to fail. They will do everything in their power to prevent the Council from hearing our testimony. And they will undoubtedly use your holding the rebels as their excuse."

"Then we'll simply have to find a way to *make* them listen," Kirk said. "Not only that, but we'll have to find a way to expose whoever is behind all this, force their hand and make them come out into the open."

"Captain, something has just occurred to me," Spock said.

"Go ahead, Spock."

Spock turned to Iano. "Lieutenant, while our minds were in contact, I received several vague impressions that I could not quite focus on, because of the pain. Who is Captain Rindo?"

"The senior police officer in command of the Mindcrime Unit," Iano replied.

"Police officer?" Spock repeated.

"Yes, that is correct," Iano said. He winced and started rubbing the head again. The pain was coming back. "The Mindcrime Unit, though it often functions independently, is technically a part of the regular police force, and as such, is under the administrative authority of the senior police commander."

"And this Captain Rindo is directly under the authority of Commissioner Karsi, whom we met along with Prime Minister Jarum when we were first introduced?" Spock asked.

"Yes, that's right," Iano said, sitting down wearily.

"What are you getting at, Spock?" Kirk asked.

"One moment, Captain," Spock said. He turned to Iano. "And what, Lieutenant, is the Board of Police Inquiry?"

Iano took a deep breath, struggling with the pain. "The administrative body charged with those high level criminal investigations involving testimony that must be presented to the Council," he replied. "Additionally, they investigate such matters as allegations of police corruption and malfeasance, as well as—"

"One moment," Spock said. "That may explain why these thoughts were foremost in your mind. When officers of the Mindcrime Unit, such as yourself, are called upon to testify, they testify before the Board of Inquiry, and the board then presents the results of its findings to the Council, is that not correct?"

"Yes," Iano said, looking up at him. "My testimony in this matter will have to be presented to the Board of Police Inquiry, and then . . ." His voice trailed off and, abruptly, as he realized where Spock was headed, a look of sudden comprehension crossed his features. "Which means that no member of the Mindcrime Unit has ever testified directly before the Council," he said. "Only to the Board of Inquiry!"

"Precisely," Spock said. "And since Captain Rindo is the senior police commander, under whose authority the Mindcrime Unit is administrated, then he has risen from the ranks of the regular police, and, unless I am mistaken, is not himself a telepath."

"No," Iano said, staring at Spock, "he is not. Captain Lovik is the senior telepathic agent, but he is only the deputy commander."

"I don't follow, Mr. Spock," Kirk said, looking perplexed. "What are you getting at? Explain."

"Simple, Captain," Spock replied. "On the surface, and from an administrative standpoint, it is all very logical, and not essentially unlike the organizational structure of Starfleet. The Patrian Council clearly cannot afford to be concerned with every minor matter involving subsidiary organizations such the police, and so the Patrian Board of Police Inquiry functions as an intermediary body, conducting all such investigations and presenting to the Council only those matters deemed worthy of their attention. However, an interesting result of this procedure is that no police officer, and perhaps more significantly, no member of the Mindcrime Unit, ever appears before the Council in person."

"Of course!" Kirk said as it all came together for

him. "And if there are no telepaths on the Police Board of Inquiry, then the board essentially functions as a buffer between the Council and the telepaths!"

"Correct," Spock said. "If certain members of the Council had something to hide, then they most certainly would not wish to be confronted with a telepath."

"Simple," Kirk said, nodding, "yet far from obvious. Deceit hiding behind basic administrative procedure. And it wouldn't be the first time. Well, we're going to have to change that. I've got an idea, but it will require the cooperation of Ambassador Jordan. Iano, how are you holding up?"

"Well enough," the telepath replied. "But the headaches seem to be coming more frequently, and my ability comes and goes with them. It's becoming more and more erratic."

"Then we don't have any time to lose," Kirk said. "We'll have to move fast. All right, everyone, listen carefully. You too, Kalo. Here's what we're going to do . . ."

"Absolutely not!" Ambassador Jordan said. "Do you have any idea what you're proposing? By all rights, Jim, I ought to have you in the brig for what you pulled with 'General Order 29'! You have jeopardized this mission enough already! What you're suggesting is completely out of the question!"

Jordan had beamed up with the rest of the landing party and they were alone in his quarters on the *Enterprise*. Kirk knew this was the only chance he had to bring him around. They were running out of time. He had no idea how much longer Iano had, and McCoy's prognosis was not good.

"Bob, listen to me, *please,*" Kirk said. "This mission was in jeopardy from the moment it began, and it was none of my doing. Believe it or not, I want to see it succeed as much as you do!"

"You wouldn't know it from your actions," Jordan said curtly.

"Everything I've done," Kirk replied, "has been aimed at helping this mission succeed. Somehow, I've got to make you see that! If you'll only open your mind long enough—"

"My mind is not closed, Jim, but it *is* made up," Jordan said flatly. "I knew you were an unpredictable maverick. You always were, even back at the Academy. I was against your being assigned to this mission in the first place, but your superiors at Starfleet seemed to have a great deal of confidence in you, and for old times' sake, I decided to give you the benefit of the doubt."

"I appreciate that—" Kirk began, but Jordan wouldn't let him finish.

"However," he continued forcefully, "everything you've done so far has only served to reinforce my original opinion. By rights, I should have you relieved of command at once and court-martialed you at the first opportunity. I've already composed my report to Starfleet and Federation Headquarters, and all I have to do is sign off on it and send it in. And frankly, right now I can't think of a single reason why I shouldn't."

"Then let me give you one," Kirk said. "You want this mission to succeed. We both know there's a lot at stake here, and bringing the Patrian Republics into the Federation would be quite a step up in your career. But that's not going to happen unless we put aside our differences and work together. Afterward, if you want to have me court-martialed, that's your perogative. I admit I misled you about General Order 29, but you forced my hand! I had to buy some time for Spock. And if I hadn't done what I did, we never would have discovered the truth about the rebels."

"Yes, I know," Jordan admitted grudgingly. "That's the only reason I'm listening to you right now."

"Look, Bob, I know you're angry, and you have a right to be, but if you can put aside your anger for a moment, just ask yourself, what possible *reason* would I have for wanting to sabotage this mission? We're supposed to be on the same team. For God's sake, *work* with me!"

Jordan took a deep breath and let it out slowly. "Very well," he said. "I'll let you make your case. But it had better be good, Jim, or I'll wind up getting tried, as well as you."

"All right," Kirk said. "Iano has determined that the rebels are not the ones with the disruptors, and our research team supports the conclusion that there must be at least *two* groups responsible for the so-called rebel incidents. We know the Mindcrime Unit was highly controversial from the beginning. We also know that the operation employed to create the telepaths has long-term lethal consequences and results in mental breakdown that endangers not only the officers themselves, but the general populace as well. The underground has tried to get that information out, but it's been dismissed as rebel propaganda. However, McCoy's evidence is incontrovertible. He *must* be allowed to present it. Somebody on the Council is involved, and they've been covering it up. Whoever is responsible has probably made a deal with the Klingons to smuggle in disruptors, not to distribute to the rebels, but to equip a clandestine special unit whose purpose has been to stage terrorist incidents and blame them on the underground, thereby increasing public support for the Mindcrime Unit and the increasingly autocratic measures of the government."

"Perhaps the Klingons have given the people responsible some sort of guarantees," Jordan said, following his logic.

"Yes, but we both know what that's worth," Kirk replied. "If the Patrian Republics join the Federation, they'll have to become signatories to the Federation Accords, and that will inevitably lead to democratic reforms in their government. Somebody on the Council is out to prevent that, and if we can expose who it is, we'll find out who's responsible for the disruptors."

"What if you're wrong about this?" Jordan said.

"I'm not," Kirk replied. "However, if this doesn't work, then I become your whipping boy. Spock will take command of the *Enterprise* and you can surrender custody of the rebels, then use my arrest and subsequent court-martial as a demonstration of goodwill to the Patrians. And I'll even cover you in my testimony at my court-martial."

Jordan thought about it for a moment as he walked over to the observation port and stared out into space. "I hope you're right, Jim," he said, "I really do. Because if you're not, we'll be charged with violating the Prime Directive and we can both kiss our careers good-bye."

"There's a lot more at stake than our careers," Kirk replied. "If we don't succeed, Bob, a lot of people are going to die. The Patrians will fall under the domination of the Klingons, and there won't be a thing the

Federation can do about it. We've got a chance to prevent that. I'd say that's worth risking our careers, wouldn't you?"

Jordan turned back from the observation port to face him. "What makes you think the rebels can be trusted?"

"Iano thinks they can be," Kirk replied. "But I'm not taking any chances. They won't be carrying live weapons, and I'll have armed crewmen watching them every second."

Jordan sighed and shook his head. "This is really crazy," he said. "And I guess that makes me crazy for going along with it."

"Then you'll do it?" Kirk said.

Jordan nodded. "All right, I'll go along." He sighed heavily. "And if this blows up in our faces, I won't let you take the rap alone. But I hope to hell you know what you're doing."

Kirk smiled. "Now that's the Bob Jordan I remember," he said. He held out his hand, and as Jordan took it, Kirk said, "Welcome back."

The Patrian Council was in session in their meeting chambers as Ambassador Jordan entered with Kirk and proceeded to the table in the center of the room. The U-shaped dais of the Council encircled them as they took their places behind the two chairs that had been reserved for the ambassador and Secretary Wing.

Prime Minister Jarum rapped his ceremonial gavel several times on the table before him and waited for the undertone from the other Council members to die down. "We are curious as to the reason for Captain Kirk's presence at this meeting, Ambassador Jordan," he said. "Why has he come in place of Secretary Wing?"

"Secretary Wing is . . . temporarily indisposed," Ambassador Jordan replied with a brief glance at Kirk. "And since Captain Kirk is directly concerned with the subject of this meeting today, I thought it best he should attend."

Prime Minister Jarum nodded. "Very well," he said. "You are welcome, Captain Kirk. Please, take your seats."

"Thank you, Prime Minister," Kirk replied. "I would prefer to stand."

"As you wish," the prime minister said. Jordan sat down in the chair provided for him.

"As I understand it, Prime Minister," Kirk said, "the issue confronting the Council today concerns the Patrian rebels currently in custody aboard the *Enterprise.*"

"Quite so, Captain," the prime minister replied. "We understand that you have come to make arrangements to remand them to our custody."

"No, Prime Minister, I have not," Kirk said. "The rebels have requested, and been granted, political asylum."

His remarks brought on an immediate outburst. All the Council members started talking and shouting at once. The prime minister had to strike the table with his gavel almost a dozen times to restore order.

"Ambassador Jordan," he said, "am I to understand that the Federation is *refusing* to surrender custody of the rebels to the lawful Patrian authorities?"

"The rebels have made a formal request for political asylum, Prime Minister," Jordan replied. "Pursuant to Starfleet regulations and the Federation Accords, we have granted that request, pending an official inquiry by a Federation court and a final determination of the rebels' political status."

This brought on another outburst of shouting, and it was a while before the prime minister could once again restore order.

"Prime Minister! Prime Minister, I would like to speak!"

"The Council recognizes Elder Harkun," the prime minister said.

Elder Harkun stood and turned to face Kirk and the ambassador. "Captain Kirk . . . Ambassador Jordan . . . while the Patrian Council would not presume to dictate terms to the Federation, neither will we tolerate the Federation dictating terms to us."

There was an assenting chorus of agreement, and the prime minister struck the table with his gavel several times until it died away.

"Elder Harkun has the floor," he reminded the Council members. "You may all speak in turn at the appropriate time." He nodded toward Harkun. "Please continue, Elder Harkun."

"It is my understanding from what you have told us that the Federation is granting asylum to these rebels on the grounds that they claim to be political dissidents," he said. "This claim is specious and thoroughly unsubstantiated."

There were several loud cries of agreement from the other Council members.

"The rebels do not represent any oppressed minority or organized political faction whose grievances and rights have been repressed," Harkun continued. "They are criminals, pure and simple, who have committed murder and violent acts of terrorism against the Patrian citizenry in an effort not to work within the system of our society, but to disrupt and overthrow it. It is not *they* who have been oppressed by the Patrian government, as would be the case with dissidents who would request asylum from third parties, rather, it is the rebels who—through acts of wanton mayhem, murder, and destruction—have been oppressing *us!"*

Once again a resounding chorus of assent broke out from the members of the Council while the prime minister hammered on the table to restore silence.

"The Patrian Council, representing the unified government of the Patrian Republics, entered into negotiations with the Federation in good faith," Harkun continued. "We had welcomed contact with other intelligent species, as represented by the Federation, and we had extended an open invitation to you, as the representatives of that body, to visit us and discuss the possibility of a formal alliance, one which could be of benefit to our respective cultures. We had accepted your offer of aid in assisting us to resolve the problem of these disruptor weapons being smuggled to the terrorists, in the hope that by working together, we could begin to establish a basis of mutual respect and understanding. We had received you here in trust, and in sincerity. *Is this how we are to be repaid?"*

Again a chorus of shouting broke out among the members of the Council in support of Elder Harkun's remarks. While the prime minister rapped his gavel, Kirk held up his hands.

"The Council recognizes Captain James T. Kirk, of the Federation starship *Enterprise*," Jarum said.

"Thank you, Prime Minister," Kirk said. "To reply

to the honorable Elder Harkun's remarks . . . first of all, we did *not* offer to aid the Patrian Republics resolve their problem with the rebels. Our aid was officially *requested* and—"

An undertone of mumbling broke out and Kirk held up his hands once again.

"And . . . we accepted, specifically and *only* on the grounds that the appearance of Klingon disruptors on Patria One represented outside cultural interference. Our agreement, gentlemen, was to help cut off the supply of these weapons, and exert our best efforts to find and confiscate those that had already been distributed."

"And even in that, Captain Kirk, you have failed!" one of the Council members called out, rising to his feet. "Through the inaction of your ship and crew, you allowed one of our vessels to be attacked by an Orion ship that had violated our space and was carrying energy weapons to supply the rebel underground!"

Angry shouts broke out once again, and Kirk raised his hands, waiting for it to die down.

"I remind you, gentlemen," he said, "that the Orion vessel in question was destroyed by my ship after it had fired on the *Komarah,* whose captain chose to take unprovoked offensive action without bothering to consult the officer I had left in command of my ship."

This did not go down any better than any of Kirk's previous remarks, and it took a while for the uproar to die down. Kirk waited tensely.

"Do I still have the floor, Prime Minister?" he asked.

"Continue," the prime minister replied gruffly.

"I stand behind the actions of my ship and crew,"

Kirk said, "and will be held responsible in any official inquiry. However, to return to the Elder Harkun's remarks: he has stated that we have been received here in trust and in sincerity. I submit to the members of this Council that this was not the case."

He raised his voice and continued over the angry reaction that followed his remark.

"What we have found since we arrived here was a government that functions in duplicity, oppresses its citizens through police state tactics, jeopardizes the lives of its law enforcement officers through lethal surgical procedures, and employs clandestine strike teams to stage terrorist acts in which innocent civilians are killed and blame is focused on the rebel underground!"

Bedlam was unleashed by his remarks. Members of the Council jumped to their feet, shouting and gesticulating, hammering their fists on the table and demanding his immediate removal from the chambers. Harkun alone said nothing as he sat and stared at Kirk. Kirk met his gaze and raised his arms for silence, but it never came, despite the incessant hammering of the prime minister's gavel.

"All right!" Kirk raised his hands and shouted, in an effort to make himself heard above the uproar. *"All right, you want the rebels? Very well, then . . . here they are!"* He flipped open his communicator and said, *"Now,* Mr. Scott!"

The perimeter of the chamber became filled with the light-play of transporter beams, and a moment later the six Patrian rebels appeared, along with Spock, Chekov, McCoy, Sulu, Lieutenant Iano, Specialist Muir, and Yeoman Jacob. They were all armed with phasers.

Their sudden appearance brought about an immediate, shocked silence among the members of the Council.

"Nobody move!" Kalo shouted, brandishing his useless phaser.

The prime minister slowly stared at the rebels with astonishment and disbelief, then turned to Kirk with an incredulous expression on his face. "Kirk, you must have lost your mind!" he said.

"No, Prime Minister, but what is on the mind of *someone* in this chamber is the entire purpose of this demonstration," Kirk replied. "Lieutenant Iano?"

Iano stepped forward and scanned the faces of the shocked Council members until his gaze came to rest on Elder Harkun. Slowly, Harkun rose to his feet.

"You," Iano said, pointing at him. *"You* are behind this! *You* are the traitor!" And then he winced and doubled over with sudden pain.

With a snarl, Harkun reached inside his robe, pulled out a disruptor and fired, aiming at Iano, but Kalo was already moving. He leaped and shoved Iano out of the way, absorbing the full impact of the blast. He cried out as his body became wreathed in the white-hot energy blast and disintegrated.

Muir and Jacob were the only ones with a clear shot. They fired their phasers simultaneously, on stun, and Harkun fell, the disruptor dropping from his hand. As they ran forward to check on him, several of the Council members tried to leave, but Spock and Chekov stepped into their path.

"Going somewhere, gentlemen?" Chekov said, covering them with his phaser. They froze.

McCoy rushed over to the fallen Harkun with his medical kit. Muir and Jacob were already there, standing over him, while Spock, Chekov, and the five remaining rebels blocked the doors.

"He's all right," McCoy said. Then he hurried over to Iano, who was slowly getting up, assisted by Kirk and Jordan.

"He gave his life for me," Iano said in a stunned tone, looking toward the spot where Kalo had fallen.

"Don't talk," McCoy said, examining him with a deeply concerned expression on his face. "Jim . . . we've got to get him back up to sickbay right away!"

"No," Iano said, pushing McCoy away. "No . . . I am going to finish what I came to do!" He turned toward the other shocked Council members and scanned their faces until his gaze came to rest on the ones Spock and Chekov had prevented from leaving. They started to back away, but Chekov came up behind them, prodding them forward with his phaser.

"They were involved in it as well," said Iano. "Councilmen Dorin, Urik, and Rahz. But Elder Harkun was the mastermind behind the plot. They were in secret contact with the Klingon Empire, who had promised them full control of the Patrian Republics. Commander Anjor was also involved, as well as Captain Lovik. The *Komarah* would rendezvous in space with Orion freebooters, who were carrying disruptors on commission from the Klingons. They would then bring the shipments back to be distributed to special teams of agents, who believed that they were acting in the interests of the government by trying to turn popular support against the rebel underground."

Sweat began to bead up on his forehead as he continued, breathing heavily. The Council chamber was utterly silent as he spoke.

"The reason the *Komarah* fired on the Orion ship

was because Anjor and Lovik were afraid their part in the plot would be exposed by the Orions in an attempt to save their vessel," he said. "The *Enterprise* had already detected the Orion ship on its scanners, and Anjor knew he could not warn them off, because any such attempt would be picked up by the *Enterprise*. He chose to fire on the ship, hoping the *Enterprise* would join him and destroy it. Instead, his own vessel was damaged, and these conspirators chose to use that as an opportunity to focus blame on the Federation officers."

He grimaced, then groaned as the pain started to return, but forced himself to continue. Sweat was streaming down his forehead.

"That's enough, Iano!" McCoy said.

"No . . . not yet," Iano replied, gasping for breath. "They were also behind the execution of the Mindcrime agents who had started to succumb to the results of the procedure. Their bodies were destroyed by the disruptors so that they could not be identified. The conspirators knew that the majority of the Council favored Federation membership, and so they . . . worked behind the scenes . . . in an effort to make . . . the negotiations . . . fail . . ."

Iano cried out and grabbed his head with both hands as blood suddenly started streaming from his nose and eyes.

"Iano!" Kirk cried out, stepping forward to catch him as he fell. McCoy rushed forward and crouched over him.

"Bones . . ." Kirk said, staring at McCoy with a stricken expression.

McCoy simply looked at him and shook his head with resignation.